Final Vow

The sixth book in the Bluegrass Brothers series

Kathleen Brooks

Books by Kathleen Brooks

Bluegrass Series

Bluegrass State of Mind

Risky Shot

Dead Heat

Bluegrass Brothers

Bluegrass Undercover

Rising Storm

Secret Santa: A Bluegrass Series Novella

Acquiring Trouble

Relentless Pursuit

Secrets Collide

Final Vow

Women of Power Series

Chosen for Power – coming April of 2014

Prologue

Rahmi, eighteen years ago . . .

Ahmed laughed as Mohtadi Ali Rahman, Sheik of Rahmi, smiled with gritted teeth as they made their way to the athletic complex. Screaming teenagers surrounded the palace gates for a chance to see the hot young royal.

Mohtadi was everything Ahmed wasn't—tall, rich, and handsome. Ahmed sighed . . . girls didn't notice him. They only noticed his athletic older brother, Jamal. Ahmed weighed less than a wet dishrag and was still waiting on a much-needed growth spurt. Ahmed was not athletic at all, much to the disappointment of his father, who served as head of security for the royal family. He was artistic. He painted and enjoyed photography more than shooting guns or lifting weights.

However, Ahmed took great pleasure in his best friend's discomfort with his role as the bachelor prince. Today was Mo's eighteenth birthday, making him officially eligible for marriage. Ever since they were just ten years of age, they'd been dreading the day they came into their majority. Ahmed's birthday was one week away and his father's constant disappointed looks worried him.

"You had better get used to it, Mohtadi. You are now the most eligible bachelor in all of Rahmi, probably the world." Ahmed laughed and slapped his friend on the back.

They had been friends since birth. They grew up playing with each other and going to the tutor together. It wasn't until they were seven that they realized they were each other's *only* friend. Their parents had planned it that way. Their intention was for Ahmed to be Mohtadi's bodyguard. However, it was often Mo who looked out for Ahmed, much to his father's continued dismay.

"The king called for me this morning," Mohtadi started as he quickly glanced back at the opulent five-story sandstone palace lined with palm trees and stone gardens as if his father might hear him.

"And?" Ahmed asked, knowing Mohtadi's father rarely paid any attention to his son unless the boy was needed in an official capacity.

"He wants me to marry a woman from Bahrain." The prince sighed and kicked a stone along the decorative gravel path.

"We knew this day was coming. When is the wedding?" Ahmed asked, resigned to his best friend's fate.

"There is not going to be a wedding. I told him no. I convinced him to let me go to university first. After all, as a lowly third son, I am not expected to inherit the throne and I will need an occupation— even if it is only for show."

Ahmed stopped walking, stunned. He couldn't believe the king would allow that. "And he is letting you go?"

"He is. I told him if he did not, I would refuse the marriage and publicly embarrass the family at the wedding and in front of the camera every chance I got," Mohtadi said with a grin.

"He could not have been happy, but you just bought yourself four more years of freedom." Ahmed was awed at his friend's courage to stand up to the king. Not many people could do that.

"That I have. I hope that is enough time to find someone to love. I wish that more than anything. My oldest brother was betrothed two years ago and he still has not met his future wife. That is not the kind of life I want."

"Where will you go to university? Here?"

"No. I am going to Cambridge. I start this fall. Hopefully, you will, too." Mohtadi broke into another smile as Ahmed pushed open the door to the athletic complex. Mohtadi had a fencing class and Ahmed had been ordered by his father to start weight training. According to his father, Ahmed was too small to be considered a bodyguard, resulting in embarrassment for the family.

"Really? That would be amazing. Has your father consented?"

"Not yet. But I requested that you go with me. He is meeting with your father now."

"I cannot believe it—England. Away from my father and able to take classes that I want. This is the best birthday yet." Ahmed stopped at the door to the weight room and shot a smile at his friend. "Thank you, Mohtadi."

Mohtadi returned the smile. "You are welcome, my friend."

Ahmed paced the length of his father's office inside the palace and waited for him to arrive. His father had finally summoned him after a week of waiting. Tomorrow was his eighteenth birthday, and he hoped that his father was going to "surprise" him with permission to go with Mohtadi to England in two months' time.

Ahmed glanced around the room at the large, dark wooden desk, the various weapons, and several accolades hanging on the wall. There were no family pictures in the office. The only picture in the room was of his father standing slightly behind the king. Someday his brother would fill that role.

The overly tall double doors opened and his father marched into the room. His short, salt-and-pepper hair matched his black suit and white dress shirt. "Son, I am glad you arrived early. I have someplace to go and can deliver the happy news quickly."

Ahmed knew better than to smile, so he stood quietly in front of the desk with his hands clasped behind him as his father sat down and looked through some papers. Ahmed tried to contain his excitement at the prospect of going to England while he waited for his father to address him again.

"Tomorrow is your eighteenth birthday. You will be a man and it is time for you to grow up," his father said, never bothering to look up from the reports he was glancing over. "As such, I have a present for you."

"Thank you, Father." Ahmed clasped his hands tightly as to not show how pleased he was at the idea of leaving his father's house.

"You are to be married tomorrow morning."

"Thank—I am sorry, what did you say?" Ahmed felt his heart stop as he stared down at the top of his father's head.

His father looked up slowly and met his son's eyes. "I said you will marry tomorrow morning at ten o'clock. Now, go and find something suitable to wear. I will see you in the morning." His father flicked his wrist and he was dismissed.

"No," Ahmed said so quietly he wasn't even sure his words had been heard until his father's eyes, filled with anger, looked up at him.

"Excuse me?"

"I said no, Father. I have no wish to marry a woman whose name I do not even know. Prince Mohtadi will be attending Cambridge and has requested I go with him—as is my place as his bodyguard." Ahmed didn't breathe and he felt somewhat lightheaded as his father slowly stood up and placed his hands on his desk.

"Listen to me carefully, Ahmed. Your position as bodyguard has been revoked. Another man, more capable than you, has already been appointed. You are a disgrace to the family. You have no talent at shooting, no talent with a sword, and can hardly lift fifty kilograms. It is clear that you cannot stand with our family in protecting the royal family. Therefore, you will make up for your deficiencies with a marriage that pleases the king.

"Rahmi needs to make a political alliance with the Kremlin. Since you are unable to physically serve His Royal Highness, I suggested that you would be pleased to serve as bridegroom to the second daughter of the Prime Minister of Russia. It sets in motion a very lucrative oil deal between our countries and gives this young Russian Federation an ally who is in good standing with the United Nations. You should be honored, yet you dare to question me?"

Ahmed instinctively cringed as his father slammed his hands down on his desk. "Father, I have never even met this woman. How am I expected to marry her?"

"It's easy. You say 'I do' and then you bed her. Now get out of here. Your brother will escort you home and stay with you until the ceremony. King Ali Rahman has been gracious enough to grant you one of the elite houses surrounding the palace as a wedding gift. You will need to thank him for it and for the marriage. Now go."

Ahmed stood rooted to the floor, staring daggers at his father's head. He didn't even know the door opened until he felt his brother's hand wrap tightly around his arm and pull him out of the room.

"I cannot believe Father would do this," Ahmed murmured as Jamal led him out of the palace.

"Why are you surprised? You should be happy that he found a way for you to be of service to the king. Congratulations, brother. Tomorrow you will become a man."

Ahmed stood in front of the Russian Orthodox priest requested by his bride's family and waited. Earlier that morning, he had learned that his bride was almost seventeen years old and had also been kept in the dark about this union until recently. Upon asking his father her feelings on the matter, his father had just laughed and told him that she was obedient.

Standing next to him, Mohtadi wore a grim smile as pictures were taken. Having a prince in the wedding had pleased the prime minister greatly, and Ahmed was sure pictures would be in the Russian papers by tonight. Music started and the doors opened. His bride appeared on her father's arm and Ahmed felt a little piece of himself die.

After the reception, Ahmed led his new wife to their house. She still had not said a word to him nor had she smiled. He'd learned during the ceremony that her name was Paulina, but that was it.

He unlocked the door and let her walk into their new house. It was a gracious gift from the king and came with a small yard in both the front and back. "We never got to meet before. I am Ahmed. Today is my eighteenth birthday," he said with a shy grin. He may not know his wife, but he might as well try to get to know her.

"I'm Paulina," she said in a heavily accented voice. "And I wish I had never met you. I'll sleep with you tonight, but only tonight and only because I would not put it past my father to ask for an exam tomorrow. Then I will move into the extra bedroom."

"But we are married. Shall we not make the best of it?" Ahmed asked. He could feel her freezing glare and decided he shouldn't have asked the question.

"No. My heart belongs to another . . . my dearest Mikhail. My father threatened to have him killed if I didn't marry you and cut off all my communication with him. But that doesn't mean I have to play the dutiful wife. It's your fault my heart has been ripped from my chest," Paulina yanked off her heavy veil and threw it on the couch. "Come, let's get this over with. Then you can continue your life as if I weren't even here."

Ahmed slowly followed her up the stairs to the large master bedroom. His bride was already disrobing when he entered. She pulled at her pins and her long brown hair fell in waves down her naked back. She was beautiful and he couldn't stop his erection upon seeing her bare bottom as she stepped out of her dress.

Paulina pulled back the covers and gave a hiss of displeasure as she saw an extra white sheet covering the mattress. Apparently her father wanted to ensure this union more than Ahmed realized.

She lay slowly down on the bed, her hair spread out on the pillowcase. Her small breasts were pert, and Ahmed wished she would change her mind about marriage. Maybe if he were gentle enough, she would realize he would be a good husband to her.

Ahmed stripped down and started toward her only to be stopped by her lip curling in disgust at the sight of him. "We don't have to do this, you know. I don't mind waiting until we get to know each other better."

"No. Do it now."

Ahmed smiled and looked down into the large brown eyes of his newborn son. Paulina had conceived the one and only time he'd lain with her. True to her word, she had moved into the extra bedroom. They didn't eat together; they didn't watch television together — they lived separately under the single roof.

The first two weeks of marriage were the worst. She frantically wrote letters and received just as many. But then they suddenly stopped. For a while, Paulina was even more withdrawn, never even leaving her room.

Ahmed let her be. He cooked dinner every night and left a tray by her door. Two months after their wedding, she actually came to him to talk. Paulina was pregnant. She wanted an abortion but Ahmed refused. He struck a bargain with her: she would have the child and treat the baby well. Upon her father's death, he would consent to a divorce. The child would stay in Rahmi and be raised by Ahmed. Her father was older with ongoing heart issues, so she eagerly agreed to the deal.

Mohtadi left for Cambridge and Ahmed was given a desk job in the Russian embassy. He had been at the office when the doctor called to let him know Paulina was in labor. She gave birth to their son at home, just as Ahmed reached her. The doctor walked into the sitting room and informed Ahmed he now had a son. Paulina had requested time to herself while the nurse bottle-fed the hungry newborn. Ahmed was kept in the living room for hours until the nurse came for him.

"He is amazing. Thank you for this gift, Paulina. What would you like to name him?" Ahmed asked as the baby boy grabbed his finger.

"I don't care. Whatever you would like. He is your son."

"He is our son. How about Kedar Valkov Mueez? It means *powerful wolf who protects*, which is suitable for my family's devotion to the royal family. I thought you would appreciate the middle name as homage to his mother's homeland." When he looked up, he saw Paulina's face had turned white. "Is everything okay? The doctor assured me you were well."

"I'm fine." Ahmed gave her a nod and then slowly scooped his new son into his arms. "No middle name. It's not done. Kedar will be his name. Now take him away while I rest."

"Come on, Kedar. I will show you your new home." Ahmed left the room and walked through the house with his son. He was a strong boy and Ahmed felt his heart swell with love. He may not have love in his marriage, but he would give his son all the love he wished his own father had given to him. "I will love you for the rest of my life and beyond, my son."

Ahmed stole into the room where Paulina slept and quietly put his son in the bassinet. Kedar had fallen asleep and Ahmed gently kissed his child's soft cheek before sneaking out of the room. If he hurried to the palace, he could tell his brother the good news and be back before Kedar woke from his nap.

Ahmed didn't bother knocking on the door to his brother's office. He was too excited to tell him that he was an uncle to even think about it. Two drawn faces looked up as Ahmed hurried in with a goofy grin on his face.

"Brother, Father. I have good news."

"It will have to wait. I need you to grab your gear and find the princess. There is word that a rebel force led by the king's cousin is approaching," his father ordered.

"Are they in danger?"

"We all are. He will try to kill every last supporter of the king's."

"My child. My son was just born," Ahmed was filled with dread. He had to reach Kedar.

"A son? Go get him. I will find Princess Baheera. We will meet you in the safe room. Hurry. They have passed the fishing village and will be here soon. We're preparing our defenses now."

Ahmed turned and ran out of the palace. Guards were taking up their posts as his father started shouting orders. Gunfire erupted from the far side of the palace so Ahmed used a hidden door in the wall to reach the street.

People were screaming and running from the downtown offices. Some stood and stared at the palace, and others hurried to their cars trying to escape the madness. His house was less than a kilometer away. He had walked to the palace earlier, something he now regretted as he saw a man turning up his front walk.

"Stop," Ahmed yelled, but the man didn't pay attention. In one quick movement, he lifted his leg and kicked open the door. Ahmed ran as fast as he could. He jumped the bushes in his yard and rushed through the front door of his house.

The world stood still as Ahmed saw the tall man holding his wife in a tight embrace. Slowly the man stepped back and pulled the long knife from Paulina's chest. As the man turned, he dropped Paulina, her body crumpling on the floor while blood bloomed across her chest.

"Who are you?" Ahmed asked, his son's cries bringing him farther into the house.

"Look at you. You are a weakling," the man spat, his voice thick with a Russian accent.

"You are not a rebel." Ahmed looked up at the tall man and took in his appearance. He was young, not yet twenty. His black hair and black eyes gave an eerie appearance.

"Very astute. I follow the money. And right now the money is paying me to overthrow this country." The man stepped closer and Ahmed looked around for a weapon but could find none. He'd have to protect his family with his fists. It was his only choice.

"And what a surprise! When I arrived here, I found this woman, who is supposed to be married to one of the famous Mueez sons, is, in fact, married to a pathetic little boy who doesn't even have a weapon on him," the man sneered.

Ahmed lunged toward the man. His fist crashed into the man's face, causing him to stumble backward, slamming into the wall. Ahmed continued to punch him as hard as he could. With one final blow, Ahmed turned and sprinted for the back bedroom where Kedar was crying.

He was halfway there when he felt a hand grab his collar and yank him to the ground. "Going somewhere? Trying to save your son? You couldn't save your wife and you can't save your country. Why do you even think you can save your son?"

Ahmed felt the breath leave his lungs as the man's boot pressed hard onto his chest. He stared up into the eyes of evil as the man pulled out his knife and pointed it at him. He opened his mouth to beg for his son's life, but the man pressed his boot harder and the words failed to come.

The man bent over and placed the blade on Ahmed's chest. "You think about that while you die. And you'll die knowing Sergei killed everything you love."

Ahmed felt the blade enter his chest. It burned as it went slowly into his flesh. The man's eyes flared and he smiled as he pulled out the bloodied blade. He got up and walked to the back of the house, following Kedar's loud cries. Ahmed tried to move but only managed to crawl a couple inches as he tried to fight the darkness enveloping him. Just before he lost consciousness, the screams of his son stopped.

Chapter One

Keeneston, current day . . .

Cy Davies and his new wife, Gemma, were glowing as they danced at their wedding. Bridget Springer smiled at one of Cy's fellow Hollywood stuntmen whom she was dancing with. Out of the corner of her eye she saw a shadow move in the trees off in the distance, but when she looked no one was there. She quietly chided herself for looking for Ahmed. It had been four months since she'd seen him or any of the royal family.

After the safe delivery of their twin boys, Mohtadi and Danielle Ali Rahman, or Mo and Dani as they were known in Keeneston, had left for the small country of Rahmi where Mo served as a prince. Bridget had heard that they received a warm welcome at the palace and the people celebrated having another generation of heirs to the throne. The rumor was that succession of the throne in Rahmi would have flipped to the king's cousin's line if there were no male heir to follow Mo and his brothers. And since Ahmed served as the head of security for Mo's family, he oversaw their protection in Rahmi.

Before he had left, he and Bridget had had a standing date for hand-to-hand combat training three days a week. She'd learned so much from him and she was now bored without him. It didn't really make sense. It's not like he even talked to her other than to tell her how to perform a move or how to correct her technique. However, she felt his absence everyday.

Because she missed her time with Ahmed, the past months had dragged on for Bridget. She had accepted a couple of small government jobs with her drug and bomb dog, Marko. Plus she had been partnered with Annie Davies at the sheriff's office. They'd busted some teenagers, checked the school for drugs, and caught some speeders. Annie had taken her to the Keeneston High School football games and she'd enjoyed seeing Cade, Annie's husband, and Will Ashton, a former NFL quarterback, coaching the boys she was getting to know on the school visits.

Will and his wife, McKenna, the new Keeneston prosecutor, were excited for the birth of their second child. After a year off from coaching, Kenna, as her friends called her, told Will to get back to what he loved. Bridget had been sitting between the two coaches' wives and had gotten hooked on high school football to take her mind off something she shouldn't even be missing.

"Cy told me all about you. Your work for the government is fascinating. I started out in the Marines before I got the bug," Cy's friend, Jayden, said, bringing her back to the present. She looked at the man she was dancing with and tried to remember what he'd just told her.

"The bug?" Bridget asked, finally taking her eyes from the shadows and putting them back on Jayden. He was handsome and he definitely had stayed in Marine shape. His brown hair was cut short and his tuxedo fit snugly over his broad muscles.

"The adrenaline bug. Jumping out of planes, driving for your life, hoping not to be ambushed . . . all got me hooked on that rush. Now I jump off buildings and drive in chase scenes."

"It does sound fun. Parachuting was one of my favorite things to do in the Army." Bridget smiled. She had joined the ROTC in college and then went on to serve four years in the Army. It's where she had fallen in love with training dogs.

Bridget felt a shiver run down her back as Jayden pulled her a little closer. The shiver wasn't from the man dancing with her. It was a feeling as if she was being watched. Casually, she looked around but didn't see anything. Right as she was turning her attention back to Jayden, she thought she saw a shadow move again off in the darkness. Her mind automatically went to Ahmed, but when she turned her head and looked, there was no one there once again.

The song ended and Bridget let Jayden escort her off the dance floor. Annie waved her over and she excused herself to go to her friend. She knew Cy had probably told Jayden about her, but there was no spark. She really needed to get over the thought hiding in the back of her head. The thought that had settled there and refused to be banished. The thought of Ahmed as something more than a sparring buddy.

"Hey, who's the hottie you're dancing with?" Annie asked as Cade looked decidedly uncomfortable with the beginning of girl talk.

"He was a stuntman with Cy in Hollywood." Bridget laughed as Annie wiggled her eyebrows. "Doesn't look too hopeful."

"Hopeful for what, dear?" Miss Lily Rae Rose asked as she and John Wolfe joined them. Using some kind of silent telepathy, within seconds Miss Lily's two sisters, Miss Daisy Mae Rose and Miss Violet Fae Rose, made a beeline toward her from various sides of the reception. They were sharks who could smell gossip, and they were circling their prey.

"Bridget doesn't think Mr. Hunka Hunka over there is anything special," Annie informed them as Cade suddenly became very interested in some imaginary lint.

"Well, some men are blessed with brawn and some with brains. I'm sure once you get him undressed, it won't really matter if he's missing the brains," Miss Violet said matter-of-factly. Bridget was pretty sure poor Jayden was now being mentally stripped, bless his heart, by Miss Violet.

"It's not that. He's fine. It's just . . ." Bridget started but was cut off by the high-pitched squeal of most the women at the reception.

Turning around, Bridget felt like doing something other than squealing. Mo and Dani, or more formally, Mohtadi and Danielle Ali Rahman, Prince and Princess of Rahmi, had just arrived and e~

were holding an adorable baby boy. What Bridget was feeling was her heart speeding up. If Dani and Mo where here, Ahmed was here, too. So, she hadn't been crazy when she saw the shadows moving. It had been Ahmed.

Bridget was swept along with the surging crowd as they encircled the happy new parents. The Rose sisters were cooing and the Davies women, along with Kenna, Dani's best friend, were hugging the couple and welcoming them back home.

"I thought you all wouldn't be back until next year. What happened? Is everything all right?" Kenna asked as she scooped up one of the babies.

"We escaped." Dani laughed. "No, Rahmi is beautiful, but the king was rather smothering and y'all know how well I do with smothering."

"Bless your heart, you said *y'all*. You really are one of us now." Miss Daisy laughed as everyone else joined in.

"It's true. While we both enjoyed being there, it is wonderful to be home. Besides, we want Zain and Gabriel to get to know their Keeneston family," Mo told their friends.

"What happened that enabled you to come home?" Paige Davies Parker, the only daughter of the Davies clan, asked. Her husband, FBI Agent Cole Parker, stood next to her with his arm wrapped around her. Bridget looked around once again for Ahmed. Would he ever hold a woman like that?

"Mo's brother, Dirar, and his wife, Ameera, were told last Christmas by the doctors in Rahmi that they thought he was sterile. Ameera is a sweet woman and I felt so bad for her. She'd been raised since birth to be a queen and to raise a king. Instead she ended up married to a second son in the royal family and couldn't even have a baby that would turn out to be the future king. It's really sad. Mo's oldest brother has all girls. During the last birth, there were complications and his wife can no longer have children. Ameera confided in me that she failed at everything she was raised to do:

marry a king and have an heir. So, we may have whispered in the right ears that coming to the fertility clinic in New York City would be a good idea. Next thing you know, Ameera started acting like me too much," Dani said, full of pride. Bridget wondered why Dani wanted Ameera, the wife of one of Mo's older brothers, to conceive so badly since Mo and Dani's sons were the ones to secure the line. Their oldest son, Zain, would be king one day.

"Oh dear," Kenna said as she tried not to laugh. The king didn't really approve of Dani's desire to be out of the spotlight.

"You know how Ameera underwent fertility treatments? Well, so did Dirar and they found out they are going to have a baby. Ignoring tradition, she told the king to shove it and went to the doctor and insisted on not only having an ultrasound, but seeing it as well. The king couldn't stand it and ended up joining her and turning into a complete mess when he saw the ultrasound of the healthy boy she's carrying," Dani told them with a kind smile on her face. For all the teasing, she and the king loved each other, even if they were complete opposites.

"So, your boys?" Miss Lily asked hesitantly.

"Are free to be raised as 'the backups' here in Keeneston," Mo said with so much happiness in his voice, everyone smiled and cheered.

Bridget stepped slowly back from the crowd and searched the shadows for Ahmed. The music started up again and thoughts of dancing with him filled her head. Would he ask her? She saw him then. Standing alone, reading a piece of paper. As if feeling her gaze on him, he looked up from the paper and directly at her. Their eyes connected and Bridget knew why Jayden had not held any appeal. She was hopelessly wishing for Ahmed to notice her.

She gave him a little smile and started to walk toward him. She'd heard all the gossip at the Blossom Café. Ahmed had never dated anyone from Keeneston, except Katelyn Jacks. She was not Katelyn Jacks anymore, but Katelyn Davies. The sweet ex-model-turned-veterinarian was married to Marshall Davies, the sheriff of Keeneston and her boss. Others had tried to get Ahmed's attention but had all been politely ignored or turned down. And who could blame them? Ahmed was dangerously good-looking. He stood just less than six feet with dark black hair that was always cut to perfection. His brown eyes noticed everything, and Bridget heated up just at the thought of what those eyes would look like if he were making love to her. Then there was his face. Strong, masculine, and it always seemed that he had a five-o'clock shadow, which just added to his air of mystery.

Some dared to whisper he still had feelings for Katelyn, but Katelyn strongly protested those rumors. From the massive amount of time Bridget had spent with Ahmed, she tended to agree with Katelyn. While he held many secrets, a secret desire for Katelyn didn't appear to be one of them. However, the trouble was she had nothing to prove it, just the hope that she could be the one for him. Taking a deep breath, Bridget put on a confident smile and stepped into the shadows.

Ahmed had been at the dance for the last half-hour. He'd seen one of Cy's groomsmen dancing with Bridget and hated it. Luckily Nabi, his mentee, had brought a Pakistani newspaper to him with a lead to Sergei. Sergei, the same man who had killed his son and whom Ahmed had let escape while helping Cy Davies save his bride, Gemma, from a mentally deranged terrorist. But he wasn't going to let him go this time. No, he was going to track him down and kill him. It was the only way he could move on with his life.

It was then he felt her eyes on him. Ahmed always knew where she was and could feel her in his heart at times. He looked up and into the crowded reception, meeting her gaze instantly. Bridget was unlike any woman he had met before. Sure, she was attractive. Her red hair streaked with blonde, blue eyes, athletic build, and the tiniest smattering of freckles made her irresistible to him.

He was all darkness to her light in more ways than one. She was tough, but at the same time, soft and kind. She was compassionate and when the men in her field laughed at her ability to do her job, she just smiled and did her job. She didn't even rub it in when she did better than they did. In turn, she was well respected by everyone he'd ever talked to. She deserved someone better than him. He'd done horrible things during his life and he couldn't ruin her by being associated with him. Sure, governments tolerated him and some had even tried to hire him away. But a man who was ruthless with no emotion was not who Bridget deserved. She also didn't deserve Sergei coming after her. And make no mistake—if Sergei found out Ahmed cared for her, he'd come after her with no mercy.

"Welcome home, Ahmed," Bridget shyly said as she fidgeted with her beautiful light-blue dress that matched her eyes.

"Thank you. Are you having a nice time?" he asked. How he wanted to dance with her, how he wanted . . . well, it didn't matter. Until Sergei was dead, there was no point to dream.

"I am now," Bridget blushed and desire raged inside her. It was obvious that, despite the fact she worked almost exclusively with men, she was not very experienced. "Does this mean we can restart our workouts?"

"I'm sorry, but no. I won't be in Keeneston long. I have business elsewhere. Speaking of which, I must be going. Goodbye, Bridget." Ahmed took a second to look her over one last time before turning away and disappearing into the night. He hated leaving her there with a look of confusion and hurt on her face, but it was for the best.

Ahmed unlocked the front door to his house and Zoticus, or Zoti, as he called the massive pit bull he and Katelyn rescued, came bounding forward with his tail wagging.

"Glad to be back home, boy?" Ahmed asked as he scratched Zoti's broad head. Zoti had not been fond of the lack of grass on Rahmi, nor the heat. The two-story historic federal house that Ahmed called home was much more Zoti's style. It was his style now, too. He had enjoyed spending time with his brother in Rahmi, but it had never been the same since that night almost eighteen years ago.

His brother had come looking for him when Ahmed didn't appear in the safe room as instructed and had saved him. He had found Ahmed unconscious and minutes away from death. He barricaded the door and grabbed his emergency medical kit. Knowing he and his brother were the same blood type, Jamal didn't hesitate as he slid a needle into Ahmed's arm and then one into his for an immediate transfusion. When he became shaky from loss of blood, he stopped the transfusion. The bandages were still soaked with blood, but it was enough to give him time to get Ahmed to the field hospital set up inside the palace walls. The fighting continued, and soon the country's citizens picked up weapons and, with a final surge of support for the king, they defeated the rebels.

Ahmed awoke the day after the skirmish ended. The knife had missed his heart by a centimeter. His father had been killed in battle and his brother was being installed as the new head of the private guard. Mo had arrived to see how his country fared and, when he heard about Ahmed, had demanded the king send him to London with him to recover.

It was then Ahmed Mueez died and just Ahmed was born. He had not been worthy of his last name and refused to use it. But someday — someday he would be worthy again.

Ahmed brought Zoti in from his walk and scooped out a bowl of food for him before walking into his office in the back of the house. He set down the Pakistani paper with the article about the train wreck that killed over a hundred people in it and began his research. To the outside reader, it was a tragedy, but there was only one high-powered person on that train and that was the giveaway. Sergei liked big statements to cover the real target. No one would think this was an assassination. Now Ahmed needed to look into who would want the minister of energy killed. If he could find that out, that person could lead him to Sergei.

Chapter Two

Bridget was deep in a dream when her phone rang and jarred her awake. She blinked the sleep from her eyes and looked at her clock. It was just six in the morning. She had gotten home from the wedding and crawled into bed just four hours earlier.

She reached over to her nightstand and answered the phone with a tired sigh, "Good morning, Daddy."

"Good morning, pumpkin. You sound as if you're still in bed. You're burning daylight," her father's gruff voice chided over the phone.

"Daylight? Daddy, it's still dark out. I think you forget I'm not in the military anymore. I'm allowed to sleep in now."

"Bah, waste of time. How was the wedding? Did you have a date?"

"Daddy, you know I didn't have a date." Bridget nudged Marko off her pillow and sat up as she turned on the light. It was no use now. She'd never be able to get back to sleep. She didn't really mind, though. She was a daddy's girl and she enjoyed talking to him.

"You're a beautiful woman. You should have a date," her father stated as if he were giving an order to one of his soldiers.

"And if I did, you would scare him away." Her father, General Richard Ward, scared everyone except her. Her dad had been the commander of the United States Special Operations Command until this past year when he'd been appointed by the president to be the

19

chief of staff of the United States Army. Congress had approved him just three months ago. That was when he and her mother, Patty, had moved from Tampa to Virginia.

Dating had never been easy because her father was intimidating with his tough attitude, rigid posture, and all-knowing glare. However, as a result of growing up on military bases with soldiers under her father's commands, she fit easily into the foul language, dirty jokes, and beer drinking often found in the military.

She had known she wanted to go into the military, but she'd been given preferential treatment because of her father when she was in ROTC at college. Soon after, she went to the courthouse without telling her parents and changed her last name to Springer, her mother's maiden name. As a result, she entered the Army as just another recruit.

"If he would be scared away by little ol' me, then he isn't man enough for my pumpkin," her father told her. And he was right, as much as she hated to admit it. "So, tell me all the gossip. Did Katelyn have her baby yet?"

As much as Bridget loved Keeneston, she was a bit of a loner. She was not really used to being herself. She had always worked with the guys and hadn't really made friends before. She and Annie had become good friends, but she didn't put herself out there much to make better friends with the Davies women and other women around her age. Bridget knew her father would worry, so she supplied him with all the town's gossip to reassure him she was happy. And she was trying to be more outgoing.

"Not yet, but any day now. The wedding was beautiful. Cy and Gemma tried to hook me up with one of the groomsmen who's a stuntman, but it didn't go anywhere."

"That's too bad," her father said, but Bridget could hear his happy smile over the line.

"Oh, Dani and Mo are back with their twins, Zain and Gabriel. Mo's older brother is going to have a baby boy so the whole group was able to come back home. Paige told me Dani and Mo couldn't be happier about it. They wanted to raise the boys away from royal life. In fact, while Dani was convincing Ameera to go to New York for treatment, Mo was trying to convince the king to allow his eldest niece to be named queen. The king, a real stick-in-the-mud, as Dani calls him, didn't approve of that. Luckily everything worked out with Ameera."

"Hmm . . . that's good to know," her father mumbled and she heard him take out a piece of paper and make a note.

"Daddy, I'm not giving you foreign intelligence anymore. Aren't you supposed to be more of an advisor now as opposed to a commander?"

"It never hurts to be aware. You remember that."

Bridget rolled her eyes. Since she was a little girl, her dad had been telling her to be aware, observe your surroundings, and memorize small details that seem out of place. Needless to say, she was hardly ever taken unaware. "Yes, Daddy. Ahmed is back, too. But he said he was leaving soon, so we won't be able to continue my lessons. I really miss them. I learned so much from him."

It sounded as if her dad growled a little, but Bridget wasn't sure. "I don't like that one bit. I told you I didn't approve of those lessons. Bridget, that man is dangerous and you should stay away from him. That's an order."

"Daddy!" Bridget felt both crushed and angry. "Ahmed isn't bad at all. He's a great teacher and I've learned so much. He is very nice when you get to know him."

"It sounds as if you're going to ignore my order. Should I be expecting you to bring him home soon?"

"Dad," Bridget rolled her eyes at his sarcastic remark, "you don't have to worry about that. Ahmed isn't interested in me." Bridget closed her eyes and cursed. She'd just inadvertently told her dad she was interested, but Ahmed wasn't.

"Well, then he's dangerous *and* stupid. Even worse."

Bridget smiled at her dad's attempt to make her feel better. "Thanks, Daddy. How's Mom?" Bridget asked, taking the conversation away from her lack of a love life. She absently scratched Marko's ears as she listened to her father delight her with tales about her mother, their new house, and what it was like working in the Pentagon. But no matter how hard she tried to pay attention, she couldn't shake the sadness of knowing Ahmed would never reciprocate her feelings.

Ahmed pushed open the door to the small eating area where he found Dani and Mo with the boys. The cheery little room was where the family had all their meals, and they usually kept a seat open for Ahmed.

"You look terrible," Mo said in a high-pitched, happy voice as he tried to convince the baby he was holding to take his bottle.

"I was up all night," Ahmed told them as he grabbed a muffin from the table and sat down.

"What a coincidence, we were, too." Dani laughed as she took a sip of orange juice while holding a baby in her other arm.

"What is going on, Ahmed? You have been acting differently since we arrived." After being best friends for thirty-six years, it was hard for him to hide anything from Mo.

"I think I have a lead on Sergei. I need to follow it. I've been working with Nabi and I feel comfortable leaving him in charge," Ahmed told them before briefing them on the information he'd uncovered. Mo looked contemplative while Dani seemed concerned.

"Of course. You have all my resources at your disposal," Mo told him, clearly understanding the gravity of the situation. He knew that this was not just some standard operation. This was personal.

"I don't understand why you have to go after him. I know he's a bad guy, but it's not your fight, Ahmed," Dani said. Ahmed gave a quick glance to Mo and with a slight nod sent a silent thank-you to him for not telling Dani about his darkest time. "You know, Bridget was so lovely last night. You two are really quite similar. Instead of chasing Sergei, you could always chase her."

Ahmed stared at the innocent look on Dani's face. "I already know her," Ahmed said sternly, wanting to warn her away from this topic.

Dani just rolled her eyes. "I mean, more than one of your in-depth background checks you do on everyone for fun."

"I didn't do one on her," Ahmed said before silently cursing himself as Dani's eyes widened and a huge smile lit up her face.

"Really?" Mo asked while he looked interested. Ahmed narrowed his eyes at his friend. But as always, Mo just ignored his glare.

"Really. Nabi handled it. It's my job to train him, after all. Because I trained him, I know he did a thorough job." That and he hadn't wanted to do it. He already cared more than he should and if she were as wonderful as he thought, it would make leaving her alone harder.

"If you say so," Mo said with a smile on his face. "I take it you will be needing the plane? Where will you be heading?"

"Yes, thank you. I'm heading into Pakistan." Ahmed saw Mo grimace. Rahmi and Pakistan weren't the best of friends.

"Try not to kill anyone . . . well, anyone who would upset their government." Mo stood up and gave Ahmed a meaningful look. "I will walk you out."

"Be safe, Ahmed," Dani told him with such kindness that Ahmed actually felt a pang of guilt for going. But he had been preparing for this for eighteen years. It was time to show Sergei the man he had become. He was no longer a scared boy, and he was prepared to fight to the death to protect the ones he loved.

Bridget wiped the sweat from her brow as she and Marko sprinted through the woods on the property Pierce Davies had given her to build a K-9 training facility. The morning sun shone through the orange, yellow, and red leaves onto the path and relaxed her as the pair exercised. The sounds and smell of fall helped to heal her pained heart.

Dani had called that morning to invite Bridget to lunch. Dani had been so nice to her since Bridget moved to Keeneston that she instantly agreed. It was then that Dani let it slip that it would be nice to have the company since Mo had a meeting with Will about breeding some horses and Ahmed had left the country. That was when Bridget felt the pain in her heart. She was acting like a love-struck teenager. It was clear Ahmed didn't have feelings for her, yet she was pining away. Well, no more. She'd grabbed her running shoes, determined to erase him from her mind and heart.

She broke from the woods and into the clearing where the new kennel was staked out and the foundation was being poured. Bridget slowed to a walk and focused on the happiness she felt seeing her dream coming true. By spring, she'd have a full kennel complete with dogs and trainers. By the time she reached her car, her cell phone rang and interrupted her vision of the future.

"Springer."

"Miss Springer, my name is Usman. I am the assistant of Mr. Rana, the owner of PK Petroleum in Pakistan. May I have a moment of your time?"

"Of course. What can I do for you?"

"There is an energy conference in New Delhi starting on Wednesday. Mr. Rana has received threats and was looking for someone who could blend into his . . . how do you say it? Group?"

"Entourage. Would you like me to pose as a secretary of some sort and provide Mr. Rana with personal protection?" Bridget asked as she grabbed her tablet and looked up Mr. Rana and his business.

"Exactly." Usman sounded relieved that she understood. "You will be needed for only a couple days. Mr. Rana will send his jet in addition to your service fee. Are you amenable to this arrangement?"

"Yes, I'll be happy to help Mr. Rana," Bridget stated. If Ahmed could just up and leave, then why couldn't she? The only relationship they had was in her head. It was time for her to put her wild fantasies to rest and move on.

Chapter Three

Ahmed looked down at the package the slim woman handed him. Tears ran from her sunken eyes down her hollow cheeks. He had tracked down the widow of the minister of energy at her sister's house in a small village three hours from Islamabad.

One look at her fear-ridden face and he knew she held the key to the puzzle. He'd been all over Islamabad talking to aides, secretaries, and journalists. They all thought it was just a derailment, which wasn't particularly uncommon for the area. However, the minister's wife had plastered herself behind her sister and started pleading for her life when Ahmed entered the small house.

Ahmed had told her, "I'm not here to hurt you. I'm here to find the person responsible for your husband's death." She had stopped her pleading and started whispering urgently with her sister. With a nod of her head, the widow had walked into her bedroom and reappeared a minute later with an overstuffed brown business envelope.

Ahmed took the package and dumped the contents onto the small kitchen table. Pictures of her husband with another woman fell out. On the back of each picture was a threat. A threat that if he didn't agree to the proposed pipeline from PK Petroleum, then the pictures of him with his mistress would be plastered all over the media.

Next came photos of his wife and infant son. Then the messages turned darker. The blackmailer threatened the life of his family if he didn't vote for the pipeline. Ahmed looked up from the table at the women. The minister's widow stared quietly at the ground while her sister held her. It had to be embarrassing to show a stranger the pictures of her husband with his mistress.

"Thank you for telling me. You are a strong woman. I promise you, I will find the person responsible." The widow gave a slow bob of her head in appreciation, but by the way her sister clutched her, Ahmed knew there was more. "Tell me the whole story, please. I am a friend." Ahmed sat down at the table, letting the women feel more at ease with his presence in their small house.

"Tell him," the sister whispered.

The widow's eyes teared up again as she kept looking at the ground. "Right before he died, I overheard a call. He was getting ready to go back into the capital when the call came in. I heard my husband turn down another bribe. He said the name Mr. Rana and then told him he was going to the papers with his threats to our family. Two hours later the train derailed."

"Who is Mr. Rana?" Ahmed asked quietly.

"The owner of PK Petroleum."

Ahmed wasn't particularly surprised. The energy business was one of the most cut-throat. He could see what happened. When Rana discovered the minister was going to expose the threats, which would most likely lead to the pipeline contract going to someone else, he had called Sergei.

"Thank you for your time." Ahmed stood up and gathered the pictures. "I can put these in the right hands to destroy Mr. Rana. But only if you want me to." The widow looked at the pictures and slowly stepped forward. She pulled out the pictures of her husband with his mistress and tore them up.

"Thank you, sir. When the police came, I tried to tell them, but they threatened us. I have nothing to lose anymore, though. My husband's brother took our house and our money. I was sent back to my family."

"Your husband should have provided for you for a year in his will." Ahmed knew the customs, but it was a male-dominated society and women sometimes were not told of their rights.

"He did. But my husband's family was not happy with our marriage. We were of different levels. They took what my husband left me. I know I could go to court, but it would do no good. Two of their sons and my husband's father are judges."

Ahmed reached into his inside jacket pocket and pulled out his wallet, taking all the cash he had and putting it on the table. "You have helped me greatly. I thank you for your trust." Ahmed took what was left of the package and left the women staring with open mouths at the thousands of dollars on their table.

"Nabi, find out everything about PK Petroleum and its owner," Ahmed ordered into his phone as he got into his car. By the time he got back to the hotel, Nabi would have all the information Ahmed would need to decide on his next move.

Ahmed tossed the car's keys to the valet and walked across the street to the bank. He pulled out more cash and was about to grab a bite to eat when Nabi called him back.

"What did you find?" Ahmed asked the second he answered the phone.

"Rana inherited the company from his father. There is a long history of corruption, assaults, blackmail, and even murders connected with this family. The pipeline is worth billions, and PK Petroleum was just awarded it this week. The government voted on it one day after the minister of energy was killed. Not surprisingly, his replacement was in favor of PK Petroleum. But, Ahmed, there's more."

Ahmed paused on the sidewalk. Nabi's voice had changed. Something was wrong. "What is it?"

"There's a huge convention in New Delhi and Rana just announced the pipeline. When he did, Bridget was standing behind him."

"Bridget? Bridget Springer? What the hell is she doing there?" Ahmed roared.

"Her highness said that Bridget was hired by Rana the day you left. She's his security. Hello? Sir?" Nabi asked into the dead line. Ahmed had already hung up. He ran to his hotel and, within minutes, was on the way to the airport. This move had Sergei written all over it.

Bridget adjusted her grip on the notebook and looked out at the packed convention hall from where she stood on the stage behind Mr. Rana. She felt the sweat trickle down her back as she wrote down her observations on a notepad. Her gun was strapped to her back under her blazer, ready if she needed it.

It was the end of October, but in New Delhi the heat was still smothering. Bridget didn't listen to Mr. Rana's speech as she scanned the crowd once again. So far the conference had been uneventful. Well, for her anyway. Mr. Rana got upset with the protesters, but they were only armed with signs.

Mr. Rana finished his speech and gave her the sign that he was ready to move. She picked up his notebook and followed him from the stage where other executives surrounded him. Bridget smiled and pushed her way through to Mr. Rana's side where she blended in with his assistants. She relaxed her body and got ready for a long wait. People always loved spending hours with the speakers, rehashing every point in the speech and going over crazy hypotheticals. It was going to be a long day.

Hours later, Bridget felt a dynamic change in the small group. They were in the massive lobby of the conference center, and Mr. Rana had just finished shaking hands with the last of his colleagues. She didn't know what changed exactly. It was just a look he got in his eyes and the way his posture suddenly puffed.

"Where to now, sir?" Bridget asked putting on her best don't-mess-with-me attitude.

"I thought it might be nice to celebrate. Just you and me." With a flick of his hand, the other assistants disappeared and she was left in the empty lobby with her client.

"I'll be happy to make a reservation for you somewhere, Mr. Rana." Bridget pulled out her phone and used it as a barrier between them.

"The kind of celebration I'm talking about does not require reservations." Mr. Rana stepped forward as though he didn't care that her contract specifically prohibited sexual advances by either party.

"Mr. Rana, I know you are a man of wealth and prominence. However, I'm not someone you buy. I don't have sex with my clients."

"We're both adults. You must have a boyfriend then. But if he can let you out of his sight, then he's not deserving."

Bridget rolled her eyes. Henry Rooney, a local attorney and walking pick-up line encyclopedia, had better lines than this. Unfortunately, she was used to this. Men saw a woman in a position of power and assumed she slept her way to the top, making her fair game for them to hit on.

"Mr. Rana," Bridget began in her best motherly voice. It tended to cool the ardor of her clients when images of their mother popped into their heads. But Mr. Rana only smiled and reached out for her. He ran his hand gently down her arm and Bridget fought the urge to deck him.

Ahmed slid to a stop outside the convention center in New Delhi. He could only hope he was in time. Was Sergei here? How in the hell did Sergei find out about his feelings for her? Pure rage settled in the pit of his stomach. He was no longer a boy who couldn't protect his woman, and Sergei was about to find that out.

He left the car parked in the street and flashed his diplomatic identification to the guard at the entrance of the conference center's property. Ahmed scanned the area as he ran across the large garden in front of the building. As he approached, he saw Bridget in the lobby through the glass doors. Something was wrong. Her posture was so rigid—it was then he saw the hand on her.

He shoved the door open so hard the glass cracked. Ahmed strode into the lobby and ignored Bridget's shocked face. His attention was on the man gripping her arm. A quick glance told him Sergei wasn't here, but the man was, without a doubt, Mr. Rana.

"I thought you said you didn't have a boyfriend," Rana sneered as he dropped Bridget's arm.

"I-I-I don't," Bridget stammered.

"Does he know that?" Rana laughed menacingly at his perceived cleverness. Ahmed ignored their conversation and strode straight for Rana. The man was trouble. The way he didn't seem concerned that Ahmed was here, but instead looked happy about it, worried him.

"The famous Ahmed. I've heard so much about you," Rana said with a slick smile on his face.

"Where's Sergei?"

"Sergei?" Bridget echoed. So she didn't know the connection.

Rana puffed up his chest and smiled again as he looked between Bridget and Ahmed. Rana, knowing who Ahmed was, only confirmed his suspicions—Sergei was involved. Ahmed grabbed Rana's suit coat and slammed him against the wall so fast Rana let out a startled yelp.

"I'll ask you only this once. Where's Sergei?"

"I don't think you have to worry. He'll be coming after you and your little bitch soon enough." Ahmed ignored Bridget's gasp. With a quick jerk, he slammed Rana against the wall hard enough for his head to make a satisfying *thunk*.

"Ahmed," Bridget's gentle voice broke through his dark haze of anger, "security is coming." He looked to the other side of the lobby to see security racing toward them.

"Tell Sergei I'm coming for him." Ahmed gave him one last slam against the wall before dropping him. "Come on, it's not safe for you here anymore." He was relieved when Bridget just nodded and started walking out with him.

"I wonder if you'll be able to protect your woman this time?" Rana laughed.

Ahmed froze at the cruel reminder of his past. He turned to end Rana's life, but Bridget was already moving. She grabbed Rana by his shoulders, and, in one quick motion, brought him down as she brought her knee up. Rana grabbed his crotch and cried out in agony as he fell to the floor.

"This woman protects herself." Bridget looked up from the crumpled man at her feet to the guards closing in on them. "Let's go."

Ahmed felt a smile tug on his lips and hurried out the door after her. He led her to his car and silently pulled into traffic. Ahmed couldn't help looking over at Bridget with wonder. She was utterly composed. She had acted as if it were completely normal for people to threaten her, guards to chase her, and to take down a man with one well-placed knee. She was one hell of a woman and he'd do whatever it took to protect her — even if that meant leaving her.

Bridget looked out the window of the car and fumed. There was one thing she couldn't stand about her job — overprotective men. Men who thought the little woman couldn't handle all the facts. She had clearly been dragged into something and yet as Ahmed drove them through the city and toward the airport, he didn't bother filling her in.

He had only stopped long enough at the hotel for her to grab her things. She had hoped he would tell her what was going on, but he hadn't said anything but, "Get your stuff." As the airport came into view, her temper started to flare. She looked over at the way he confidently drove the car out onto the private runway and stopped before the jet. It pissed her off that he seemed to think there was no need to explain what was going on.

Bridget got out of the car and grabbed her luggage as Ahmed talked to some men who had approached the car. The door to the plane opened and Bridget climbed the steep stairs and smiled at the pilot. She said hello, took a seat, and stewed.

It didn't take long for Ahmed to come through the door. He took the seat opposite hers and glanced out the window as the plane prepared to take off. "Is there anything you'd like to tell me?" Bridget asked.

"No." Bridget blinked and then narrowed her eyes at him.

"Excuse me," she said with a deadly softness to her voice.

Ahmed raised his eyes to meet hers and narrowed his own eyes in return. She had to admit he was good with that stare. Unfortunately for him, she grew up with the king of icy glares and they didn't intimidate her. "I said no. It's doesn't involve you, so drop it."

"Drop it? It sure sounded as if he threatened my life. I think that makes me involved."

"I'm not discussing this with you." Ahmed stood and picked up a large envelope that had been sitting on the table between them. "I have work to do. Have a nice flight, Miss Springer." Bridget stared in shocked silence as he walked into the back room of the plane and shut the door.

Sergei hung up his phone and smiled. So, Ahmed was in love. Rana had told him about the look on Ahmed's face when he found them together. There was no doubt in Rana's mind that Ahmed and this Bridget woman were involved.

It would be fun to take her from Ahmed, just as Ahmed had taken love from Sergei long ago. The happy memories of his youth tortured him when he closed his eyes at night. He was no longer that person with ambition to go into the law. A naïve lad with hopes and dreams had died after Ahmed entered his life. That boy ceased to exist and now only hardened revenge filled his soul. What luck that after all these years Ahmed finally had something Sergei could take from him.

When Sergei was in Kentucky, he had heard about the pretty new addition to the small town. He had placed some bugs in that insipid restaurant and endured hours of nonsense to learn of Ahmed's every move. But then there had been bets placed when Bridget had starting taking some classes with Ahmed. It was cute really. She looked sweet and innocent with her cheerful hair and freckles, wanting to learn self-defense. She was just the type to make a man fall to his knees. Her innocence would be irresistible to men like Ahmed and Sergei. Ahmed would want to protect her. Sergei just wanted to screw her until that innocence was gone.

He looked around the large tent he was staying in and grunted to himself as he picked up his bag. It was time to pay Keeneston a visit.

Chapter Four

A hmed rammed his fist into the punching bag over and over again. He and Bridget arrived back in Keeneston three days ago, and he hadn't been able to sleep yet. Every time he closed his eyes, he thought about his wife falling to the floor and the sound of his son crying.

When Ahmed had gone to school in England, he had started lifting weights with renewed determination. He'd enrolled in martial arts and boxing classes along with taking numerous psychology classes at Cambridge. But it hadn't been enough. With a couple of well-placed phone calls from Mo, Ahmed had been given permission to train with MI6 in London.

He'd learned a lot by the time he finally went back to Rahmi. He had been trained in warfare, fighting, and interrogation techniques, to name just a few things the best of British intelligence had taught him. His brother had hardly recognized him. He'd gained close to sixty pounds of muscle and had grown three inches. Gone was the youthful appearance and gone was the artist—replaced with a warrior.

It was that warrior spirit that refused to let him slow down. He had to be prepared for Sergei. Revenge would be his and he wouldn't stop until Sergei was dead. He hadn't forgotten about Rana and smiled as he slammed his fist into the bag. He had exposed Rana to the world for the murder of the minister of energy. The Pakistani government had pulled the contract and opened an investigation into the blackmail of the minister and the derailment of the train.

Bridget had called and had stopped by, but he had refused to talk to her. He hadn't wanted to see anyone right then. His mind was too focused on the past. Too focused on the weakling he had been. Ahmed slammed his fist into the punching bag again and again, beating the demons that haunted him. No more. He would never be that scared, helpless boy again.

"Ahmed!"

Ahmed jerked his head up from where he was pummeling the bag to find Tammy Davies standing on the top of the stairs leading down to the basement. She rested one hand on her slightly rounded belly and gripped the railing hard with her other hand. Her wide eyes showed her shock at his appearance. He hadn't shaved since he got back from New Delhi. He hadn't had time. His normally well-kept hair was hanging loose around his face and a lock had fallen into his eye.

"What are you doing here?" Ahmed sniped.

"The Rose sisters were worried about you. Miss Violet made you a basket of your favorites. She says you haven't been in the café since you got back and she was worried you weren't eating. I can see why now. You look horrible. Have you eaten anything since you got back?" Tammy asked with concern.

"I don't know. I've been a little busy." Ahmed knew that was a lie. Food hadn't held any appeal to him for days now. The only thing fueling him was his hatred and need for revenge.

"Ahmed, you were there when Pierce and I needed you. Let us return the favor. What can I do to help you?" Tammy asked gently as she slowly made her way down the stairs.

"You can go home. I don't need any help."

"Haven't you learned yet that we're your friends and friends help each other?"

"I don't need friends and I don't need help. Go away."

"Ahmed," Tammy gasped. When he looked back up, the little sprite of a woman with her blonde, spiky hair was storming toward him. "You can pull this crap with Bridget and the rest of this town, but not with me. If I have to, I will drag that incredibly hot ass of yours upstairs, strip you naked, and throw you into the shower. It's a tough job, but someone has to do it."

Ahmed fought the smile. Tammy barely reached his chin, yet there she stood with her hands on her hips and eyes flashing with pure determination. She'd had a crush on him when they'd first met, but their relationship had quickly turned platonic. Quite honestly, she was more of a sibling to him than his brother was. "I think Pierce may take issue with that."

"He'd understand. Besides, these darn pregnancy hormones have me all over the place. He'd probably thank you for taking me off his hands for a while. Now, move it."

"Where am I moving it to?" Ahmed pulled off his gloves and took a deep breath. His stomach rumbled and Tammy just gave him an "I told you so" look.

"Upstairs. Shower. Shave. Then you're taking your friend out to lunch. I'm starving." Tammy turned on her heel and headed back upstairs knowing he'd follow.

Ahmed followed Tammy down the sidewalk and into the café. He just wanted to get this over with and get back home. He wanted to see if he could hack into Rana's network to get a lead on Sergei.

The café was packed and as soon as he entered he saw Bridget sitting in the back with Annie. He didn't notice the way the place suddenly went quiet or the way he was suddenly surrounded by three white-haired ladies until it was too late.

"Ladies," he said with a hint of warning in his voice.

"We need to talk. But first you need to eat. Bless your heart, you look awful." Miss Violet shoved him down into a chair, and Miss Daisy placed a plate of fried chicken in front of him.

"Eat," Miss Lily ordered. Ahmed narrowed his eyes and felt Miss Violet's wooden spoon crack against his head.

"Don't sass us. Now eat. And if you get up before that plate is clean, I'll have Marshall arrest you," Miss Violet ordered.

Ahmed looked behind him and saw Marshall Davies, the sheriff, along with two of his deputies, Noodle and Dinky, guarding the door. Willing to risk another hit with the spoon, he narrowed his eyes and glared at them. Noodle and Dinky shifted uncomfortably but held their ground. Marshall just glared back. Those damn Davies men. They were an odd bunch. So much like Ahmed, yet they had the joy of life in them. Wives, children, happiness . . . It was what his life should have been.

The chair across from him scraped and Cy sat down casually. "What's up?"

Ahmed just stared at him. Cy's Hollywood good looks were deceiving. He was the most dangerous person in the café besides himself. "Don't."

"Cut the crap, Ahmed. Everyone here knows something's up. What can we do to help?"

"Nothing. You of all people should know better than to ask," Ahmed hissed under his breath. The whole freaking town was trying to listen.

"Now that you mention it, I remember I asked you for help and you gave it. It's about time I returned the favor."

"Fine. I need some bank records." If Cy could get that for him, he'd have more time for training.

"Done." Cy stood up and walked out of the café as soon as Ahmed gave him the information.

Ahmed raised his eyes and met Bridget's concerned gaze. He should talk to her, but he couldn't. Every time he thought about her, images of his wife filled his head. Except with those images, it was Bridget's body falling to the ground while Sergei stood smiling over her as she bled to death.

He shook the image from his mind, ate his chicken at a record pace, and ignored everyone else who came and talked to him. Shoving the empty plate across the table, he stood up and looked around. "Happy?"

Miss Violet pursed her lips but gave him a quick nod. "Be back tonight for dinner or I'll hunt you down myself." Ahmed ignored her but then a broom crashed down on his head. Dammit. These women were going to give him a headache.

"Did you hear my sister?" Miss Lily asked with her hands on her hips.

"Yes, ma'am."

"Good. Now, get whatever is struck up your craw out and tell us what's going on. We just want to help. You're part of this town and we help our own."

"You got dinner. Don't push it." Ahmed turned and strode to the door. He was halfway there when he felt the broom crack into his head again. He stopped and took a deep breath. When he looked up, he saw Marshall's laughing face.

"She'll do it until you give in and tell them. You're about to experience a type of interrogation no training has prepared you for."

"Get out of my way, Sheriff." Ahmed was itching for a fight. He knew at least it would be a challenge with Marshall. As if sensing it, Noodle and Dinky took a step away from them. Marshall kept his relaxed pose, but the smile froze on his face.

"If you need to blow off steam, I'll be happy to help you with that, but being an asshole to your friends isn't called for. I'll say this once. We're here to help. You've helped us all numerous times in the past, and we are happy to repay the favor. If that help is just someone to fight, then I'll be happy to oblige you. But if you don't want another broom to your head, you better curb the attitude."

"You have no idea what this is about or what I need to do. Now get out of my way."

"Are you going to make me?" Marshall's relaxed posture was gone as he stepped into Ahmed's face.

"Let him go, Marshall." Marcy Davies, Marshall's mother, said from a booth.

Ahmed heard her stand up and walk toward them. He felt her soft touch on his arm and looked down at her. "You're not alone in this. But we will let you go for now. Just know you're never alone." Marshall moved away from the door and Ahmed gave her one last look before storming out.

Bridget sat with a death grip on her knife and fork as she watched Ahmed bite off anyone's head who dared to talk to him. When he stormed out of the café, she felt the whole place start to breathe again. Soon she could hardly hear Annie as people speculated about what was going on with Ahmed. They still loved him. They were still worried about him. They were all wondering how to help him. But how do you help the man who had just treated them so dreadfully?

She dropped her knife and fork, which effectively cut off Annie's speculations. He'd shut her out ever since New Delhi. He refused to take her calls. Refused to see her when she knocked at his door. She'd had enough.

"I think it's time I had a little talk with our resident grouch."

"You go, girl," Annie said with a smile as Bridget dropped some money on the table.

"Damn straight." Ahmed was looking for a fight; well, so was she.

Bridget pulled her car to a stop in front of Ahmed's house. Anger and righteous indignation fueled her through the front door Ahmed had mistakenly left unlocked. Zoti trotted forward and wagged his tail. She knew where he'd be. There was a gym in the basement. She gave Zoti a quick pat and threw open the door to the basement. She heard him working the bag before she even started down the stairs.

Not bothering to announce herself, she walked down the steps. She even ignored him when he stopped to stare at her in surprise. She walked over to the bench and picked up the spare set of gloves and shoved her hands into them. She turned toward him and before he could say a word, she punched him in the face.

"Is this what you need?" she shouted. Ahmed took the shot and she could see anger darken his eyes, but he didn't move. She swung again, connecting with his jaw. "You think you can just shut everyone out?" This time he did move. He raised his hands and they faced off.

"You need to learn when to back off. This is not any of your business," he said in his cold voice.

"And you need to realize you're being an asshole." Bridget dodged a punch and connected with his stomach. He didn't even grunt as he advanced on her with a flurry of punches.

"You have *no* idea what Sergei has done! None!"

"That's because you won't tell me." Bridget took a shot to her shoulder and shoved him back.

"It is personal. He has to die and I have to be the one to kill him. He has been allowed to hurt too many people." He dodged her attack and took her feet out from under her with a quick kick-sweep.

"I can help you, but you're shutting everyone out." Bridget rolled, grabbed his legs, and pulled him down onto the mat with her. He grabbed her leg and flipped her under him.

"That's because it is my fault he is still around. I should have killed him a long time ago. But *you* need to back off. You need to forget all about me. Stop calling me, stop coming by . . . just stop." Ahmed pinned her to the mat and sat straddling her as sweat dripped down his face.

"I can't," she snapped, looking up at him.

"Why not?" Ahmed yelled back in frustration.

"Because I'm in love with you." Bridget took advantage of his stunned silence and, with a quick thrust of her hips, sent Ahmed flying over her head. She turned and pinned him to the ground before he reacted.

"You can't be. No one can."

"That's just because you're too scared to open yourself up to it." She pushed off his shoulders and stood up. She ripped the gloves from her hands and stormed up the stairs with the admission of love causing her body to shake. She had grown interested in him when she had studied him in the military. She had felt a connection to him that she discounted as admiration. But when Mo had introduced them, she had been instantly attracted to his mystery, kindness, and loyalty. Over the course of their meetings, she'd slowly fallen in love with him. But she was a proud woman and she wasn't going to beg. No, it was his turn to beg.

"Oh no, y'all drank the whole thing," Morgan Davies groaned as she looked at the empty pitcher of the Rose sisters' special iced tea. Morgan, who was married to the eldest Davies brother, Miles, had stopped by after work to see how Bridget was doing.

Bridget was surprised. Morgan had been friendly, but she and Miles were the quietest couple in their group. Morgan told her Annie had called and reported on the scene at the café. Having married a man who was the silent type, Morgan came to offer her support. It appeared everyone had known about the crush Bridget thought she had hidden so well. Or at least all the Davies women knew about it.

Within the hour, all the Davies women were at the apartment. Gemma brought the tea and those who weren't pregnant had happily poured a glass. Soon Bridget was spilling her heart. Surprisingly, she felt better. A lot better.

"Katelyn, you look a little off. You okay?" Paige asked.

"Yeah. This kid has decided to stay in a little longer. My bladder makes an excellent pillow." Everyone turned to the knock at the back door. "Oh, that's Marshall. He's here to pick me up." Katelyn hoisted herself up and gave Bridget a hug. "I'm so proud of you. There's a lot we don't know about Ahmed, but I have a feeling he'll come around. Just know that when he does, it'll be the hardest thing he's ever done.

You've already put him in his place. Just make sure you're there for him when he comes to you."

Bridget gave a little smile and walked Katelyn to the door. "Thank you. I had never thought of it like that. I don't think it'll happen, though. He's not interested in me. I've just been too involved in my schoolgirl crush to realize it."

"If you say so," Katelyn said with a look that told Bridget she didn't believe a word of it.

"We'd better get going, too. You call us if you need anything at all," Annie said before stopping and giving Bridget a hug.

Bridget waved goodbye to the group of women and locked the door. It took heartbreak, but she had gained friends. Real friends. Tonight she felt as if she were truly a part of them. She made her way to the bedroom and closed the door. Marko had fallen asleep an hour ago and was snoring away on the bed. She kicked off her pants and pulled her shirt over her head then padded into the bathroom and turned on the shower. Stepping under the hot spray let her muscles relax.

Ahmed took a sip of beer and dropped his head against the back of his couch. What had happened today? He'd been ambushed by the town and beaten up by the woman he loved. And she said that she loved him.

What had he done when she had the courage to confess her love? He'd sent her away. But, he had to. He couldn't put her in danger. He had to keep her safe and the only way to do that was to keep her away from him.

Zoti's head shot up and a low growl resonated from his throat. Ahmed's eyes snapped open and he pulled his gun. Zoti got off the couch and slowly made his way to the door. His nose sniffed the air and he growled again. Someone was outside.

Ahmed hugged the wall, avoiding the windows as he made his way to the front door. He barely moved the curtain and looked out into the dark night. He didn't see anyone. He opened the door and looked out and then down. He felt the blood rush from his head as he stared at the blanket folded around a picture. The picture was of Bridget and the blanket that was wrapped around it was his son's.

Chapter Five

B ridget leaned her head under the spray and washed the
shampoo from her hair. The shower had relaxed her a bit, but
it hadn't given her any ideas for erasing Ahmed from her
mind. Slowly, she became angry with herself for not being able to
move on from the feelings she had developed over the hours they'd
spent together every week.

Water trickled down her body as she reached for the conditioner
and froze. The house's feel had changed suddenly. It could have
been the squeak of the door or the creak of a floorboard, but it was
enough to cause Bridget to step out of the shower, grab the gun from
the sink, and dart behind the bathroom door. Where was Marko? She
only prayed that the intruder hadn't harmed him. It was strange that
he hadn't barked.

She watched the doorknob slowly and quietly turn. The door
swung open and stopped just before it hit her. A shadow entered the
room and stopped. She couldn't see who it belonged to but suddenly
a hand was on the door and it was slammed shut.

"Drop the gun," she said coolly as she leveled the gun at the
intruder's heart.

"With pleasure," Ahmed lowered his gun and slid it back into his
holster as he rocked back on his heels. Bridget felt his eyes travel the
length of her naked body. His eyes darkened and she flushed as she
saw his reaction to her. Maybe he wasn't so unaffected after all.

Bridget lowered her gun while ignoring the fact she was nude. She'd been in war with men. Modesty went out the window when you had to go to the bathroom in the desert without a palm tree in sight. "What are you doing sneaking into my bathroom? I could have killed you."

"Most women don't take a gun into the shower with them," Ahmed replied as his eyes dropped down her body once again. Marko trotted into the room and nudged Ahmed's hand, demanding an ear rub. Her traitorous dog was so not sharing her pillow tonight.

"Well, I'm not most women," Bridget said a little breathlessly.

The way he looked at her was enough to set her afire. "No, you certainly aren't," he said with a hint of admiration in his rough voice.

Bridget swallowed hard, refusing to lose control. She had to remember he was the one putting the distance between them, so she shouldn't fling herself onto him.

"Then can I ask what you're doing in my bathroom with a gun? Do you normally break into women's apartments while they're in the shower?" Bridget saw his eyes momentarily flash before his impenetrable mask fell back into place. "Oh my gosh. You've done this before," she accused as she put her hands on her hips and stared him down.

"That situation was very much like this one. The woman was in danger."

"The only danger I'm in is of shooting you."

"You can do that after I take you someplace safe."

"I'll do it right now if you don't start explaining yourself, Mr. Badass. You think you can just come into my house and order me around? I'm not some mindless little girl who does what daddy orders. I can take care of myself."

Ahmed reached into his pocket and pulled out a folded picture. He held it up and unfolded it. Bridget looked at the picture of herself smiling at her back door. It was from tonight when she was saying goodbye to the girls. "This was at my front door wrapped in a blanket—my murdered son's blanket."

Bridget didn't blink. She didn't even swear. Instead she let out a breath and gave a slight nod of her head. "I'll meet you in the living room."

Ahmed looked at Bridget standing confidently in the nude with nothing but a gun on and didn't move. She'd just dismissed him, but he was having trouble leaving. He'd spent the last eighteen years of his life learning how to control emotions and desires, but right now all his training was going out the window. He wanted to kiss Bridget with every ounce of pent-up feelings he had. He wanted to cup her breasts and caress them with his tongue. She was perfect. Her breasts were larger than he thought. She must have hidden them under sports bras. And the curve of her hips begged him to place his hand there and pull her close.

When Bridget let out an impatient sigh, he snapped out of his daydream and reluctantly left the room. It took everything he had not to strip and join her in the shower. Just one more reason he really needed to kill Sergei.

Ahmed reluctantly walked out of her room and ended up pacing in the living room as he waited for Bridget. Not only was he sexually frustrated, he was also more worried than he would care to admit. He and Bridget had spent hours and hours together every week for months. Just her presence had seemed to comfort his wounded soul and give him hope for a future he had never dreamed he could have. He was being forced to face his past failures. He hadn't been able to keep his wife and son alive and now Sergei was challenging him to keep Bridget alive.

He turned at the sound of bare feet padding down the carpeted hall and saw Bridget coming toward him. Her athletic frame was highlighted by tight black running pants and a fitted, light-pink, deep V-neck T-shirt. Her long wet hair had been pulled back into a single braid that hung down her back.

"Tell me about your son." Bridget sat down on the couch but Ahmed couldn't tell this story while sitting.

He paced in front of her and then stopped as he looked out the back window. "I was married on my eighteenth birthday." He didn't need to look at her to know she was surprised. He heard it in the way her breathing suddenly halted. "It was an arranged marriage between two overbearing fathers. I didn't want her, she didn't want me," Ahmed began. He started pacing again as he told her of his wife who hated him and the child he had only gotten to hold once.

"And this," Ahmed raised the blanket, "was my son's blanket. I had swaddled him in it myself. I found it on my doorstep with this picture of you inside it. It's a clear sign that Sergei is coming after you. He's challenging me to protect you because I failed to protect my wife and son."

"But why is Sergei coming after me? Sure, I helped you with his previous boss, but could he really know that? Does that mean everyone who helped rescue Gemma is now in danger?" Bridget asked. He finally looked at her. He should have known better than to expect her to leap into his arms asking for protection. Instead she was calm and completely sensible.

"He had Rana hire you to get a reaction. And with the reaction he got, Sergei knew . . ." Ahmed stopped before confessing his own feelings for Bridget.

"Knew that I loved you and therefore would punish me," Bridget completed as she stood up. "And that's what Rana meant when he asked if you could protect me."

"Yes and no." Ahmed looked at her. She had said she loved him, but would she still after all this was said and done?

"What do you mean?" Bridget stepped closer to him to pick up the picture of herself.

"Yes, this is what Rana meant. No, it wasn't about your feelings." Ahmed pulled out his phone and called Nabi. "I need two men over at Bridget's for the night—front and back," he told Nabi before hanging up the phone.

"I don't need people outside protecting me. I'm perfectly capable of protecting myself. And what do you mean it's not about me?"

"I know you're capable of protecting yourself. It's why I'm going against all my instincts and letting you stay here instead of throwing you over my shoulder and taking you someplace safe."

Ahmed couldn't stop himself from stepping toward her. He brushed a loose piece of hair from Bridget's cheek and cupped her face in his hands. Looking down at her he could see the battle of emotions on her face. She loved him and that knowledge bolstered his determination. "Bridget . . ." He said her name with the love he felt but couldn't voice.

"Yes?"

Ahmed ran his thumb over her cheek and when she tilted her head toward him he did something he hadn't done for eighteen years. He gave in to his desire. Lowering his lips, he gently placed them on hers. When she stepped into his arms, her hands hesitantly on his chest, he could no longer stop himself. It would be impossible to stop at one brush of the lips as he felt her soft body and warmth against his hardness.

His hands delved into her hair as he tilted her head farther in order to deepen the kiss. Ahmed ran his tongue along the seam of her lips, and when she opened to him he took full control of the kiss. She tasted like heaven. After living in hell for most of his life, he didn't want it to end.

Ahmed pulled her close to him and ran his hands down her back. Bridget moved her arms to his back and clung to him as she unconsciously pressed against him in need. Excitement coursed through him. He had to have her closer to him. Ahmed gently pushed her back against the wall and let some of his body weight press against her as he explored her with his hands.

With one hand Bridget grasped his hair and the other she ran over his shoulders. He felt one leg hook against his waist and he ran his hand up the back of her thigh until he was able to caress her bottom. Ahmed thrust himself forward and Bridget moaned into his mouth while he grabbed her other leg. She wrapped her legs around him and he pinned her to the wall with his lower body holding her up by her bottom.

"Ahem."

In one quick move, Ahmed dropped Bridget against the wall and covered her with his body while drawing his gun. He felt her steady herself with a hand to his shoulder, but when he saw her gun was similarly drawn and held out to his side he knew the tap was to let him know she had his back. It was a common technique used in the military.

"I am sorry to interrupt, but no one responded when I knocked. I got worried."

"Mo?" Bridget asked as her head popped up.

"Nabi told me you needed security and I wanted to see if there was anything I could do. But, it seems Ahmed has things well in hand."

Ahmed lowered his weapon and glared at his best friend. He felt a shove and realized Bridget was trying to get around him. He took a step forward and Bridget stepped out and slid the gun into the small of her back. How had he not felt that? He had been so caught up in the feel and taste of her that he had become oblivious to his surroundings. He could have gotten them killed. Ahmed felt the anger and resentment build. He had failed this test and he had failed himself yet again.

"Please, come in," Bridget said politely as she straightened her hair.

"No," Ahmed said shortly. "I have business with Mohtadi that I need to discuss in private. Goodnight." Ahmed gave her a quick bow of his head and shoved his friend out the door. He'd never been so angry with himself. He could have gotten her killed tonight if Sergei had shown up.

The crisp night air soothed him as Ahmed tried to calm down. All those years of training and he'd thrown them out the window the second she looked at him. How was he going to keep her safe while keeping his distance?

"Care to tell me what was going on in there?" Mo asked quietly, knowing Ahmed's posture was radiating with anger.

"Sergei threatened her." Ahmed handed him the photo and the blanket. "And I was too busy giving in to my fantasy that I dropped my guard. I've never let that happen since . . ."

"Since your son was killed. I take it this is his?" Mo asked with sadness.

"Yes."

"Well, I'm glad I came then. Your brother called. There are rumors of my cousin Sarif growing unhappy again. He's heading to the UN to make an appeal to grant him the right to control Rahmi."

"On what grounds?"

"He is trying to claim that my grandfather was born second and his own father was, in fact, born first. I'm so relieved my boys will not face this. Grandfather was born eighty-seven seconds before Sarif's father, but he has always said it was a lie. That the nurses got the order mixed up on the birth certificates. However, Grandfather was a smart man. When he was just a teenager, he knew this would eventually happen. His twin was resentful of being only seconds away from the crown and not having any of the power that went along with it.

"My grandfather persuaded my parents to find a very favorable marriage for him. Hence, he ended up marrying a queen. But my grandfather also gathered the doctor, nurse, and his parents to write out affidavits stating they knew him to be the first-born. Prayers were said and it was observed the baby had a birthmark in the shape of Rahmi, which they took as a sign that he would be a good ruler. A birthmark that not only my Grandfather had, but my father, my brothers, and I all have along with my sons. However, Sarif's side of the family did not inherit this birthmark."

"Does Sarif know about this?" Ahmed asked.

"No. And that is why your brother called. He wants you to go to the UN and stop Sarif before he makes his address. It's just an embarrassment to my father and during this turbulent economic time, he doesn't want oil investors thinking we're weak."

"And since Rana has been arrested, Sergei is looking for an employer at the same time Sarif is trying to overthrow your father."

"Exactly. How much do you want to bet they have teamed up again? They made a strong run at the throne before. I'm afraid they will try again. So is my father." Mo let out a frustrated sigh.

"I take it the jet is waiting." Ahmed made his way to his car and glanced around to make sure the guards were in place.

"Yes. I will make sure Bridget is protected while you are gone. And Ahmed, be warned. Sarif is dangerous. He's fueled with a level of hatred and resentment we cannot even begin to know."

Ahmed shook his friend's hand and got into the car. As he started the engine, he looked up and saw Bridget in the window. He wished he could tell her his true feelings. Someday this would be over; he just hoped he would emerge from this upcoming battle alive.

The knock at the door interrupted Ahmed's packing. It was a gentle knock — not one he was familiar with — and it certainly wasn't Bridget's. If she found out he was leaving, she would be beating down the door to find out where he was going. He zipped his suitcase and went to answer the door.

Ahmed hid his surprise at finding Marcy Davies standing at his front door. She held out a plastic container filled with cupcakes and smiled.

"Mrs. Davies? What can I do for you?" Ahmed asked.

"Oh, I hope I'm not disturbing you," Marcy said as she walked by Ahmed, through the living room and into his kitchen, all while taking in his house in one quick glance.

"You could never disturb me. Now, what can I do for you?"

Marcy grabbed a cupcake and shoved it into his hand as she made her way to the couch. She looked up, smiled at him, and patted the cushion next to her. "I have been thinking about you a lot recently, but after that incident in the café, I just felt compelled to see you. It occurred to me that while you have been here for everyone in Keeneston, and certainly my family, I have never heard about your family. I assume that is because you don't want to talk about them. But then again, you aren't what I'd call chatty."

Ahmed felt his lips quirk. "True."

"I don't even know if you have a mother or father," Marcy said, but by the way she stared him down it was clear it was actually a question.

"No. My father died in a rebellion when I was eighteen, and my mother just a short time before that."

"Well, you've taken care of my sons and now it's time for me to take care of you. Let me tell you a story." Marcy settled back into the couch and eyed the uneaten cupcake until Ahmed took a bite of it.

"It's good. Thank you."

"You're welcome, dear. Now, when I was sixteen years old, I met the most amazing man. He was tall, dark, and handsome. Not to mention the way he could sit on a horse. Do you know what the trouble was? He was with a Keeneston Belle," Marcy sneered. "Not just any Belle, but the queen bee. So when another boy asked me to the prom, I agreed. I thought it was the universe telling me Mr. Tall, Dark, and Handsome wasn't for me.

"The day before prom was our final exam for home economics. We had to prepare a dinner and then the teacher and the senior men from the prom court would judge it. I set my fried chicken down in front of Mr. Tall, Dark, and Handsome, and he took a bite then looked up at me. The way my toes curled and I couldn't look away told me the universe was wrong—this was the man for me, period. Do you know what I decided to do?"

Ahmed shook his head. He had no idea what this story was about and why she was holding him hostage with cupcakes and kindness. "What did you do?"

Marcy smiled and patted his knee. "I fought for him. I sent him brownies — and my brownies are magic — with a note from a secret admirer. The note had just enough hints that he could guess, but not know for sure, it was from me. Then I dressed for the prom and ignored him."

"What?" Ahmed wasn't expecting that.

"That's right. I was nice and looked drop-dead gorgeous. I strutted around prom with all the confidence in the world while he couldn't help wondering if I was the one who sent the note. Now, the Belle actually played into it by being caught making out with the star of the basketball team, who happened to be my date," Marcy explained and Ahmed just stared. "After a very public breakup, Mr. Tall, Dark, and Handsome was about to leave. I couldn't let that happen now, could I?"

"No?" Ahmed guessed.

"That's right. So I grabbed a cheese ball and threw it at him. Hit him right in the back of the head." Ahmed felt his eyes widen in surprise. "See, I couldn't run after him in the heels I was wearing. He turned slowly and I smiled. When he came over, he asked me to dance. I said I would only if he stopped being so stupid and saw the woman standing before him. The one who was not a Belle, was a good cook, and who had a slightly wild side. If he could take a chance on getting to know the real me, then I would take the chance of dancing with him."

"I take it you danced?" Ahmed asked.

"We did. And then when we were sitting in jail that night we talked about life, feelings, and love," Marcy sighed happily.

Ahmed did a double-take. "I'm sorry to interrupt. Did you say jail?"

"Oh, yes. We left the prom after that one dance and he took me to the lake right outside of town. We might have had a beer or two as we sat looking at the water while we got to know each other." Marcy smiled as she remembered that night. "Then he got the idea for us to strip down to our underwear and go swimming. And well, other stuff. Anyway . . . when we got out, I didn't want to put my dress on over my wet undergarments. And as he walked me home on the empty highway, Sheriff Mulford drove by. He was a stickler for the rules so I argued my bra and panties were actually a bathing suit, trying to get out of public indecency charges. Little did I know back then it was illegal for a woman to walk down the street in her bathing suit without a police escort — or a club. Sheriff Mulford booked me into jail and told Mr. Tall, Dark, and Handsome to go home. He didn't want to leave me so he punched Sheriff Mulford right in the face and was booked with me. That's when I knew I was in love."

"Mrs. Davies, I'd love to say I understood the purpose of this very interesting story, but I don't," Ahmed admitted.

"I'm getting there. We spent the night in jail, which I ask you not to mention to anyone," Marcy smiled innocently and Ahmed wondered what else she wasn't mentioning. "We talked and I took a chance and told him how I felt about him. Forty years later, we're still going strong."

"Mr. Davies punched the sheriff?"

"Sure did. Just to stay with me in jail. He's very romantic like that. Now, as to why I'm here. If I hadn't taken a chance and thrown that cheese ball at him, we might not be married today. The way you and Bridget look at each other is the way Jake and I look at each other. And since you don't have a mother to take you aside and tell you to never let go of love once you find it, here I am. And if anyone is capable of fighting for love, you are."

"I'm sorry to disappoint you, but I'm in no position to even contemplate love," Ahmed said stiffly as he stood up.

"You don't contemplate love, Ahmed. You grab it with both hands and hang on." Marcy stood up and patted his shoulder. "And eat those cupcakes, dear. You need them."

Ahmed walked Mrs. Davies to her car and shook his head. He didn't know which to be more surprised about. The fact that she and Jake fell in love in jail or that she actually came and gave him a lecture on love. Too bad he had to disappoint her. He wasn't good enough to love after all the things he'd done. Besides, he had a plane to catch and a man to kill.

Chapter Six

Standing at the window, Bridget looked out into the night as Ahmed drove away. She had been breathless with passion just moments before and then he just walked away. She was completely embarrassed. Had she been that bad? She knew she didn't have that much experience, but it had seemed pretty wonderful to her. However, right now there was something she needed to attend to, and it was even more important than trying to figure out men.

Bridget picked up her cell phone and dialed her father. When it went to voicemail, she tried the office. It was the middle of the night, but she knew her father could be at the office for days at a time when there were emergencies.

"Pentagon. Office of the Chief," a tired woman answered.

"Bridget Springer for General Ward," Bridget tried to say politely as she tapped her fingers on the kitchen island.

"I'm sorry, but the general is unavailable at this time. Can I take a message?"

"I don't mean to be difficult, but this is his daughter and I need to speak with my father."

"I'm sorry, but . . ."

"No. It doesn't work like that. At least go tell him I'm on the phone before you decide if he'll talk to me."

Bridget heard the woman grit her teeth. "Hold." Bridget tapped her foot and waited. Her father's secretaries usually knew to put her through no matter what. It was a policy that he had since she was a little girl. "I'll put you through, Miss Springer." The secretary didn't sound particularly happy about it, but before Bridget could apologize for the urgency, she was being patched through.

"What is it, pumpkin?"

"I need your help. Sergei has targeted me," Bridget told him before explaining the picture Ahmed had brought to her.

"I told you I didn't want you involved. I'm sending someone for you."

"No, Daddy. I know you don't want to hear this, but I'll do whatever it takes to help Ahmed, whether he likes it or not."

"Pumpkin . . ."

"Daddy, I'll do this with or without your help."

She heard her father step out of the room he was in and into a quiet space. "There have been some developments here. I'm working with the president's men. We know Sergei has entered the US. We just didn't know why. With what you're telling me, we know he was in Kentucky this evening, but our intel is saying he'll be at the UN meeting this week. Delegations arrive in the morning and will be here for the week," her father explained.

"Is that why you're in lockdown?"

"Yes. We're coordinating security with the Secret Service for the best way to capture him. We've heard rumors of Sarif Ali Rahman contemplating an overthrow of Rahmi. Considering what happened last time he did that, we think the two have teamed up again."

"I need to help. I have to find Sergei. My life isn't the only one dependent on it."

Bridget heard her father sigh and then the noise started again. "Agent Woodberry, I'm assigning Bridget Springer to your team."

"The dog lady?"

"The dog lady," her father confirmed.

"Bridget, meet with Agent Woodberry tomorrow at the UN. Bring Marko. I might as well put you to work."

"And conveniently have me guarded by the Secret Service." Bridget almost felt like stomping her foot. Some fathers grounded their children, but her father stuck government agencies on her. It was like she was fourteen all over again when she snuck out of the house to go to a party one night. The next day there was an off-duty military police officer trailing her.

"That's my best offer."

"Fine," Bridget said as she rolled her eyes.

"Pumpkin?"

"Yes, Daddy?"

"He'd better be worth it, 'cause right now I'm going to kill him for putting you in this position. Just promise me you'll be safe."

"He's worth it. And he didn't put me anywhere I didn't put myself. Thank you, Daddy." Bridget hung up the phone and went to pack a bag. Ahmed may think he was protecting her, but she wasn't going to sit back and wait for Prince Charming to save her. No, this princess was going to kick a little ass.

Ahmed blended into the shadows surrounding the embassy. He had spent the last two days observing the comings and goings of the Surman embassy and hadn't been able to catch a glimpse of either Sarif or Sergei. The first day he arrived he'd tried to talk to Sarif, but they wouldn't allow him past the gate.

Sarif was scheduled to talk tomorrow at the UN and time was running out. He was going to have to break into the embassy to find Sarif tonight. Ahmed looked up at the six-foot cement fence topped with a decorative iron railing. Cameras sat on every corner, and he was pretty sure there were motion detectors attached as well.

He had found a weakness at the back gate. Every night a dry cleaner's truck came in. The guards didn't bother to check inside the van. He figured he could leap in a couple blocks from the embassy. Stepping from the shadows, he started down the street opposite the embassy. A car's engine slowing caught his attention and he ducked back into the shadows.

A black SUV with dark-tinted windows came to a stop at the back gate. The window rolled down and Ahmed froze. Sergei. The gate opened and Sergei drove through. Ahmed looked down the street and saw two more SUVs approaching. Keeping to the shadows, he sprinted toward them. The first SUV pulled to the gate and was waved through. Ahmed reached the second SUV as it slowed to turn into the drive. Ahmed ran up from behind it and before it could slow to a stop, he yanked the back door open and grabbed whoever was sitting there.

The man was so surprised he fell from the SUV as the others started screaming. The guards at the gate aimed their weapons and fired as Ahmed dragged the man into the street. He struggled, but Ahmed just pressed the knife into his side hard enough to draw blood. "Cooperate and I won't kill you." Ahmed knew he had him when the man screamed as he dug the knife deeper. It was hard to find good mercenaries these days.

Ahmed tightened his hold and hauled the man into the dark before the others could even get out of the car. He dragged his captive between the buildings until he reached his car three blocks away.

"What are you going to do with me?" the man asked as Ahmed raised the trunk and stuffed him in.

"We're going to have a little talk." Ahmed slammed the trunk closed and got into the car. Darkness knotted in his stomach. Before Sergei, he never would have imagined doing what he was about to do. Now it was second nature. And that exact reason is why Bridget deserved someone better than him.

Hours later, Ahmed dragged the unconscious man from the abandoned building and tossed him into the passenger's seat. His mouth was covered with duct tape and his hands and feet were bound. He wouldn't be waking up anytime soon. Now Ahmed just needed to figure out what to do with him. It wasn't like he could walk a bloody and unconscious man into the police station. He had fought the darkness in him that called for death. Images of Bridget stopped him. She would have been disappointed in him. Somehow that thought had stopped him from killing the man; instead, he'd just knocked him out and shoved him in the car.

It really hadn't taken that much persuasion to get the man to talk. Ahmed knew the schedule and how many guards were there. He also told him they were most worried about obtaining Saudi Arabia's permission to attack Rahmi. Sarif was meeting with the representative from Saudi Arabia the next morning and if he got their blessing, Sarif would go forward with his speech in the afternoon. Since Sarif was refusing to talk to him, Ahmed would just go to the Saudis. Without their support, Sarif's rebellion would be dead in the water.

The Saudi embassy was close to the city's main State Department building, which was close to the UN. Ahmed made up his mind and turned down First Avenue. He could drive by and dump the man there. Surely he was on some terrorist list and the State Department would happily take care of him.

Ahmed approached the UN and spotted Bridget immediately. What was she doing here? She smiled at one of the agents and he felt her eyes move to the street. It was as if they were drawn to each other. He was hidden from view by dark tinting, but he still felt her see him.

Slamming on the brakes, Ahmed knew what to do. He fought the urge to leap from the car and kiss Bridget, showing her how much he'd missed her. He hadn't realized just how much he had fallen into the void of revenge until he thought of her . . . his light, his hope, and his dream for the future.

Bridget arrived at the UN with the Secret Service for the third morning in a row to help sweep the UN building for bombs. She hadn't heard from or seen Sarif, Sergei, or Ahmed. She was beginning to think her dad had sent her here to keep her safe. She just hoped Ahmed was safe. He was battling demons and she couldn't help worrying that he would do anything to achieve his revenge.

"Springer," Agent Woodberry called to her from across the stage of the UN, "are we clear?"

"Yes, sir. All clear."

"Good. The vice president is arriving soon. We need to meet the teams out front." Bridget tossed Marko a tennis ball and played with him as she made her way out front.

She stepped out into the cold fall morning and approached the street with Agent Woodberry. As she stood talking with him, she saw a car driving down First Avenue. She didn't know why she was drawn to it, but as Agent Woodberry talked, she kept her eye on it. When the tires squealed, she darted out into the street with her gun drawn. Something wasn't right. The door opened and a man was shoved to the ground. In the split second before the door shut, she saw him. It was Ahmed.

"Springer, get back!" Agent Woodberry called as he shoved her behind him and yelled the details of the car into his radio.

Agents stopped traffic and surrounded the man in the street. Bridget pushed her way forward and looked down at him. She breathed a sigh of relief when she saw his eyes start to flutter. "Isn't he one of Sergei's men?" Bridget asked innocently. She knew the answer. That's the only reason Ahmed would have this man.

"Sergei?" Agent Woodberry said with wonder. He was only one of the most wanted men in the world and to nab an associate of his would be major in terms of his career. "Quick, call the director and tell them of our capture," Woodberry said as he hauled the man up and waved for a car to be brought around.

"McDowell, you're in charge of the vice president's arrival. I'm taking this bastard in."

Bridget tried not to smile. While they would look into the car that dropped him so nicely wrapped at their feet, they would never find Ahmed. And further, the man they arrested would rather face Sergei than Ahmed so he'd keep his mouth shut. She had wondered if she would find Ahmed and now she knew she didn't need to worry. He'd find her.

Chapter Seven

Ahmed stood still as he waited for the representative of the sheik. After a phone call from Mo to the ambassador of Saudi Arabia, Ahmed had headed over to the embassy to meet with him. He stood in the luxurious sitting room and glanced around at the pillowed couches with gold accents. A large table sat next to a fireplace with a roaring fire inside. The table had an ornate chair at the head that he assumed was for the sheik or his representative.

The door opened and Ahmed turned and bowed to the group of men who entered. "Thank you for agreeing to see me."

"Of course. Rahmi is a neighbor of ours. What was so important that it could not wait?" the representative asked as he took a seat in the elaborately carved chair at the head of the table.

Ahmed bowed his head, asking permission to sit. The man lowered his chin to his chest quickly and Ahmed took a seat. "I'm afraid it is in regard to King Sarif. We have heard he intends to speak at the United Nations this afternoon to lay out his case for a coup in Rahmi."

"We have heard this, too."

"But, what you haven't heard is there is evidence his claims to the throne are nothing more than delusions of a greedy and irresponsible man longing only for power." Ahmed kept his eyes locked with the representative and then handed the package of copied documents to one of the men surrounding the room.

The man took the package, walked around the table to his boss, and handed it to him. The room was silent except for the sound of each page being placed on the table as the man read through the package.

"This is very interesting, Mr. Ahmed."

"It's just Ahmed. His Royal Highness King Ali Rahman felt he could trust you and your sheik with this information. His Royal Highness does not like to discuss such family matters in public. I am sure you understand."

"Yes. His Highness does understand and does not wish to be involved in family squabbles. He has enough of his own to deal with."

"King Ali Rahman is sympathetic to that and wishes to keep our relations strong. His daughter speaks highly of your country since she married one of the sheik's sons and the king wishes me to convey that should the sheik desire to meet, he'll be more than welcome at the palace."

With a nod from the representative, Ahmed stood up and gave a slight bow before turning to leave. "Ahmed, the Sheik of Sheiks also bid me to invite you to our palace should you tire of life in the United States."

"Thank you for such an honor." Ahmed bowed again. The sheik had been trying to lure him away from Rahmi for years. It was now almost a joke between them. As Ahmed headed out of the room, he heard the representative order one of his men to call King Sarif and tell him the sheik had withdrawn his support for Sarif's appearance before the UN and to cancel their meeting.

Ahmed dialed his phone as he walked down the street, waiting for Mo to pick up. "It's done. Saudi Arabia is withdrawing their support. And tell your father to invite the sheik to the palace. I got the impression it would be a welcome break from his own family matters."

Bridget pulled the collar of her jacket up and pushed herself farther down the cold, damp path. The sun had set hours ago, but the path in Central Park was lined with lampposts as she and Marko ran off the frustrations of the day.

Just as she thought, Ahmed had left no clues as to his identity. Secret Service had found the car just a mile away. It had been wiped clean and left with a full tank of gas. The owner of the car had been identified as eighty-three-year-old Zelda Barkowitz of Upper Manhattan. After meeting with her, Agent Woodberry's ego had been deflated. While he'd been credited with the capture of the man with ties to Sergei's terrorist group, he had been thwarted in identifying the driver of the vehicle.

Bridget had been left with the group of agents who looked after the vice president during his speech. Afterward, she had finished her security detail and had heard from agents that the terrorist they captured was unwilling to talk about the driver of the car. Bridget had smiled as she said goodnight and headed back to her hotel.

She'd opened the door, flipped on the lights, and let out a frustrated breath. She felt foolish as she looked around her empty room, as a part of her had expected to find Ahmed sitting in the chair waiting to see her. Marko had grabbed his toy and started to leap around the room with pent-up energy. Bridget, too, had pent-up frustration not knowing Ahmed's whereabouts. So, she'd put on her tennis shoes and had taken Marko for a run.

Marko trotted happily by her side as they shot out of Central Park and ran down Fifth Avenue. It was only a little over a mile and a half to her hotel from there and Marko was happy for the opportunity to stretch his legs even more.

Bridget weaved her way around the people walking down the sidewalk as she drew closer to her hotel. She slowed to a walk as the hotel came into view. Marko nudged her leg with his head as his tongue lolled out of his mouth.

"Come on, big boy. Let's get you some dinner and me a shower."

Bridget pushed through the door and the two of them rode the elevator to her room. Opening her door, she once again felt disappointed when she found it empty. After feeding Marko, she stripped off her shirt and made her way to the bathroom, leaving her running attire strewn along the floor.

The hot water felt great after her run. She was surprised, though, that Ahmed hadn't come yet. She had been so sure that he would find her. The longer she thought about it, the more she talked herself out of it. He hadn't bothered to tell her where he was going or even that he was leaving.

The shower curtain rustled and Bridget smiled as she turned. Ahmed had finally come. The curtain was pushed open and a black nose poked through, followed by Marko's happy face. He looked up at Bridget and she heard his tail thump the tiled floor.

"I guess it's just you and me tonight."

Bridget turned off the water and got out of the shower. Her stomach rumbled as she dried her hair and got dressed in a light sweater and a pair of jeans. "I'll be right back, boy," she cooed to Marko as she shut the door to his crate.

The restaurant in the hotel was filled with a mix of lawyers, businessmen, politicians, security, and tourists. She waved at the table of Secret Service men who had been brought up from Washington for the week and took a seat at the bar.

"What can I get for you?" the bartender asked as he checked her out.

"Two burgers to go, please." He gave her a smile and went to place the order. Bridget kept glancing at the entrance. She knew Ahmed wasn't coming, but she couldn't stop hoping she was wrong. She wanted to feel him to make sure he was safe. She wanted to find out what she could do to help. There were few things worse than not knowing the whole story when she was involved in it.

"Here are your burgers. Are you sure you don't want to stay for a drink? My shift ends in fifteen minutes," the handsome bartender asked. Bridget felt herself blush. She wasn't used to men asking her out.

"What? Springer's getting hit on."

"Shut up, Sweeney." Bridget stood up and gave the bartender an embarrassed little smile as the table of agents whooped with laughter. "Thanks for asking. Goodnight." Bridget flipped off the table of agents making kissy noises as she walked by them. And her friends wondered why she hadn't dated much.

"I'm back," Bridget called out to Marko as she pushed the door open with her shoulder, balancing the burgers.

"What are you doing here?"

Bridget's eyes shot up and met Ahmed's angry eyes.

"How did you find me?" he accused.

Bridget refused to recoil at his anger. "I'm working. What does it look like I'm doing?"

"You knew I was here. I saw you this morning. You weren't surprised at all when I dumped Sergei's man at your feet."

"You're not the only one with sources. And I'm trying to help you. Unfortunately, you're too blinded by revenge to notice I could be an asset to you."

"I don't need your help. I work alone." Ahmed pushed away from the window and strode toward her.

"Not when it involves us, you don't." Bridget held her ground. He may look as if he could explode at any moment, but she knew there was a caring heart buried underneath all that anger. His freezing glare and deadly voice didn't scare her. Instead it pissed her off.

"There is no us. You're only putting yourself in danger coming here. You need to go home right now."

"I know exactly what I'm doing. Can you say the same? And you can forget about me going home. I'm staying until *we* catch Sergei."

Ahmed stopped in front of her and stared her down. Bridget just stared back, ignoring the fact he was standing close enough for her to feel the heat radiating off him. "Why are you doing this?"

"Simple. I told you I love you. Do you think I'm so weak that I'd just sit at home while some crazy man is out there trying to kill us? I was taught to strike first, and if you're not going to work with me, I'll just do it myself."

"It's not your fight."

"It is now, so get over this lone-wolf act. I love you. You're not alone. Now deal with it," Bridget yelled. She felt steam practically blowing from her ears as she pushed past him.

Ahmed grabbed her arm and pulled her back. Bridget's hands curled into his shirt to keep from falling. She felt his heart beating and the dips and ridges of his body under her hands. Bridget swallowed hard, her mouth suddenly dry as she looked up into his dark eyes. Gone was the anger; gone was the steely determination of revenge. In its place was a look of such kindness Bridget felt she'd melt.

He lowered his head toward hers, gently brushing his lips against hers. His hold loosened until he was trailing his fingers lightly down her arms. He wrapped his arms around her and pulled her close. Reaching up, Bridget cupped his face and made him look at her. His eyes were tired. His five-o'clock shadow tickled her hand as she traced his bottom lip with her thumb. Right then she knew she had made the right decision. Ahmed had been alone for so long he didn't know how to ask for help. The conflicted man she held needed help even if he didn't want to admit it.

Ahmed turned his head in her hand and placed a kiss on her palm. Bridget raised her lips and kissed him. He may not love her; he may not even be capable of love. But she had enough love for them both. She felt his muscles relax under her touch as he lost himself in the kiss. Their tongues slowly explored each other as their hands traveled over each other's arms and back.

When Bridget ran her hand down the ripples of his stomach toward his pants, his kiss turned from soft exploration to a demanding lover. Bridget's heart pounded as she, too, grew demanding. She freed his shirt from his pants and pulled the black, tight, long-sleeved shirt over his head so she could finally see what she'd been feeling. His hands were on her then, fast and eager, as they slid under her sweater.

"Springer? Come on, open the door. I hear you in there. Are you getting naked for me?" Bridget and Ahmed froze, and she groaned the second she saw his eyes cloud over and felt his muscles tense up. She felt him practically growl.

"Don't move, please. It's just assignments for tomorrow," Bridget said in the calm voice she used when trying to reassure the dogs she trained. "Coming," she snapped, all the while keeping her eyes locked on Ahmed's.

"He's a dead man."

"No, he's just an idiot. He's harmless."

He shook his head and she knew she had lost him. "I can't be distracted like this. Go home. Please." He turned and walked through the connecting door she hadn't even realized had been opened. Within seconds he had disappeared behind closed doors and locks.

"Springer, stop primping and open the door. I'll screw you no matter what you're wearing . . . or not wearing."

Bridget yanked open the door with such force he stepped back a bit. "Dammit, Sweeney, what do you want?"

"Here are your assignments for tomorrow. What, are you on the rag?" Sweeney smirked. She was sure he'd been the guy in college who popped his collar and thought he was so awesome. He'd been riding her hard during the whole assignment—teasing her at every opportunity. He asked where she hid her tampons and who she'd slept with to be up here playing with the big boys.

"No, I'm just tired of putting up with your bullshit. Insecure men with small dicks who don't know how to use them are a pain in the ass." She slammed the door in his face and fell back onto the bed in a huff. One good thing about being private security was if she got fired, she wouldn't be court-martialed.

Ahmed smirked as he listened to Bridget unload on Agent Sweeney. He had been tempted to make the man disappear, but she seemed to be handling him all on her own. He tossed his shirt onto the chair by the bed, kicked off his shoes, and finished what Bridget started. Once naked, he paused at the connecting doors once again. She was just a couple of inches away from him and the thought made him reach for the doorknob.

He shook his head and let his hand drop. Sergei was after her, and if he lost his focus, he knew what would happen to her. He had to keep his distance. Whenever he touched her, he forgot about Sergei and the danger they were in. The darkness faded and emotions he'd buried long ago tried to make their way out.

Instead of going to her, he turned his back on the door and walked to the bed. He lay down with his hands behind his head and stared at the door. With the deal between Saudi Arabia and Sarif dead in the water, Sergei would get busy with a new cause. Fortunately, Ahmed was pretty sure that new cause would be him. Ahmed had left enough evidence of his visit to the embassy that it would be easy for Sergei to find out it was Ahmed who had killed Sarif's chance for the throne. He'd done it on purpose, hoping it would cause Sergei to turn his full attention to him. It was time the two of them ended this. He wasn't sure why Sergei had decided to come after him eighteen years ago, but it didn't matter anymore. It was time for it to end, and the only way that was going to happen was for one of them to die.

Sergei swept the table with his arm, sending the phone, papers, and a laptop flying. That bastard had done it again. He'd somehow turned the Saudis against them. Sarif had just come into the room in the embassy Sergei was using to plan the takeover of Rahmi and told him that it was Ahmed who was spotted at the Saudi embassy meeting with the sheik's personal representative this morning. Minutes after the meeting, Sarif had received the phone call that the sheik had decided to support Rahmi. In fact, the sheik was going to be visiting Rahmi to meet with his friend, King Ali Rahman, next month.

To make matters worse, one of Sergei's men had been abducted last night and then tossed on the street in front of a group of Secret Service agents. There was no telling what the man told the Americans. It really was hard finding reliable men.

"Come. Pack everything up. It's time to leave this place. It's too dangerous to stay. There are too many questions about why I cancelled my speech this afternoon. We'll leave for home in the morning," Sarif ordered.

"Are you wishing to terminate my contract?" Sergei asked. With a flick of a wrist, some men started packing up the room.

"No. I think I need you more than ever now," Sarif said cryptically as he walked out of the room.

Chapter Eight

When Bridget worked for the government, she reverted back to military time. She was awake by zero five-hundred and dragging Marko out from under the covers to go for a walk. When she stepped outside in the dark of the morning, delivery trucks were roaring past the hotel, taxis were lined up, and people were trudging down the sidewalk with coffee in their hands.

Bridget walked past the embassies near the United Nations as Marko kept his nose to the ground and sniffed every tree they passed, deeming them too inferior to lift his leg on. A cold wind swept down the street and Bridget buried her chin into her scarf and shivered.

"Come on, Marko, or you'll have to hold it all day. Our first assignment starts in an hour." Marko just grunted and walked to the end of his twenty-foot leash to investigate the next tree.

"So, you're the one he's chosen." Bridget shivered at the sound of the voice that exuded pure hatred.

She turned and saw a man standing near her in a black overcoat and hat. A scar ran the length of his cheek and his black eyes reminded her of a rat's. "And you must be Sergei."

"And you will be dead soon."

Bridget smiled to hide the fear that was pummeling her body. "We'll see about that. Personally, I'm putting twenty on it being you.

What can I do for you this morning?" Sergei studied her, clearly trying to intimidate her with his silence. "Well, if you don't want to talk, maybe you can pick up that poop. It's always hard to do with a leash in your hand." She saw Marko kicking at the small patch of grass out of the corner of her eye. But the reaction she got from Sergei was worth it. He looked pissed.

"American women," he spat. "You think you're our equals. You think we're here to serve you. I don't know how he can even tolerate you after he had a real woman. It'll be such a pleasure when I finally come for you. I will enjoy it greatly. Too bad today is not that day. But soon."

Sergei turned and started walking down the sidewalk when Bridget called out to him. "You're wrong, you know. I don't think I'm your equal. I think I'm better than you. Marko, *stellen!*" Bridget dropped the long training leash and Marko took off as soon as she gave the attack command. She smiled at Sergei's shocked face as he took off running.

Bridget ran after them, but Sergei slammed a gate to an embassy and disappeared on the grounds before they could get to him. "Good boy," Bridget said as she scratched behind his ears and looked up at the embassy. It was for a small Middle Eastern country near the Persian Gulf called Surman. Interesting. Very interesting, indeed.

The last day at the UN was exhausting. Half of the people had left early and the remaining were annoyed that the others didn't think they needed to stay. It turned into one big political whine-fest.

Bridget had kept her eyes open all day but hadn't heard a thing about Sergei or his men. She also noticed that King Sarif was nowhere to be found. Finally she saw Agent Woodberry and flagged him down. "Woodberry," Bridget called as she headed toward him. She cringed when she saw Sweeney standing with him, but it was a small price to pay for the intel she wanted.

"Springer. You've done a great job this week. Thank you. I'm glad you joined us. Anytime you want to again, we'd be happy to have you."

Sweeney grinned as if he had just learned a great big secret and leaned over to the agent next to him. "I think we just found out how she got assigned here," he whispered.

Woodberry ground his teeth and Bridget just glared at Sweeney before turning back to Woodberry. "Thank you, sir. I was just wondering if you had learned anything about Sergei from the man you captured."

"Unfortunately not. The CIA learned he left the country this morning. Unfortunately they didn't find that out until an undercover operative saw him this evening in Rome."

"What's in Rome?"

"My guess? A meeting between the king of Rahmi and the Italians. They're meeting to discuss oil exports. The joke is a trade between oil and wine — you know the king loves nothing more than a good red wine," Woodberry said.

"That he does. Lucky for him his son married his favorite winemaker's daughter. I think it's made him partial to Italy." Bridget smiled as she remembered the king with Dani's father.

Sweeney nudged the agent next to him again and looked behind Bridget. Woodberry straightened up and Bridget just prayed it wasn't another sniveling diplomat. She didn't think she could take any more of them.

"Hey, Springer, here's your chance to sleep your way up another level," Sweeney laughed before straightening up and assuming the cocky-gent appearance.

"Go fu . . ."

"Miss Springer," the deep voice interrupted from behind. Bridget stiffened.

Sweeney's eyes widened and his face turned red with anger. "I guess you already have," he hissed and turned toward the newcomer. "Sir, Banks Sweeney. It's an honor to meet you."

"It won't be when I'm through with you. Woodberry, you're the head of this unit, aren't you?"

"Yes, sir."

"I want a formal investigation on this man. From what I just heard, we have a serious problem with professionalism, and I'm willing to bet there are women agents all over with complaints just waiting to be taken. Sweeney, is it? Remember one thing, women are to be respected. If you can't do that, you have no place representing the United States government. Springer, we need to talk," he said to the back of her head.

Bridget shrugged at Sweeney's outraged face. "What? He has a point." Sweeney lunged at her, and Bridget lashed out with a right cross that sent him to the ground. "Thank you, I've been wanting to do that all week."

"She hit me. You all saw that. She can't get away with that."

Woodberry grabbed him by the jacket and hauled him up. "I saw you trip over your own feet and fall flat on your face. What about you men?"

"That's what we saw, too, sir," the men surrounding Woodberry said with smiles on their faces. Apparently men didn't like Sweeney either.

Bridget said goodbye to Woodberry and the others before making her way over to the man who had come to see her. He stood in his uniform beside a black town car. "Hi, Dad."

Her father smiled and wrapped her up in a tight hug. "It's good to see you, pumpkin."

"It's good to see you, too." She smiled, and Marko leaped up to rest his paws on her dad's stomach as he rubbed Marko's head.

"And it's good to see you, too, Marko."

"What are you doing in New York? Is everything okay?"

"Everything is fine. I just wanted to see my daughter. Has that Sweeney guy been bothering you? You could report him, you know."

"Dad, if I reported every guy like Sweeney, I would never be able to work because I'd be filling out paperwork every day. I can handle them. I'm a big girl," she said, smiling up to her dad.

"I know. But no matter how big you get, you're still my little pumpkin. And, I have news for you that your mother insisted I give you."

"Mom did?"

Her father let out a tortured sigh. "Your mother can ferret out information better than most of my men. Anyway, she discovered I knew Ahmed left for Rome this morning and told me I had to tell you."

"Rome. He followed Sergei."

"I made the mistake of telling your mother you stood up to me about Ahmed, and she said for me to make arrangements for you to fly to Rome. If I don't, then I'm on the couch with no dinner or dessert. She threatened me as she made her homemade apple cobbler."

"What could a man do?" Bridget grinned.

"Exactly. There's a New York Air National Guard plane waiting for you at Stewart Air Force base. They have a pit stop for refueling in Rome and can take you when they leave in the morning."

"What about Marko?"

"Your mother wants to see her granddog and I want regular updates. If I don't get them, then I'm sending in the Marines . . . literally."

Bridget flung her arms around her dad and hugged him tight. "Thank you, Daddy."

Her father grunted as he hugged her back. "He better treat you right. I'll kill him if he hurts you."

"I know and I appreciate it. You're the best." She kissed his cheek and hugged Marko before preparing for her trip to Rome.

Ahmed kicked the stand to his Ducati and slid off his helmet. He looked down the packed narrow street as he walked down the gray cobblestone sidewalk toward a small café. He took a seat and brought out his phone to call his brother as the waitress poured a cup of coffee.

"Hello, Ahmed. Thank you for taking care of Sarif for us. His Royal Highness is very relieved since we're leaving tomorrow for a meeting."

"Of course. But I fear it's not over. Sarif flew out with Sergei and his men. They made a stop in Rome on their way home. Interestingly, Sergei and his men stayed in Rome."

"Sarif took Sergei to Rome?"

"Yes. What is it?" Ahmed asked as he sat forward in his chair at the worried tone in his brother's voice.

"The king and I are to arrive in Rome tomorrow morning for a meeting. I do not think this is a coincidence."

"So that is why he is here. You need to cancel the trip. I think Sergei is here to assassinate the king." Ahmed tossed down a couple of euros and headed for his bike. "Where is the meeting?"

"At the Quirinal Palace. But, Ahmed, His Royal Highness will not cancel this trip."

"At least try. If all else fails, then I will see you here tomorrow and help you protect him."

Ahmed revved the engine of his Ducati and tore off down the street toward the palace. He had a lot of surveillance to do and would, he hoped, be able to figure out how to prevent Sergei from putting his plan into action.

Bridget smiled at the waitress as she set the cappuccino on the small bistro table. "*Grazie.*" Bridget breathed in the aroma of the little coffee shop and took a sip of her drink before closing her eyes in satisfaction.

The sound of a metal chair scraping the cobblestones interrupted her brief moment of bliss. "You're late," Bridget said smugly as she took another delicious sip of her drink.

"You're following me," Ahmed said grimly. "I told you to stay away from me. How did you find me this time?"

Bridget smiled sweetly. "And if you remember, I told you I don't care what you say. This involves me and I'm going to help. I also think I already told you I have my own sources. Those sources not only told me you were in Rome but that Sergei is also here, most likely to assassinate King Ali Rahman." She didn't even blink as she saw his hands tighten around the armrests of his chair. Instead, she took a sip of her cappuccino and smiled serenely at him.

It had hit her while she was sitting in the back of a National Guard cargo plane that Ahmed was so used to using his reputation to scare people away from getting close to him that only Mo had been truly allowed in. Bridget knew she wasn't the smoothest with men. She tended to speak her mind and had discovered some guys didn't appreciate that. Additionally, she didn't have much experience with men in a romantic way, but was going to fight for the love she felt for Ahmed the only way that made sense — by being herself. She would love Ahmed no matter what. She just wished he could return her feelings.

She had a feeling there was so much more to Ahmed and if anyone could understand his dark side, it was she. He just had to trust her enough to tell her. He wasn't the only person to see or do horrible things. When Bridget had been hired as personal security during the war, she'd fought right alongside the men on the front lines. In fact, her convoy had been ambushed and she had spent three hours fighting off insurgents. She understood what it meant to fight for her life.

"So you picked this café, why?" Ahmed asked as he relaxed his hands and shooed away the waitress who was approaching them.

"I'm scoping a spot for an attack on the king. I think I found it, too."

"The top of the café," they both said at the same time, never taking their eyes off of each other.

Bridget's lips twisted as she tried not to laugh at Ahmed's frustration with her. In a quick, unguarded moment, he looked both ticked off and impressed. She lifted her little white china cup and took another sip of her drink. A gentle breeze rippled through the air and her napkin floated to the ground. Bridget leaned forward to reach for it as something pinged off the table, shattering one of the beautiful tiles and sending a shard into her bicep.

"Get down!" In one fluid movement, Ahmed was out of his chair and had pushed Bridget under the heavy metal table as little pings bounced off the top. "You're hit." Ahmed grabbed at the blood on her arm and Bridget realized he had gone white.

"Ahmed," she grabbed his hand and made him look at her. "I'm fine. It's just a little cut. Now, that has to be Sergei or one of his men, and personally, I care a lot more about getting that bastard than a little blood."

"Are you armed?" Ahmed asked as he pulled a gun from the small of his back. Bridget just raised an eyebrow and pulled out her weapon. "Stay behind me," Ahmed ordered as he rose from under the table and fired off a round at the top of the café. Bridget took advantage and made a dash for the café's entrance.

Ahmed cursed as Bridget ran for the door. He should have known she wouldn't listen to him. Sergei must have seen Bridget head for the door because the bullets stopped flying. Pedestrians were screaming in fear and in the distance sirens wailed.

Bridget was already through the inside of the café and out the back door by the time Ahmed entered the building. He saw her dart into the alley and saw a black-clad arm snap out from behind a dumpster and hit Bridget right across the chest, taking her down to the ground. Fear ripped through Ahmed as he shoved people out of the way and overturned little tables while pushing his way through the café.

He burst through the door and Bridget took full advantage of the distraction by kicking up as hard as she could. The man grabbed his crotch and fell on top of her. In a quick move, she had him on the ground and was wrenching his arm behind his back. Ahmed skidded to a stop and took a deep breath. She was remarkable. It was one thing to see her in training, but she was a thing of grace and beauty while taking down a man twice her size. The only trouble—it wasn't Sergei.

"Didn't your mother teach you not to hit a girl?" Bridget asked as she slammed his head into the concrete.

"He's going to kill you," the muscle-head laughed. Before Ahmed could leap on him, Bridget slammed his head down again and applied a little more pressure to the arm she had pinned behind his back.

"Me?" she asked so sweetly Ahmed almost laughed . . . almost. "Why would he want to do a thing like that to little ol' me?"

"Because of him," the man said as he spat blood from his mouth.

"Well, that isn't nice. Why don't you tell me where I can find Sergei so I can have a little talk with him? Maybe we can resolve this because I'd hate for him to kill me," Bridget said in a deceptively sweet tone.

"I've already called him. He'll find you tonight," the man warned. The sirens came to a stop and the sound of boots pounding through the café had Ahmed slipping their guns into the dumpster. He may have immunity, but foreign officers tended to get a little annoyed when they caught him armed.

"*Mani in alto!*" the officers shouted. Ahmed raised his hands in the air with his diplomatic papers in his hand.

"*Arrestare quest'uomo primo,*" Bridget shouted over the noise. She knew Italian? Was there anything this woman couldn't do? "Arrest this man first," she shouted in English when the officers continued to point their guns at her and yell.

"Excuse me. We are a diplomatic envoy sent to stop an assassination attempt on the king of Rahmi. We caught this man and are claiming the right to deport him immediately. Here are the papers," Ahmed said with a cold tone of authority.

One officer reached down and cuffed the man Bridget was straddling as another man reached for the papers Ahmed held out. "This says you have diplomatic immunity. She does not. Arrest her," the officer ordered in heavily accented English.

"Let her go," Ahmed said in a deadly voice.

"No. And if you do not move away I will arrest you, too, diplomatic immunity or not." The man yanked Bridget to her feet and Ahmed saw her grimace as the cuffs were put on.

Ahmed narrowed his eyes and with a shrug decided to make it worthwhile. He brought his arm back and slammed it into the officer's face, sending him to the ground. No one was allowed to hurt his woman. No one.

"Take them both to jail," the officer yelled as he struggled to stand up.

"Ahmed, why did you do that? I will be out in no time," Bridget whispered as they were shoved into the back of a police car.

"A woman once told me a jail cell is a great place to get to know someone," Ahmed said with a grin as the door to the police car was slammed shut.

Chapter Nine

Ahmed didn't cringe when the iron door to the jail cell slammed shut. The Italians had agreed to their request to be put in a private cell together as they waited for the Rahmi embassy to be called. Bridget had handed them a card with a smile and thanked them for arresting that horrible man who tried to kill her. The officers had grinned like idiots and while Ahmed did not speak Italian, he knew they were flattering her by the way she blushed at their comments. The thought of trying to see how far his diplomatic immunity would go did cross his mind while he watched them fawn over her.

"You really didn't need to do that. I'll let you in on a secret," Bridget said as she took a seat on the bench against the far wall. "This isn't my first time in jail."

Ahmed felt his eyes widen. She'd been in jail before? "I'll let you in on a secret, too. It's not my first time either." He smiled as he relaxed on the bench beside her. He felt her staring at him and it was only then that he realized the smile was lingering on his lips.

"It looks good on you, you know? The smile," Bridget teased as she bumped him with her shoulder.

"It's good to finally have a reason to smile," he said as he slid his arm around her shoulder and pulled her closer.

Her body fit perfectly against his while he traced tiny circles on her arm with his thumb. It wasn't as if he had been celibate. There'd been women over the years. But only for a night or two, and he certainly hadn't held them next to him like he was doing now. Everything was different with Bridget. He felt a strange combination of both peace and fire raging throughout his body as he held her. All those nights alone and wishing for someone to love were rushing to the surface because of this woman.

"Bridget, why aren't you afraid of me?" Ahmed asked while resting his chin on the top of her head. He stroked her hair, a little redder now as winter approached, and wondered about this woman's motives. Most women found him irresistible because he didn't chase them and filled their quota for dark and mysterious. They never knew his dark side and he would never show them that part of him. Bridget, though, had caught glimpses of it and hadn't run in terror. In fact, she kept pushing him to show more.

"You're caring, loyal, and protective of your friends. And you love dogs. What's to be afraid of?" she asked in return, snuggling closer to him.

"Probably the not-so-legal ways I go about my job, the things I've seen and done . . ." Ahmed trailed off as he thought about the men he'd had to kill, the days and nights of torture he had endured — it had changed his soul just as much as losing his son had.

"Maybe that's because I've been to those places, too. It's not something I talk about, just like you. But I've been caught in ambushes and stuck out in the desert forced to protect an injured comrade and myself. I also spent some time in an Afghan jail. By the way, this jail is so much nicer. I'm not that person, though. Sure, those things helped to shape me, but they aren't who I am. Just like whatever you've been through may affect you but it doesn't define you." Bridget pulled back and looked into his dark eyes. He looked back at her and felt for the first time someone could reach his soul. If there was anyone who could maybe understand him and not hate him for his dark side, it had to be her.

"Bridget, there's so much to tell . . ."

"*Signorina* Springer. You are free to go. There is a man on the phone for you," a young guard with appreciative eyes and a wide smile said, holding the cell door open. "Not you, *Signor*." Ahmed narrowed his eyes and glared as Bridget stood up and headed for the open door.

He softened his face when she turned around and gave him a wink. "Need me to bail you out?"

"I'm sure Mo will have me out by the time you get off the phone." Bridget gave him one last smile and then took the phone from the guard.

"Hello? Oh, hi." Ahmed felt his jaw tighten at her happy voice. "I know. I'll try to behave." She laughed, turning her back to Ahmed.

Another officer hung up his phone and nodded to the guard by the jail door. "He's free to go." Ahmed tried not to smile. He knew it wouldn't take long for Mo's father to convince his friend, the Italian president, to release him.

"Thank you again. I love you, too," he heard Bridget say into the phone before handing it back to the guard.

Ahmed felt as if he'd been kicked in the stomach. He thought she didn't have anyone special in her life. It was one of the reasons he felt he had time to defeat Sergei. Some stupid part of his brain thought she was his, even though he hadn't declared his love for her yet. He had thought he could do what he needed, and she'd be there when he was ready. Wait, she'd kissed him and told him she loved him . . . and he hadn't said it back. Had she decided he wasn't worth waiting for? Well, he'd show her. He was tired of sitting on the sidelines of life. Tired of watching his friends find love as he had to push it away. It was time to fight for it. It was time to stop letting Sergei dictate his life. Bridget was his. Now he just had to prove to her he was worth taking a chance on.

"Good, you've been sprung. So, what's our game plan?" Bridget asked when she saw him standing next to her.

"The plan is to meet me in the hotel lobby at seven." Ahmed turned and walked out leaving her standing there surrounded by smiling guards. He had to call Jamal and then plan a date.

Bridget strapped on her bulletproof vest and slid her Glock into the back of her pants. She checked the small Sig at her ankle and the knife hidden in the vest before tugging a black sweatshirt over all her gear.

She froze when she heard the knock at the door. She picked up one of the guns that she couldn't hide on her body and approached the door silently. "Who is it?"

"I have a delivery for *Signorina* Springer from *Signor* Ahmed," the voice called from the other side of the door. Bridget leaned forward and looked through the peephole. She relaxed when she recognized one of the hotel staff and opened the door.

"*Grazie*," Bridget said as she took the big white box with a red bow on top.

Bridget closed the door and walked to her bed. She untied the big bow and slid the lid off. She pushed aside white tissue paper and her mouth dropped at the sight of the red dress. With shaky fingers, she lifted the small card with a handwritten note from Ahmed, asking her to wear the dress tonight.

She put the note down on the bed and lifted the dress from the box. It had a corseted bodice and an A-line skirt that would glide along the floor. She pulled the boxy black sweatshirt off along with her vest. No way that was going to work with this dress. Bridget placed her weapons on the bed and slipped into the dress.

The soft fabric caressed her body as she walked to the mirror to check out the new look. She glanced at her watch and then to the weapons lying on the bed. She had fifteen minutes to do her hair, put on makeup, and try to fit as many weapons in the dress as possible.

She had just slid her knife into a sheath on the outside of her thigh when there was another knock at the door. She picked the gun up from the bed and made her way to the side of the door again. "Who is it?"

"It's me." With that smooth deep voice, Bridget didn't have to ask who "me" was.

She lowered her gun and opened the door. Ahmed stood wearing a tuxedo and holding a red rose. Bridget licked her lips unconsciously at the sight of him before her. He looked sinful in a tuxedo, and she couldn't decide if she liked the sight of his broad shoulders, flat stomach, or muscled thighs better. Maybe he would just let her rip it off. If only she had dated more, then she might be able to read his signals better. In reality, she had no idea what she was doing and felt as if she were constantly arguing with herself about whether she should let him make a move or just jump him.

"You look stunning, my dear." Jumping him was definitely the way to go. "For you."

Bridget smiled as she took the rose and felt her heart speed up. Was he finally feeling something for her or was this just a pretense to catch Sergei? "Thank you. I could only fit one gun and one knife in this dress. I feel practically naked." Bridget laughed nervously as Ahmed looked her over slowly. She felt her breathing falter as his eyes lingered on her breasts and then slid lower. "Um, so are we off to get Sergei?"

"No. Not tonight. At the last moment, my brother convinced the king and president to move the meeting to an undisclosed location. They will be safe from Sergei. Tonight you won't even need the gun, and I am trying to figure out where on that delectable body of yours you have hidden it."

Bridget gulped as she felt his words wrap around her. She brought her hand up and fanned her face as she tried to regain control of her body. "Then what are we doing?"

"I'm taking you on a date."

Ahmed placed his hand on the small of Bridget's back and guided her to the red velvet chair in their private box at the *Teatro dell'Opera*. Tonight he would show her that he could be the man she deserved. By the end of the night, she wouldn't even remember that man on the phone.

"The opera—I've only been once and I've always wanted to go again. What are we seeing?" Bridget asked with excitement as she took a seat close to the banister.

"*The Marriage of Figaro*. It's one of my favorites. I'm just glad we didn't get kicked out of the country before we could see it," he smiled at her again and leaned back in the chair next to her. Two smiles in one day. She was having an effect on him.

Turning her head, Bridget looked around the box and then out the golden archway toward the stage. "It's about to start. It looks packed. I'm surprised we don't have other people in here with us," she whispered as the lights dimmed and the large red velvet curtain opened.

"I bought the box. I wanted to spend the night with you—and only you," Ahmed said in a low voice. He looked down at her smiling up at him, her breasts rising with every intake of breath. He'd have to find out where she kept that gun.

"Me? Alone? Why?"

Ahmed smiled again when Bridget fumbled her words. She hadn't dated anyone since coming to Keeneston and her unassuming innocent reactions had him hard in seconds. He knew she was not experienced enough to purposely tease and yet he had to fight his basal desire to claim her for the entire world to see.

"So I could do this." Ahmed cupped her chin and brought her lips to his. He kissed her gently trying to control the desire surging through him. If he knew she only wanted him, then he'd take her against the wall in the shadows at the back of the box as Figaro and Susanna sang of their wedding.

Instead, he moved slowly, parting her lips and tasting her. Ahmed let his hand slide under her gown. He moved it up her leg and smiled against her mouth when he felt the knife. It turned him on even more as she clutched his arm while he slid his hand over the leather of the sheath toward her arching hips.

Ahmed pulled back and looked down at her. Her lips were parted and slightly swollen from his kisses. She still clung to him, looking at him with complete trust that had him gripping her thigh with fierce desire. "Before we put on a better show than the opera, turn and keep your eyes on the stage," Ahmed ordered with a voice graveled from passion.

He watched as she swallowed hard and nodded before turning to the stage. The look of disappointment emboldened him as he, too, turned to look at the stage. But when he moved his hand toward her center, her eyes widened and she shot him a smile before looking back toward the stage. He didn't think he could take her in the back of the box, but he could have her in one way tonight.

As Bridget's breathing quickened, so did his. The sight of her flushed cheeks against her serene expression had him filled with desire. He knew he put that blush on her cheeks, and as the aria reached its crescendo, he felt Bridget find hers. Her hand gripped his upper arm as the crowd cheered the singer on stage.

Bridget took a shaky breath as she tried to calm down. Ahmed had just, well, he'd just . . . wow! She didn't think she'd be able to put together a coherent sentence for the life of her right now.

She kept her eyes on the stage and almost jerked when she felt Ahmed's fingers lace with hers. Bridget looked over at him then. His brown eyes were soft as he leaned down and placed a tender kiss on her lips. Oh, if she thought she was in love with him when he didn't talk much and their way of flirting was sparing, this side of him was too much. Roses, kisses, and opera . . . she wasn't just falling in love — she was diving headfirst from the tallest building.

Bridget glanced at Ahmed one more time as he watched the opera. His thumb was absently rubbing her knuckles and he looked, well, happy. His face, normally so tense, was relaxed and he even had a slight smile on his lips.

At intermission, they strolled through the grand opera house. His hand never left hers. The second half of the opera flew by with much laughter and excitement. The patrons applauded as the red curtain closed and the lights came on for the final time.

"That was wonderful. Thank you so much for bringing me." Bridget smiled as she stood up.

"The night is not over yet," Ahmed whispered as he slid her wrap over her shoulders.

"What's next then?"

"You'll have to wait and see."

"Now that's my man of mystery," Bridget teased, slipping her hand through his arm.

"I like that."

"Being mysterious?"

"No, being yours. It's something I'd be proud of. Much more than anything else I've done in life." Ahmed covered her hand with his. They had stopped in the middle of the opera house lobby and stood looking at each other while the other patrons streamed by them.

They may not be the words of love Bridget wanted to hear, but they were still the sweetest words ever spoken to her. "Take me back to the hotel," she said over the pounding of her heart.

The door to the room banged open as she and Ahmed fell into his room. Her hands were pulling off his bow tie while she kicked off her heels. Ahmed shrugged out of his jacket and slammed the door shut. Bridget was too busy working on the buttons of his shirt to notice the table set with candles, champagne, and chocolate-covered strawberries.

She pushed the shirt from his shoulders and licked her lips in anticipation of exploring his body. Muscles rippled under her touch as she ran her hands from his shoulders, down his chest, and over the ridges of his abdomen. Above his heart was a large scar that had been stitched up a long time ago. The smaller white scars that were scattered across his body only seemed to enhance his features. Before she could reach for his belt, his hands were on her. He pulled her arms behind her and held her wrists loosely together in one of his hands.

The action thrust her breasts up toward him as he feasted on her mouth. His free hand slid up her rib cage and kneaded a breast. His fingers found her erect nipple as he buried his face in her neck. Bridget's head rolled to the side as he nipped and then kissed her. She was breathing him in—his presence was almost overwhelming. He was everywhere, except the one place she wanted him.

"Bridget?" Ahmed asked as his hand found the zipper to her dress.

Bridget knew what he was asking—permission to do what she had been dreaming about since she first met him. "I know you aren't good with emotions, but I love you. I love you enough for us both. Make love to me, Ahmed."

Ahmed didn't say anything in response but the sound of her zipper being undone and the fierce primal growl that came from him were his answer. The dress fell to the floor and Ahmed stepped back. "So that's where you hid your gun."

Bridget looked at the hunger in his eyes and the smile on his lips and felt emboldened. She sat down on the bed and leaned back against the pillows. She saw his eyes darken, and in one swift move, he was naked. Clothes could never do him justice. His legs were thick and strong. A small trail of dark hair led from his navel straight to his . . . hello!

Bridget gulped as he climbed onto the bed. His arms were braced on either side of her as he looked down into her eyes. He slowly lowered his head and kissed her. "Now, Ahmed. I need you now."

Chapter Ten

Ahmed didn't want to move. Bridget was curled against his chest sound asleep as the plane prepared to land at the Lexington airport. They had not slept much the night before. This morning, they had both received phone calls from their respective sources alerting them to the fact Sergei had left Italy after King Ali Rahman and the president had disappeared to hold their meeting.

Jamal had said the king was reluctant to have the meeting in private—he did like the pomp and circumstance of formal state visits. After Jamal had arrived and interrogated the man Bridget caught, the king gave in and held the meeting in private late that night. They were gone from Italy by the morning and would already be safely back at the palace in Rahmi.

"Bridget? Dear, we're landing," Ahmed said gently while he rubbed her back. She stirred in his arms and Ahmed was struck again with the fierce desire to protect her. She may look, and quite honestly be, tough when she was working, but when she was in his arms, she was simply the woman who held his heart.

"We're home already?" she asked sleepily as she sat up.

"Yes. I'll drive you back to Keeneston if you'd like."

"Um, Ahmed?"

"Yes, dear?" he asked as he continued to run his hand down her back. He loved the way his name sounded from her lips.

"I'm not . . . I mean . . . I don't really know what to do now. With us."

Ahmed placed his finger under her chin and raised it, forcing her to look him in the eye. How could someone so kind and unsure of her feelings be so confident and secure in her abilities in the field?

"I've never really been an *us* before. It sounds nice. I believe it's customary for new couples to dine at the Blossom Café. Shall we have lunch there?"

Ahmed couldn't believe he'd offered to do something so public. Sadly, he knew Miss Lily, Edna, or, most likely, John Wolfe would ferret out the information, and he'd lose the upper hand by the end of the day. For some reason, he felt inordinately pleased to be able to walk into the café with Bridget beside him. And unless John had spies in Rome, no one would have a clue they were together. Ahmed felt almost like laughing at the idea of surprising them.

Bridget beamed and Ahmed smiled back at her. "I'd love that . . . if it's not too much for you? You've seen what they do to new couples, right?"

"Please. I've been interrogated by far more experienced people than a group of senior citizens," Ahmed joked while the images of Cy and the rest of the Davies men succumbing to the pressure from the Roses lingered in the back of his mind.

Ahmed opened the door and held out his hand for Bridget. She placed her small hand in his and they walked to the cheery yellow door of the café. He didn't want to brag, but the most amazing woman in the world was on *his* arm. He smiled down into Bridget's nervous face and almost laughed. He'd seen her take down a man twice her size just the other day and now she was nervous to face her friends. He found it adorable.

"Don't worry. I'll always be here to protect you," he said to her as he reached for the door.

"I can protect myself, thank you. Besides, it's not me I'm worried about," she said cryptically as they stepped into the café arm-in-arm.

Ahmed looked up and felt his smile slip. Every person in the café had frozen in place. Forks, spoons, and sandwiches were hanging midair as the patrons stared at them. More particularly, stared at his hand holding Bridget's. No one moved. No one spoke. The only sound was of Miss Violet's spatula clanging on the floor.

Ahmed looked around and found Mo and Dani, with shocked expressions on their faces, sitting at the big table full of their mutual friends. Bridget squeezed his hand as she plastered a nervous smile on her face. He made eye contact with Miss Daisy and swallowed hard when her eyes narrowed. Her pen was still poised over the pad as she prepared to take Will's order.

"We're dating," Ahmed blurted out under the scrutiny. He'd told his brother about this town and its ability to put government agencies to shame, but you just couldn't understand how scary they really were until you went up against them.

"Oh, bless your hearts," Miss Daisy exclaimed as she dropped her pen and hurried to beat her sisters to hug them.

"We couldn't be happier," Miss Lily cried as she joined her sister.

"You have to understand what a surprise it was to see you together. It didn't register. Neither of you has ever shown any interest in anyone before. Well, we're just happier than pigs in mud." Miss Violet dabbed her eyes on her apron as she pushed Mo out of the way to get to the couple.

Ahmed refused to let go of Bridget as they were enveloped in hugs and congratulations from the town. Finally Mo and Dani made their way through the crowd. "We are so very happy for you, my friend." Mo shook his hand and Ahmed couldn't help but think how different this was from the night before his wedding eighteen years ago when Mo had consoled him. "You deserve this happiness."

"And you too, Bridget. We're very happy for you *both*." Dani smiled as she kissed Ahmed's cheek and gave Bridget a hug.

Ahmed felt Bridget pull her hand away as she was wrapped in a hug from Annie. "I think you pulled off the surprise of the year," Cade said, shaking his hand as Bridget and her best friend laughed.

"Come join us for lunch and tell us all about how this happened," Katelyn said with a sweet smile as she rubbed her belly.

"Yes, I can't wait to hear all about it." Kenna grinned while Will shook his hand.

"Thank you. We will." Ahmed let out a breath and felt relaxed again. It was strange how he and Mo had been outcasts when they first came to the town. But with a force of nature named Kenna behind them, they became a part of Keeneston. He may have been born in Rahmi, but this was his home. He had felt like a failure in Rahmi. He had been constantly compared to his brother and mocked for being a weakling who preferred to take pictures rather than fire a gun. He'd changed after Sergei. He'd not only turned into his brother; he'd become better than his brother. He'd allowed himself to be consumed with the need to prove himself. But for the first time, he was thinking of putting it all behind him and starting a life with Bridget — after he killed Sergei.

Ahmed held out a chair for Bridget and then took a seat next to her. It was hard to keep his hands off her as they placed their orders. He let Bridget tell of their meeting in Rome and even smiled when she got to the part about how hard it was to hide a gun in the dress he got her. It took him a moment to realize his tablemates had stopped talking and were staring at him again.

"Honey? Are you okay?" Pierce asked Tammy. "You're all red."

"I'm fine," Tammy gulped as she used her hand to fan herself.

"You look flushed, too; is it the baby?" Marshall worriedly asked Katelyn.

"Maybe it's hot in here — Kenna, you're red, too. It doesn't feel hot in here, does it?" Will asked. The men shook their head and the women nodded theirs.

"Pregnancy hormones," Gemma said as she, too, fanned her face.

"Yes, that's it," Tammy giggled.

"Did I miss something? I just hate missing the latest gossip." Ahmed didn't have to turn around to know who owned that overly sugary voice. "Bill and I just got back from a convention."

"Hi, Bill," Cole said from across the table. Ahmed would have turned around, but two over-inflated beach balls were sitting on the top of his head at the moment. "Hello, Kally."

"It's Kandi." Ahmed felt her boobs bouncing against his head as she stomped her foot in annoyance at Cole. He heard the slight sound of a knife being unsheathed next to him and almost grinned. Bridget was coming to his rescue.

"I could fix those for you right now. It looks like you need to let a pound or two of air out of those puppies. Hold still. It'll only take a sec." Bridget raised her knife and Kandi jumped away from Ahmed with her eyes full of terror.

"Please do. I've been having nightmares of being smothered to death by them," Bill sighed. Ahmed finally turned around and saw the dark circles under Bill's eyes.

"Hi, Mr. Rawlings. Do you need a table?" Summer asked as she bounced up to him. The perky waitress had been out to find a husband for the past two years. Ahmed was just glad he would no longer be in her crosshairs—not that she'd been brave enough to even talk to him, but he'd seen the way she had eyed him.

"Yes, thank you, Summer." Bill looked around and then let out a long-suffering sigh again. "Kandi, get your tits off Henry. Our table's ready."

Bridget choked on her drink as she heard Bill call his wife. The whole table erupted in laughter. Bridget laughed even harder as she saw the tears rolling down Paige's cheeks.

"Did you see Henry's face?" Paige asked as she laughed even harder. Bridget had. When Henry had gone to stand up, he bumped his head into Kandi's bazongas, forcing him back into his chair.

"Oh gosh," Katelyn cried as she grabbed Marshall's arm. Bridget and the table just laughed harder as Henry almost ran from the café.

"Ow," Marshall yelped and everyone stopped laughing as they realized the look on Katelyn's face was one of pain, not humor. "What's the matter?"

"I'm in labor. I laughed so hard I went into labor," Katelyn giggled when the contraction passed.

"You need some pillows to lean back on?" Miles asked seriously, but the glint in his eye gave him away.

Katelyn snorted while Marshall looked frozen in place. "I think a ride to the hospital would be better. Thank you, though, Miles." Katelyn stood up and so did everyone else except Marshall.

"Bro, come on. Your wife needs to be driven to the hospital and you have that car with the cool sirens on it." Miles's sarcastic remark had Morgan smacking his arm.

"You realize I'll hurt you if you're like this when I go into labor," Morgan mumbled as she helped lead Katelyn around the table.

"I'm calling your grandparents. We'll all meet you there after we pick up the dogs. Marshall, snap to it." Paige thwacked him against the back of his head and finally got him moving as she waited for Mrs. Wyatt to pick up the phone.

"I'm going to be a father," Marshall murmured as he stood up. "Oh crap, I'm coming. Do we need the sirens? Of course we need the sirens." Marshall answered his own question as he took his wife's arm from Morgan.

Marshall stopped by the door where the Rose sisters were already in full baby-prep mode, by organizing phone trees and casseroles. He leaned down and kissed Katelyn so gently and reverently that Bridget felt a longing she'd never felt before. She wanted that. Would Ahmed ever want a wife or a baby after what happened before?

"I love you," Marshall said to Katelyn as some of the women in the café teared up.

"I love you, too. Can I play with the siren now?" Katelyn smirked. "Thank you all," she called out to the café. She was met with well wishes as Marshall helped her to the car.

Ahmed came to stand beside Bridget and slid his arm around her waist. She leaned into him and wondered if they had a future together. While she told him she had enough love for them both, she wished for more. She wished for a man to love her and she just didn't know if Ahmed could.

"I'll take you home if you're ready. I have some work I need to do. But I'd like to see you tonight."

Bridget looked up at Ahmed and gave him a soft smile. "I'd like that."

Ahmed stalked into the security office that was housed in the cottage next to Mo and Dani's house. Nabi quickly stood and handed him a set of papers. Ahmed scanned them and tossed them onto the table.

"Leave," Ahmed said simply to the other guards in the room. To his credit, Nabi didn't flinch as he and Ahmed waited for the room to clear.

"How credible is this information?" Ahmed asked when everyone was gone.

"Very. It comes from my father." Nabi's father worked with Jamal and was known for his solid sources. "There's something else. I hope you don't mind, but after you told me Miss Springer was in danger and we started watching her, I thought about why she was in trouble."

"Because of me," Ahmed said without hesitation. He wouldn't betray his guilt or his worry about Bridget to his apprentice.

"I know that—but how did Sergei even know to target Miss Springer? He had to have a reason to have Rana hire her in the first place." Ahmed just nodded. He'd been thinking the same thing. "While you were gone, I let myself into Miss Springer's apartment and searched for bugs after I did the daily sweep of the main house."

"What did you find?"

"Nothing. But, as I walked out of her apartment I stopped on the street to think. It dawned on me then. Where do you go to get information on anything happening in the town?"

"The café," they said together.

"I found three bugs. One in the kitchen and two in the dining room," Nabi told him as he pulled out his cell phone and showed him pictures of the bugs.

"Did you leave them?"

"Yes. I thought it better Sergei doesn't know we found them. It could somehow help us in the future."

"Good thinking. You've come a long way this past year." Ahmed tried not to laugh as the compliment left a shocked and then excited look on Nabi's face. He was a good kid. The only thing Ahmed had found that scared him was when the town pressed in on him. But the boy had held his ground both times.

"Thank you, sir."

"Have you found anything on Sergei's location?" Nabi's excitement faded and Ahmed had his answer. "Keep on it. Hack the satellites if you have to. I know the U.S. government must have an idea where he is."

"I've contacted everyone I know in the underground world trying to find him. Between your name and my father's, I have a lot of informants looking for him. We'll find him."

Ahmed looked at his watch. "I have to pick up Bridget for dinner. We'll be at my place. Come get me if you find anything."

Nabi gave him a determined nod. "We won't let anything happen to Miss Springer. She's one remarkable woman."

"That she is. Thank you, Nabi." Ahmed headed to his car as the other guards came back into the cottage.

As Ahmed drove toward town, he thought about how Nabi had arrived in Keeneston. Nabi's father was Jamal's top man back in Rahmi. Jamal had called Ahmed a year ago to discuss one of the king's visits to Keeneston. During the conversation, he had complained about the overly serious pup who wanted to be the next

Ahmed. Jamal has scoffed at it since Nabi was tall and rail-thin and too green to be of any use.

Ahmed had felt for him. He knew what it was like to want to please and have no one pay any attention to you except to criticize. So he had told Jamal to send Nabi to him. After spending some time with the boy, Ahmed had discovered that Nabi had a knack for finding information. He took his job seriously, and as he kept to Ahmed's fitness routine, he kept growing stronger and more confident. Nabi was also, much to Ahmed's chagrin, almost as good a shot as he was.

He parked his car on Main Street and stepped out. He looked down the street and saw the café lights were off. Katelyn must not have had her baby yet. Everyone was moving on with life — getting married and having children. Ahmed felt as if he were running in mud. He was torn between finding a future with Bridget and living in the past. Revenge had been the only thing that had kept him going for all these years. What would he be without it and how could he expect to just forget it? No, Sergei had to die.

Chapter Eleven

T he old federal-style house Ahmed lived in was in direct contrast to his outer appearance. It was filled with bright colors and beautiful pictures. Zoti thumped his tail from where he lay on the couch as Bridget made her way toward the kitchen. Ahmed had been different when he'd picked her up. It was as if he were somewhere else. He'd been quiet, but every touch conveyed something more.

A plate of cheese and two glasses of wine sat on the island in the middle of his kitchen. She took a seat on one of the stools and watched him stir some kind of sauce. "Smells great."

"Thank you. I guess I'm still thinking of Italy. I thought I'd make some pasta tonight."

"It's perfect. It's so nice of you to cook dinner for me."

"With Katelyn still in labor, the town is pretty much shut down. Plus it's nice to be here with just you. I have gotten used to having you all to myself. I have to share when we're at the café, and I really do not like to share." Bridget almost forgot how to swallow her wine as he gave her a heated look before flashing a smile that had her melting.

"I guess I'll tell my other dates that."

Ahmed's hand tightened on his wine glass. "What other dates?"

Bridget burst out laughing.

"Funny. How should I get my payback?" The laughter died in her throat at the sound of his silken voice as he stalked toward her.

"By cooking me dinner?" she asked lamely as she tried to swallow.

"I'm suddenly hungry for something else." In one swift move, Ahmed lifted her onto the granite countertop, his lips coming down onto hers. He spread her legs and stepped between them, immediately pulling her against him. She could feel how hungry he was for her as she rocked against him. When her breasts filled his hands, she no longer cared about dinner.

Bridget lay on the couch with her head in Ahmed's lap as a movie played, unwatched, on the television. She was so used to taking care of herself; it felt strange to be taken care of. No man had ever cooked a romantic dinner for her before. And certainly, no one had ever made love to her the way Ahmed did.

"Ahmed?"

"Yes, my dear?"

"Were you happy before Sergei came into your life? What were you like?"

"I was happy, but I was also naïve."

"And then Sergei changed all that?"

"No, my father did when he forced me to marry Paulina. I went from living life to just trying to survive it. When Kedar was born, I thought I had something to live for again."

"And then Sergei took him from you." Bridget paused, thinking about what Ahmed must have gone through. "Did you go after him then?"

"No. Mo took me to England. I learned, I trained, and then I went after him when Mo told me Sarif was harboring him."

"You went to Sergei?"

"Of course. I was young and angry. I thought since I'd become a man and trained with the best soldiers in Europe, I was unstoppable. I was on a mission to teach Sarif and Sergei a lesson. I thought I could kill them both, even though King Ali Rahman had forbidden it. Mo begged me not to go, but I didn't listen."

"What happened?" Bridget asked as a feeling of dread came over her.

"Sergei captured me. I was chained in a room with no food. I was tortured for days. Then he made a mistake. He thought I was so weak I couldn't fight, so he didn't chain me back up. When the guards came in a little while later, I managed to escape."

"And so your need for revenge grew." Bridget understood, but she didn't like it. The first rule of being a good soldier was to leave your emotions at the door. It was why men didn't like working with her at first. They thought she would get emotional in battle. "You're never going to let him go, are you?

"Not until he's dead. It must not have been easy for you either. There aren't too many men who do what you do, let alone a woman."

Bridget allowed him to change the subject. "It hasn't. But it's also rewarding. I had to get used to the hazing, the teasing, the objectifying."

"How did you do that?" Bridget felt him tense under her. Talking of something that happened to her years ago bothered him more than talking about being tortured.

"I didn't turn them in. I didn't complain. I kicked their asses during training and on the job. I was a good soldier, but as a woman I was not allowed to be on the front line. I knew I could do more good in combat situations by working private security. Working with my dog on the front lines for one month I saved more lives than I had in the four years I was in the service.

"By then I had proven myself, and the other soldiers treated me as just one of the guys. I know more dirty jokes than any person should. I could also teach Henry some pick-up lines he could never come close to thinking of," Bridget laughed. Ahmed relaxed again and she snuggled closer to him.

"Where is Marko?"

"My parents are taking care of him. I knew I would be traveling a lot right now and Marshall said the sheriff's department didn't need him at the moment, so he got to go with my dad and be completely spoiled."

"Where are your parents?"

"Outside D.C. in Virginia. They just moved there a couple months ago for my dad's job."

"What does he do?"

Bridget was about to tell him about her father, the general, when Zoti leaped off the couch a moment before there was a knock at the door. "I'm sorry, my dear. Will you excuse me?"

Bridget sat up and watched Ahmed open the door. Nabi stood there with some papers and leaned close to Ahmed, whispering. Ahmed said something back and then turned to her.

"What is it?" she asked.

"Nabi will drive you home. I have some work I must see to." He leaned down and kissed her. "Thank you for a wonderful night. I'll see you tomorrow at the regular time for hand-to-hand training?"

"Yes, but what is it?"

"Nothing, just something for Mo."

Bridget lowered her voice so Nabi wouldn't hear. "You know that's not the truth. What is it?"

"Nothing you need to worry about. You know I'll take care of everything. Good night, my dear." Ahmed kissed her forehead and turned to Nabi. "Please see her safely inside." And with that Bridget watched Ahmed stride from the house and into the darkness.

Ahmed took a deep breath to stop the anger flowing through him. One of Nabi's sources had come through with a bit of gossip he hoped Ahmed would pay for. Nabi, knowing Ahmed never paid for information, threatened the man instead. He had caved and given Nabi the information he'd heard. There had been a request to find and kill a very specific dog: a dog belonging to one Bridget Springer.

If the owner could be captured, then there would be a bonus. But only if she was alive.

It wouldn't take much to make it disappear. A couple of well-placed calls with a carefully made threat or two would have people getting worried about fulfilling the request. To make sure, Ahmed was getting on a plane and taking a quick trip to New York City. The source of this information was there and had the ear of some very nasty people. Rats really. They preyed on the weak, but when someone stronger threatened them, they scattered back into the shadows where they belonged.

"I have already called for the pilot. He will meet you at the airport. Take the helicopter to the plane; it is faster," Mo said as he walked out of the shadows next to his house.

"Nabi told you?"

"He thought you might want to apply some pressure to let everyone know you were serious about leaving Bridget alone. Ahmed, it's time. You need to find a way to end this. You know what's next, don't you?" Mo put a hand on his shoulder and Ahmed gave a barely conceivable nod. The same image that had been haunting him in his nightmares flashed into his head. It was the image of Sergei pulling a knife from Bridget's heart.

"I won't let it get that far. He'll never get close enough to take her from me. I'm not sitting back waiting anymore. I'm going after him, even if it means I never come back. I just have to find him."

"Hopefully, you will find something in New York. Keep me updated. As always, I am here if you need me."

"Thank you. I don't want Bridget to know I'm gone. She'll worry. Or worse, she'll follow. If I'm not back by the time she visits tomorrow, make something up, please."

"I will look after her. Be safe, my friend."

Ahmed opened the door to the helicopter and turned it on. He'd be in New York in just a couple hours. After he finished with that little rat, no one would come near Bridget or Marko again.

Nabi refused to let Bridget into her apartment. She was fuming as she stopped behind him on the metal stairs leading to her kitchen door. He pulled out a gun and then motioned for her to hand him the keys.

"Is this really necessary?"

"Please, do not worry. I will protect you tonight," Nabi proclaimed to her as if he had just told her the nightly special at the café.

"You will protect me? From what?" Bridget snorted.

"Intruders. Ahmed asked me to see you safely home. Making sure your home is safe is part of that assignment—including changing this dead light bulb. It is hard to see anything. You could fall down the stairs," Nabi explained to her as if she didn't know that.

"Would you like to borrow my gun? It is more powerful than yours," Bridget said sweetly as she pulled out her gun and smiled at Nabi. "It's okay. Most men don't know how to admit a woman is better at protecting someone than they are. I can wait a minute while it soaks in."

"Oh, it is not that. I know how very accomplished you are," Nabi reassured her.

"Then what is it?"

"Simple. Ahmed would kill me if I didn't make sure everything was safe inside. I really don't want to make him mad."

Bridget let out a sigh. "Fine. I know how he gets. All quiet and pouty."

She heard Nabi snort. "Pouty? You may have seen him irritated. He gives this face, right?" Nabi gave his impression of Ahmed when he was exasperated and Bridget tossed back her head and laughed.

"That's it exactly."

"Well, that's not him mad. When he's mad, he sets his jaw, narrows his eyes, and becomes so silent and stiff, you'd think he was a statue until he makes his move on the person who upset him. Trust me, you don't want to be that person." Nabi unlocked the door and then paused. Bridget stopped laughing as Nabi cocked his head. "Someone's coming."

Bridget didn't have a chance to say anything. Nabi was surprisingly fast as he shoved her through the door and slammed it shut. He pushed her into the kitchen and to the floor behind the small island. "Stay here."

Nabi crouched down in her dark apartment and darted for the kitchen door. He pressed his back against it and cocked his gun. The sound of feet climbing the stairs reached her ears. Bridget checked her magazine to make sure it was full for the multiple people making their way toward the door and stood up so she could aim at the door.

There was the sound of someone pressing against the glass and then she heard muffled voices through the thick door. The doorknob turned and she saw Nabi pushing against the door. "Does anyone have a key? They unlocked the door."

"No. They must have found my hide-a-key," Bridget whispered as the door was pushed open a crack before Nabi was able to slam it shut.

"On the count of three, I am going to roll away from the door. It'll pop open and they'll fall through. Cover me, okay?" Nabi asked as he pushed the door closed again. Bridget gave a single nod and bent down. She used the island for cover and the counter to steady her aim. "One-two-three!"

Nabi leaped away from the door and it flung open. There was screaming as the dark figures fell into her kitchen in a heap. "Freeze," she and Nabi yelled as they leveled their guns on them.

"Okay, but if Daisy Mae doesn't move, she's going to squash the cupcakes."

"And I'm sorry, dear. I'm afraid I spilled some leftover soup on your floor."

"At least I saved the casserole."

Bridget lowered her gun and flicked on the lights. She was greeted with the sight of a tangled mess of Rose sisters balancing food in their hands. "You know, you could have knocked."

"We looked in the window. No lights were on so we figured you were with Ahmed. We were just going to leave this extra food on the counter for you," Miss Violet explained as if it were no big deal Nabi was standing there with a gun still in his hands.

"My, that's a small gun you have," Miss Lily clucked at Nabi as she went about cleaning up the spilled soup. "Have you seen Edna's big gun? That's a real gun."

Nabi put his gun away and smirked as he took the cupcakes from Miss Daisy and set them on the counter. "It's not the size of the gun that matters. It's how you use it."

"That's just something the salesperson tells you to make you feel better, dear," Miss Lily said sympathetically as the grin fell from Nabi's face.

"I've always liked a little size," Miss Violet stated matter-of-factly while putting the casserole in the refrigerator.

"Me, too. I like the weight of it in my hand," Miss Daisy told Nabi, handing him a cupcake with a pink napkin.

Bridget didn't know what to do. She wanted to laugh, she wanted to gasp, but in the end, she caught Nabi's blanched face and a giggle escaped. Then another and another until she was bent over slamming her hand against the counter as she gasped for breath.

"What is it, dear?" Miss Lily asked. Bridget looked up and saw Nabi's look of horror and three innocent faces looking back at her and broke out into a new round of laughter. She could only shake her head in response to Miss Lily's question as she tried to stop laughing.

"What's all the food for?" Bridget finally managed to ask after taking some deep breaths.

"Katelyn and Marshall had a baby girl. This is what was left over from the party we had in the waiting room. You know those nice nurses are so excited every time someone from Keeneston has a baby."

"Does she have a name?" She knew Ahmed and Katelyn were good friends so she wanted to make sure she got all the details to tell him after he finished with whatever it was he was doing for Mo.

"Bless her heart, she's precious. They named her Sydney. She is a healthy seven and a half pounds with a head of blonde hair like her mama and what looks to be hazel eyes just like her daddy," Miss Violet said as she clasped her hands to her chest.

"I thought Ahmed would be there," Miss Daisy stated casually.

"Mo had something he needed done," Nabi filled in quickly. So quickly in fact that it captured Bridget's attention.

"Well, thank you, ladies. This food is fantastic and I'm so happy for Katelyn and Marshall. But," Bridget covered her mouth and gave a fake yawn, "I'm beat. I'll make sure to stop by the café to find out how little Sydney is doing tomorrow."

"Oh, yes. We're taking them breakfast in the morning. Not good for a new mom to eat hospital food. We'll bring her something nourishing." Miss Violet fussed as they headed for the door, escorted by Nabi.

Bridget thanked them again for the food, gave them each a hug, and closed the door before Nabi could escape. "Okay, spill it."

"Spill what?" Nabi asked nervously.

"What's Ahmed doing?"

"Just something for Mo. You know, diplomatic stuff," Nabi told her as he walked into the kitchen to grab another cupcake. "Here, try this. Amazing."

Bridget stepped forward and took the cupcake he was offering. "I know it's more than that. Something's going on that you all don't want me to know about."

"I'm sorry, but I'm bound by confidentiality with his Royal Highness. I cannot talk about diplomatic relations."

Bridget rolled her eyes. She'd get it out of him.

"Here. Have a napkin."

Bridget reached for the napkin, but it fell from Nabi's hand right before she could grab it. She bent over to pick it up and, by the time she straightened back up, the kitchen was empty and she heard the sound of a door slamming. She ran to the door and flung it open. "Coward," she yelled into the night as Nabi made a dash for his car.

Her butt started vibrating so Bridget closed the door and dug into her back pocket for her cell phone as she eyed the plate of cupcakes. "Springer."

"Ah, Miss Springer. It is so nice to talk to you again," the cold Russian voice said through the phone.

"Sergei. How are things in hell? Hot?" Bridget asked as she reached for another cupcake.

"You'll find out soon enough when I kill you."

"Sergei, Sergei, dude, you need new lines. I'm trying to enjoy this great cupcake and you're all about death. Have you tried yoga? Chocolate? Getting laid? Anything to improve your disposition."

"I plan on screwing someone very soon. You, while Ahmed is helpless to watch." Sergei's voice was even colder, but she had heard the slight crack. Bridget smiled; she was pissing him off.

"There we go with the threats again. Did you not get enough hugs when you were a child? Is that it?"

She heard Sergei take a deep breath. "I'm looking forward to killing you slowly. I've very good with a knife," Sergei laughed and Bridget felt the hair on her arms rise. "I'll see you soon, real soon," he laughed again with no trace of humor.

"Okay. I'll save a cupcake for you," Bridget said nonchalantly. The phone line went dead and she chuckled. She shoots, she scores. Bridget 2, Sergei 0.

Sergei threw his phone onto his bed. That insufferable woman! He would kill her slowly now and make Ahmed watch. Ahmed had taken everything he loved and now Sergei was even more determined to do the same to him. If Ahmed thought the torture he had escaped was bad, he wouldn't even be able to imagine what Sergei had in store for him now.

He paced his room and thought about that bitch. If she and Ahmed were a couple, then the best way to tackle them would be to separate them. If he could draw Ahmed away from her, then he could strike on two fronts. He could get Ahmed away from

Keeneston and have someone get Bridget and bring her to him. Then when the time came to end Ahmed, he could bring out the final bit of torture . . . Bridget. He could see it now. Ahmed weak and dying as blood drained from his body. He would bring Bridget out and kill her right in front of him, just as he had done to Ahmed's wife. It would be full circle. Sergei smiled. Full circle—that's it. He knew how to draw Ahmed out.

Sergei picked up the phone, dialed the number, and waited. "Sarif. It's time to go home." After all, it should end where it began.

Chapter Twelve

A hmed tossed his keys on the counter and hurried to his room. His clothes were covered in blood and Bridget was due at any moment for training. The New York trip had been everything he expected. He'd found his way into the underworld and made his point—Bridget was not to be touched.

He stripped off the black shirt and threw it in the trash. No amount of dry cleaning in the world could save that shirt. He shucked his pants and hurried into the shower. When the red water ran clear again, he got out and applied a salve to his raw knuckles. He slipped on a pair of athletic shorts and headed into the kitchen right as Bridget knocked on the door.

Ahmed took a deep breath and opened the door. His breath caught at the sight of her on his porch. The sun was shining down and the red highlights in her hair seemed to be glowing.

"Hi. How was work?" she asked as she walked into his house.

"Good," he smiled seeing her gaze linger on his bare chest. He wasn't completely unaffected either. She was in tight black pants that hugged every curve. And from their past workouts, he knew she wore nothing but a tiny tank top under her fleece jacket. It had been hard to contain himself during the previous lessons when they weren't together. But now that he'd had her, all he wanted was to have her again. Especially when he knew all his worries and fears disappeared when he was inside her. "You got home safely?"

"Yes, but you may want to buy Nabi a bigger gun. I fear he might be having inadequacy issues due to the small size of his, um," Bridget cleared her throat, "gun."

"I'll talk to him and see if that's what he wants." Ahmed led the way down the stairs and wondered what that was all about. He stopped wondering when Bridget unzipped her jacket to reveal she'd only worn a sports bra.

"Ready?"

Yes, he was. In more ways than one. "Yes. Let's practice what to do if an attacker gets you on the ground."

"Like this?" Bridget grabbed Ahmed's shoulder and stepped forward, hooked her leg behind his, swept out his leg, and pushed him to the floor. Ahmed grinned, looking where she had his arm in a hold and her knee on his chest.

"I was thinking more like this." Ahmed grabbed her leg and yanked it out from under her. He straddled her hips and placed his hands loosely around her throat. Her legs were bent at the knees and Ahmed wished it was her on top like this. "Escape," he said in a rough voice as he looked down to where she was taking a deep breath.

In a quick move, she reached across her chest and grabbed his arm while capturing his foot between her calf and thigh. She bucked her hips and pushed with her arms so that Ahmed fell to the side. Bridget used that momentum to roll him on his back then smiled triumphantly from where she sat on top of him. "Like that?" she asked, wiggling her bottom.

Ahmed groaned and knew he had already lost. She was cradling his erection between her thighs and enjoying the power she had over him. And he was more than content to let her have all the power she wanted as long as she kept touching him.

"Just like that," Ahmed said as he gave her a wicked grin and ran his hand up her rib cage.

"Where did you go last night?"

Ahmed's hands paused at the underside of her breasts. "I had to do something for Mo."

She slowly pressed down with her hips and rubbed against him. "You're not telling me something. What is it?"

"That I missed you. I've been thinking about this all night." Ahmed grabbed the underside of her bra and pulled it up until it trapped her arms. His mouth was on her breast and his hands wrapped around her back before she could ask another question.

Bridget freed herself from the constraining sports bra and rocked against him as he teased her nipple to a tight point. "Fine. Don't tell me. We'll both have our secrets then."

Ahmed heard the words but didn't care what they meant right now. He didn't want her to know he had killed someone last night to protect her. He didn't want her to know he did it in front of other men who had dared to question his ability to stop them from hurting her and turning her over to Sergei. Going after Marko was one thing, but these men didn't want to stop with the dog.

"I love you," he heard her gasp when his fingers pressed between her legs. Her head was thrown back and Ahmed knew he'd do anything to keep her safe. Going after Sergei was the only way to do that—even if it meant dying himself.

Bridget sat on a stool in Ahmed's kitchen and watched him pour two glasses of wine. Their lovemaking had been different, more desperate. She knew he was keeping something from her the second she saw his scraped knuckles. And the desperation and fierceness in his moves told her something bad had happened. He didn't want to talk about it and she was too afraid of losing him if she pushed too hard, so she let it go.

Her thoughts kept going back to her conversations with Sergei. Why was he tormenting her? Why did he want her to know she was going to be killed? Was it to upset Ahmed into doing something foolish? "Ahmed, why do you think Sergei seems to be personally out to get you?"

Ahmed set down the wooden spoon and took a sip of wine. "I've thought about that, too. It started off as a political rebellion. Russia and Rahmi had tense relations. Having someone close to the Russian prime minister marry someone close to King Ali Rahman was a show of respect and a desire to work together.

"It all revolves around oil and related technology. The Russians are way ahead of us in that respect. They've been doing it a lot longer. After the marriage, their scientists showed us how to process the oil better, how to build sturdy pipelines, and so on. In return, the Russians got a political ally in the UN. We are way too small a country to be their competitors, but our votes were very important to them coming out of the Cold War."

"Why would Sergei care about that?"

"I don't think he did. Another thing Russia exports are mercenaries. The king's cousin, Sarif, had been gathering support for an overthrow since he was sixteen years old. When my father brought this information to King Ali Rahman, Sarif was married off to a queen of a small country with no real power in the international community. The queen had been desperate for an ally and King Ali Rahman agreed to military protection in return for Sarif being named king consort. King Ali Rahman had hoped Sarif's new duties would keep him too busy to worry about Rahmi. But it didn't work. Sarif had tasted power and wanted more. He hired Sergei, and I think he came after me because of my father."

"Your father?"

"Even though I wasn't anything like my father, I was part of the inner circle. He came after me and tried to kill anyone close to the royal family. Then when I went after him again, I made it personal. It had to grate on him that I had survived the first assassination attempt and then escaped when he caught me. Plus it looked really bad to his prospective employers."

"And just like you can't let it go, neither can he. You're the one who got away."

"Exactly. I'm the only black mark on his record, as he is on mine. And now he's after you. It has to end soon. My brother in Rahmi is getting nervous that something is in the works. After Italy and the UN, he's preparing for a fight."

"What's your brother like? You don't talk about him much. And you never talk about your father."

"My father and I never saw eye to eye. My brother and I get along better now that we're both accomplished. He handles things in Rahmi. I handle things here. You told me your parents are in D.C.; what are they like?"

"My mom is very quiet and sweet-natured. She's the one who will trap a spider and take him outside. I'm a total daddy's girl, though, even with my dad being super traditional and very fond of rules. I hated them growing up, but I understand them now that I'm older."

"What do they think of your job?"

"They're okay with it. Proud, but they worry, too. Sometimes it's hard to get my dad to understand what I'm doing. However, he always ends up supporting me."

"They sound perfect, and I'm proud of you, too. You're too brave by half," Ahmed joked, walking around the table and wrapping her up in a hug.

Bridget enjoyed the feel of him as she rested her head against his chest and wrapped her arms around his waist. "What are you planning and how can I help you?"

"Thank you, my dear. Unfortunately, I don't think you can give me the help I need."

"What kind of help is that?"

"Just satellite images of Sergei's suspected compound in Egypt," Ahmed laughed. "Come on; I think we should shower before we go over to Dani and Mo's for dinner."

Bridget just smiled and let him lead her back into his bedroom. She had a feeling Ahmed was going to get lucky tonight in more ways than one.

Ahmed was taking forever to leave. Bridget pretended she needed extra time to get ready and tried to get Ahmed to take Zoti for a walk before heading over to Dani and Mo's. Finally when she said she just needed to put her hair up, he left with Zoti. She threw her hair in a ponytail in five seconds and dug out her phone to call her father.

"Hello, pumpkin."

Bridget cringed at the stern tone in his voice. Her father was not happy. "Hi, Daddy," she tried for cheery in hopes of thawing her father's bad mood.

"I'm starting to get worried every time you call. Terrorists falling at your feet, you in an Italian jail—what's next? Calling to tell me you've been shot?"

"I know. I'm sorry, Daddy. Well, not really, but it sounds as if I should be." She heard her dad chuckle and knew he was just worried about her.

"What do you need this time?" her dad asked, all-knowing.

"Satellite images of Sergei's suspected camp in Egypt," Bridget said as if she were asking for an apple pie recipe.

"Those are classified. I can't give you that. I've given you plenty, but this is too much. This man is putting you in harm's way. He's putting you in danger and you want me to leak you classified information? This has gone too far, pumpkin."

"Oh, hush, dear. Give her the information or she'll just go there," her mother's steady, soft voice said from the background.

"No. Not this time. Can't you see this man is using you for your connections?"

"Daddy, he doesn't even know you're my father. He's hardly using me. There has to be a way we can make this legal . . . like a joint operation," Bridget suggested.

"What's his plan?"

"I don't know. He's tired of waiting for Sergei so he's going after him."

"I'll need to talk to the president. We've been trying to get eyes in the camp for months, but they're good. We haven't been able to get a clear picture of any of the leadership. Maybe if Ahmed, and *only* Ahmed, goes in and shares everything he finds with us, then we *may* be able to back him up with drones—unofficially, of course."

"And if he gets caught?" Bridget asked while she held her breath.

"Then the U.S. will have no knowledge of this and there will be no backup. He'll be on his own. Do you still want me to continue with this?"

"Yes. He'll find a way to get those images and I'd rather he have the potential for backup than to go in there completely alone."

"I'll email you if I get anything. But, pumpkin, I don't want you near this. This isn't New York or even Italy. This is an unstable country with no get-out-of-jail card."

"Thank you, Daddy. Someday when you meet him, you'll understand why I'm doing this."

"Someday when I meet him, I'm putting his head through the wall for putting you in this situation in the first place," her father mumbled.

Bridget heard the front door open and knew she had to hurry. "Gotta go. Give Marko and Mom a kiss for me. I love you." Bridget hung up, picked up her bag of clothes, and walked into the living room.

"You can leave your clothes here, unless you want me to take you home tonight. I was hoping you would stay here."

"I can do that. I wanted to check on the training facilities before work and you're closer than I am."

Ahmed put a hand to his heart and looked wounded. "You're only with me because I'm closer to your property. That hurts."

"There are many reasons I'm with you and I think you know that's not one of them. Now, who's going to be at this dinner?"

"Kenna and Will, Henry and Neely Grace, and Tammy and Pierce."

"Their law office? Then why are we going?"

"They invited us. I know I don't date much, but isn't that what couples do?" Ahmed teased as he helped her into her coat.

"I guess. I'm still getting used to being a couple. But, I like it." Bridget rose up on her toes and placed a quick kiss on Ahmed's lips.

"I do, too." Ahmed wrapped his arms around her and kissed her thoroughly. Yes, she definitely liked this relationship thing.

Chapter Thirteen

Bridget nervously held onto Ahmed's arm as they headed down the long hallway to the space Dani had converted from a formal sitting room to a comfortable living room. Bridget knew the people waiting for them were friends; however, she'd never been half of a couple before. What if she did something wrong?

It came down to love. All the couples here were so perfect because they each loved one another. Every fiber of Bridget's being knew she loved Ahmed. She loved the person underneath his rough exterior that only a few were allowed to see. That's the man she fell in love with. Her heart ached for him, knowing she was one of the few he'd ever let completely in. After hearing about some of his past, Bridget believed only Mo held that privilege. She just didn't know what she had to do to have him trust her completely.

Lately Bridget had been telling herself she had enough love for them both, but when compared to the couples waiting, it was clear it couldn't work like that. The couples in the living room ahead of them stood side by side, each giving and receiving all the love they had. They were true partners, lovers, and soul mates. She knew Ahmed was that to her, but no matter how she tried to ignore it, what they had was not the same as what these couples shared.

"Is everything all right, my dear? You aren't nervous, are you?" Ahmed asked quietly as they approached the door.

Bridget heard the happy voices from within and Ahmed must have felt her stiffen as she compared their relationship. "I'm fine." She saw Ahmed simply raise a brow questioningly. At least he didn't press her further. So she plastered on a smile and entered the room.

"I don't know how you did it. Ahmed is like a big brother to me, even though I don't know his last name. When is his birthday or what is his favorite food?" Tammy laughed as the girls sat around snacking on some chocolates.

Bridget looked over at Ahmed standing quietly between Will and Mo as the men talked. Tammy had just summed it up. He was a big brother to the whole town and they all loved him for it. They all sensed his goodness, but he held himself apart.

Bridget shrugged her shoulders and gave a little smile as Tammy continued talking excitedly about them. The more Tammy squealed about Bridget and Ahmed's relationship, the more Bridget's heart sank. The fluffy fairy tales Tammy was spinning were too good to be true—not that she didn't have dreams of those exact things. But the more Tammy talked, the more Bridget realized she couldn't settle for anything less than the love these couples had.

"I think you're embarrassing Bridget," Kenna said politely when she realized Tammy was the only one talking.

Bridget sent her a thankful look and went back to chewing her lip.

"Have you heard the latest on Miss Lily and John?" Kenna asked, hoping to change the subject.

"No, what?" Dani asked as she moved to sit on the edge of her seat. After years of Miss Lily sticking her nose in everyone's relationships, the town was having a field day with the Miss Lily and John saga.

"Last week he asked her if she wanted to move in together." The other women gasped at John's blunder. Miss Lily would not appreciate that. She was as old-fashioned as could be when it came to dating.

"Is he still alive?" Bridget asked. Miss Lily might be small, but she packed quite a wallop with her broom.

"Wait, it gets better." Kenna giggled. "He accused her of using him as her boy toy." The women laughed so hard the men turned and stared at them. Kenna wiped the tears from her eyes and continued her story. "She told him if he wasn't ready to commit to her fully, then he could get lost. There are rumors of Miss Lily having found love before. In fact, it was such a grand love she could never find another like it."

"That's so sad," Bridget said as she glanced at Ahmed. If he couldn't love her, would she ever be able to find love again?

"Bets are flying at the café," Kenna continued. "John was seen at the seniors' dinner at the church last night sitting at a table full of women. When Miss Lily walked in on Roger Burns's arm, it apparently became quite the to-do. John confronted her at the banana pudding and called Mr. Burns a fuddy-duddy who is old enough to be her father."

Tammy choked on her drink, "I guess that could be true. I mean Mr. Burns is knocking at the door of one hundred, isn't he?"

"Sure is," Dani agreed. "What happened next?"

"Miss Lily told him she needed a man who was more mature so he would understand a woman like her could never live in sin."

Bridget giggled and then burst out laughing as she looked at the four of them sitting on the edge of their chairs in a circle eating chocolate and gossiping. "Oh my gosh—we're them. We've turned into the Rose sisters!"

Kenna, Dani, and Tammy looked around at each other and realized what they looked like sitting with their heads together and laughing. "We just need the white hair," Tammy joked as she rested her hand on her baby bump.

"And weapons. I'm good at hitting people with a purse," Kenna teased.

"I'm good at shooting people," Bridget put in. She could talk about weapons.

"You're Edna," Dani shouted before the girls all leaned against each other, pleased with their comparison.

Ahmed only half listened as the guys talked about the current football season. He had played rugby when he was in England so he ended up watching that more than football. He had sensed Bridget's nervousness when they first arrived, but she seemed to relax during dinner. And now the women were sitting in a tight circle with their heads together as they laughed.

She was gorgeous as she threw her head back and laughed. He didn't deserve her. The dark days and nights that had stretched out into years had affected him in unspoken ways. He could never be the man she deserved. That knight in shining armor all girls dream about. No, he was the dark knight from nightmares. Who could love that?

The truth slammed into him so hard he almost lost his balance. He had to let her go. Will looked at him questioningly but Ahmed waved him off. He just needed some air. As the conversation continued around him, he felt as if he wasn't of this Earth anymore. He had to let her go or he'd drag her into his nightmare.

Ahmed made his way to the balcony and breathed in the cold air. There was a reason he couldn't tell her he loved her. He didn't know how to love. He only knew how to kill. He'd spent the last eighteen years of his life destroying any feelings he had in order to protect himself and everyone else. No one could get close to him or they died. And now he was in the exact same position once again. He let Bridget get close to him and she was in danger.

Bridget had to admit, she'd had a good time. She said goodbye to everyone and Ahmed had escorted her to his car. She could tell Ahmed was unhappy about something, though. "Is everything okay?"

"I'm taking you home," Ahmed said in a hard voice.

"And getting naked?" Bridget teased. Her smile faded, though, as Ahmed didn't react. He kept his eyes on the road and clenched his jaw. "Where are we going? Your house is that way," Bridget pointed the opposite way Ahmed was driving.

"I told you, I'm taking you home."

"Don't you want to get a bag? And I left mine at your house."

"Nabi picked it up and has already dropped it off at your house. I don't need a bag. I'm not staying."

Bridget felt as if she'd been punched in the stomach. She looked over at him, but he just kept his eyes on the road. He refused to look at her as she felt tears stinging the back of her eyes. "What did I do?"

"You loved me. Goodbye, Bridget."

Ahmed stopped the car in front of Southern Charms and waited for her to get out. Numbness settled over her and she had nearly forgotten how to breathe. Bridget blindly grabbed the door handle and staggered out into the night. She made her way around the back of the building and up the steps before she could drag in a ragged breath.

Tears blurred the stairs as she climbed them, refusing to cry out loud. All she wanted to do was wrap Marko in her arms, but she didn't even have her best friend with her because of Ahmed. Marko was gone so she could help Ahmed. So she could show him she was worthy of his love. She felt like a fool.

Ahmed slammed his front door so hard it splintered down the middle. Zoti darted off the couch and cowered under the table as Ahmed stormed into the kitchen and grabbed a bottle of bourbon. He ripped off his tie and tossed it onto the counter before turning up the bottle.

The amber liquid warmed his mouth as he took one drink after another. A part of him knew he should be begging Bridget to forgive him and another part hoped Sergei would appear on his doorstep right now to kill him . . . anything to end this vendetta.

Ahmed saw Zoti and felt even worse. He'd hurt the woman he loved and scared his dog. He *did* deserve to be killed. He bent down and gently reached out for Zoti who wagged his tail and nuzzled him kindly. Ahmed wrapped his arm around Zoti and ignored the knocking at the door. He didn't want to see Nabi. Ahmed knew he'd ask why he'd been ordered to take Bridget's bag to her house tonight when it was clear he'd come back home. Nabi had been spending too much time at the café.

The door opened and Ahmed had his gun in his hand before the handle had even turned. "Get out, Nabi, or I'll shoot you."

"Then you'd be hung for killing a member of the royal family."

"At this moment, I don't think I'd care. You can get out, too. Don't think being my prince will prevent me from kicking your ass."

"Then let's go," Mo shrugged out of his jacket and took off his tie.

"You're on." Ahmed gave Zoti a pet and led Mo down into his training room. He peeled off his shirt and slid on the gloves as Mo slowly unbuttoned his shirt and set it on the bench. He tried to be patient, but he just had to hit someone soon. "Let's go, Your Highness."

"You broke her heart, didn't you?" Mo asked quietly as he squared off in front of Ahmed.

Ahmed threw a punch that had Mo staggering backward. "It was for her own good."

Mo kept his calm and delivered a jab that Ahmed easily blocked before going on the offensive again. He delivered punch after punch and just wanted Mo to go down. "And what's good for you? What about the person you have beaten down inside of you since Sergei entered your life?" Mo countered and landed a solid punch on Ahmed's jaw.

Ahmed took the hit and then landed a hard punch to Mo's face, snapping his head back. Blood dripped from the cut on his lip as Ahmed hurled punch after punch at him. Mo protected his head and waited out the flurry of punches.

"That person doesn't exist anymore. He can't. He was nothing. No one loved him because he was weak. I'm not that man anymore. I can protect my own now."

Mo finally made his move and slammed his fist into Ahmed's stomach before he delivered an uppercut to his jaw. "That's right. You can protect your own, including the woman you love. And you were never nothing. You were my only friend. My best friend—you always will be."

Mo held up his hands and tossed his gloves on the floor. He grabbed his white dress shirt and slid it on over his sweat-soaked body. His lip was swollen along with his eye and he had a bright red mark on his cheek. Finally the anger left Ahmed. His best friend just took a beating to help him out.

"You, too. I wouldn't have survived without you. Dani's going to kill me when she sees you."

"Probably. But you deserve it. Now you better find a way to win Bridget back."

Chapter Fourteen

B ridget awoke with the headache from hell. She'd eaten all the cupcakes the Rose sisters had left and cried until there were no more tears. Then she'd gotten mad. How dare he treat her like this? And then she'd passed out cold after the sugar high wore off.

Now her head was pounding, her eyes felt like sandpaper, and she was starving. Bridget staggered into the bathroom and groaned. She looked awful. Her eyes were red and puffy. Frosting was dried onto her cheek and chocolate crumbs were smashed into her hair. She needed coffee badly. Too bad she didn't have any. It looked like a trip to the café was inevitable.

The shower was hot and steamy when she got in and washed the evidence from last night's pity party from her face and hair. If she could face down stone-cold terrorists, then she could face a café full of neighbors. Bridget kept repeating that to herself as she dried off and got dressed for the day. She was on call with Annie and it would be good to spend the day with her best friend.

She walked out the door and told herself once again it would be fine. She was strong and she'd accepted that Ahmed had hurt her. She was a strong, independent woman who didn't need a man to make her life complete.

Ahmed hung up the phone with the florist and paced his living room. He'd never had to say he was sorry for anything these past eighteen years and he didn't know where to start. He'd ordered chocolates, flowers, and now he was wondering if he needed to run into Lexington for some jewelry. However, Bridget didn't strike him as a jewelry girl, maybe a gun. Yes, a gun. One of the new . . . The knock at the door had him hurrying to answer it. He had Mo's French cook working on a romantic meal for her when he would beg her to forgive him. "Cy? I thought you were taking a honeymoon," Ahmed said in surprise.

"We did. We left right after I got you those bank records. I got home late last night and guess what? My phone's been ringing off the hook. Apparently you decided to finally take the leap and started dating the perfect woman. And then out of nowhere, decided to dump her. Am I up to speed?" Cy asked rhetorically as he pushed his way into the house.

"Come in," Ahmed said dryly.

"I wasn't asking. What's going on and why did you turn your back on the best thing that could happen to you?"

"I know you, the golden boy, don't hear this much, but it's none of your business."

"I picked Bridget to come to Keeneston last Christmas and now I feel responsible for her. Not only that, but you and Miles are the only ones here who have some inkling of what I've done. If anyone can understand you, then it should be me," Cy said as he tossed his jacket on the back of the chair and took a seat on the couch. "I'm not leaving."

"I can see that." Ahmed let out a breath and took a seat in the chair across from him. Cy smiled in victory and it was tough for Ahmed to remember that under his friend's Hollywood good looks and winning smile was a cold-blooded spy.

"I take it Bridget is who you told me about on the plane before we jumped to rescue Gemma."

"Yes," Ahmed said quietly.

Cy leaned back and stretched out his legs. "Talk."

Ahmed closed his eyes for a second. It wasn't easy to do. "I buried that side of me years ago when Sergei killed my wife and son. What happened was . . ."

"I know what happened." Cy waved him off. "You don't have to go into it if you don't want to."

"You know?"

"I am a spy, you know. A good one. The only thing I don't know is why Sergei came after you in the first place. But, more pertinently, I want to know what happened with Bridget."

Ahmed knew he shouldn't be surprised, but he was. "You know about my family. Do you know about my capture?" When Cy gave him a quick nod of his head, Ahmed actually felt relieved. Cy knew and would understand his perspective without having to relive those horrible times. "I vowed retribution. I promised myself that Sergei would pay for what he did to me, to my family. I have spent every waking moment turning myself into the most physically and mentally fit soldier I could be so I could channel my anger and exact my revenge. I detached from everyone so Sergei could never use another person to hurt me again.

"Then what do I do? I fall in love with someone close enough to Sergei's sphere for him to be able to manipulate and use her to torture me. Last night, all I could think about was the danger she would be in. I would drag her into this hell with me and she deserves so much more than that."

Cy leaned forward, rested his elbows on his knees, and took a deep breath. "You're not the only one with a dark side. I've gone to places for my government that stole parts of my soul. I've killed, I've tortured, I've . . ." Cy took a deep breath to steady himself.

"I know. You're not the only spy around," Ahmed said sarcastically to spare Cy from reliving his own nightmares.

"Thanks. But the darkness I felt overtaking me, snuffing out who I really was, started to fade when I met Gemma. I can laugh again, for real. Not the fake laugh I used to fit in. I feel the pressure leaving and I see a future. A happy one. You had that with Bridget, didn't you?"

Ahmed only nodded. He had felt the cold darkness seeping back into him the second she got out of the car last night. "Is it fair to her to drag her down this path with me? It'll only show her the beast I am and the weak boy I once was."

"We're not beasts. We're men who would do anything to protect those we love. And she knows that. She has her own darkness. It's why I was drawn to her and sent her here. Her unit had been ambushed and she'd lost half the men in her unit. She shielded the injured with her body and held off the rebels until backup could arrive two hours later."

"She's told me some, but she's so full of life that it's hard to believe."

"Did it occur to you she's just good at hiding it? Physically, I would choose Bridget to have my back any day. But she's looking for that light, too, just like you are. And from what I heard, you both found it in each other. Instead of pushing her away, it's time to bring her close. She'll give you the answers that you think killing Sergei will give you. By the way, how did Sergei know about Bridget?"

"Nabi found bugs in the café," Ahmed said absently as he thought about what Cy has just said.

"I'll take care of them. I know a way to rig them so whoever is listening has no idea I've messed with them. They'll still be live, but unless you're yelling directly into them, you won't be able to make out any clear words. You need to get cleaned up and get your woman back."

Cy stood up and Ahmed held out his hand. "Thank you. I knew I wanted her back but was still worried if it was the right thing to do."

"That's what friends are for." Cy slid into his jacket and gave the cracked door a look before turning around to face Ahmed. "Oh, and I might wear a Kevlar vest if I were you."

The sunny day and crisp chill in the air refreshed Bridget as she waved to people and made her way to the café. She opened the door and forgot everything she had just told herself when three white heads clucked around her and pulled her down for a group hug.

"Oh! Bless your heart."

"I still can't believe it."

"How are you doing?" the three Rose sisters all asked as she suddenly found her head smashed against Miss Violet's bosom.

Bridget pulled free and stood up to face the crowd of onlookers. "I'm fine. But I won't be if I don't get some coffee," she laughed all the while her heart broke.

"Sure thing, dear," Miss Daisy said so sympathetically that Bridget knew they didn't believe her for a second.

"You poor thing." Bridget felt shivers run through her body as Kandi flounced into the café. "It must hurt knowing you aren't woman enough to keep Ahmed. Or are you just that bad in bed?" Kandi laughed as if she said something funny and everyone in the café cringed.

Kandi strutted past her, hitting Bridget in the arm with her luggage-sized purse. She had zeroed in on Henry sitting alone in the middle of the restaurant working on his computer. "See, B, you gotta take control. Men like that. You grab them." Bridget's eyes went wide in surprise as Kandi bent over, grabbed Henry's collar, and kissed him. Henry tried to leap back, but Kandi had his collar in a death grip as she devoured him.

Bridget and the rest of the patrons cringed when Kandi deepened the kiss and Henry floundered about trying to get free. Even the Rose sisters stood transfixed. Bridget picked up a glass of ice water from a nearby table and poured it on Kandi's head. She sputtered like a drowning cat and leapt away from Henry who promptly fell backward out of his chair, spitting to clean out his mouth.

"You bitch! I was trying to help you . . . you, you ice queen. No wonder he left you," Kandi screeched as she leapt at Bridget, her long nails clawing at her.

There were moments in Bridget's life when she had wanted to lose it. Holding a dying comrade, arguing with her father, dealing with sexist men in her work—but she had always held it together. But not today.

As Kandi came at her, she picked up a bottle of maple syrup and squeezed it straight into her face. The café cheered, but suddenly fell silent. Bridget steeled herself and turned to face who she thought would be Ahmed. Instead, she was met with Bill's angry face.

"I'm sorry, but she deserved it," Bridget said as she raised her hands in the air, still holding onto the syrup bottle.

"I know she did. She was taking our kids to school and I thought I would surprise her by picking up breakfast. Imagine my surprise when I walk by and see her tongue down Henry's throat."

"It wasn't me," Henry called from where he was crawling away from Kandi on hands and knees.

"Oh, I know it wasn't," Bill said quietly. "It was my *wife*."

"He kissed me, Billy-Willy. You know men just throw themselves at me." Kandi begged him to believe as she used her fingers to wipe syrup from her eyes so she could see. The patrons snorted their disbelief and some even laughed.

"That worked the first ten times, but not now. I'm such an idiot. Let's see how you like it." Bill started looking around. "Who's single?"

"Bridget is," Miss Violet called out mischievously.

Bridget felt her eyes widen as Bill focused on her. He wasn't an unattractive man. He was softer than Ahmed with a bit of a belly and his light brown hair was thinning. He wasn't the type of man Bridget normally thought of dating, but he was a nice guy. And he had a steady job that didn't involve gunfire. Plus he seemed to really love his children. Maybe she needed to look for a Bill of her own.

"You and Ahmed split?" Bill asked with wonder.

"He dumped her," Miss Violet called out again.

"Sorry, he's almost as much of an idiot as I am. But, I need to make a point to my wife." Bill grabbed her then and Bridget's mouth fell open in surprise. Bill took advantage and kissed her as Kandi shrieked.

Bridget felt his hand skim down her back and cup her bottom and when she went to protest, Bill's tongue darted into her mouth. Bridget didn't know what to do, so she just stood there. She was single and it looked as if Bill was about to be. However, she was disappointed. Sure, he was a good kisser, but nowhere near Ahmed's toe-curling, get-me-naked level. Would anyone ever be able to measure up to Ahmed? Bridget almost snorted as Bill continued to kiss her as passionately as he could. No one could live up to Ahmed.

The only hint of trouble came with the intake of thirty people's breaths. Bridget felt a cold darkness settle over the café and broke the kiss just in time to see Ahmed step inside the door and stop. "Bill, I'd run if I were you," she said sweetly as she gave his arm a pat.

Bill turned around and panicked. He stumbled against the table, knocking it into a syrup-covered Kandi who, while trying to get out of the way, slipped on the spilled water. With a quick, ear-piercing shriek, Kandi's arms flailed and down she went. Bridget watched in horror as Bill turned to see his wife hit the floor. Then he quickly turned around to watch Ahmed stalk toward him, completely ignoring Kandi flailing on the floor.

"I'm sorry, but she said she was single," Bill pleaded as Ahmed let out a barely audible growl. Bill backed up and hit the table now lying on its side and gulped. Bridget and the rest of the café stood in silence, transfixed by Ahmed and his murderous eyes, a terrified Bill, and a maple-syrup-covered Kandi sobbing in a puddle of water on the ground.

"I got twenty on Bill peeing his pants," Miss Lily whispered.

"I'll take that. I bet twenty on him being dead before he has the chance," Miss Violet whispered confidently.

"That's not fair, Violet Fae. You saw Ahmed outside and still told Bill to kiss her. You were just rigging the odds," Miss Daisy complained.

"Put my twenty with Miss Violet," Ahmed said coldly as he reached out to grab Bill's collar. Bill screamed and leapt backward, right into the table. He teetered for a minute and then tumbled over the table, landing hard on top of Kandi. He bounced a couple of times on her twin inflatables and then finally came to rest.

"Ahmed, that's enough. Bill's right—we're not together and he can kiss me if he wants to. In fact, I can kiss anyone I want." Bridget scanned the room and with a smirk leaned down and planted a big kiss on Old Man Tabby. "Now, are you going to beat up Mr. Tabernacle, too?" Old Man Tabby sat stunned until a little smile came across his face. It quickly faded when he looked up to Ahmed.

"Let's talk outside," Ahmed said quietly, suddenly realizing he was making a scene.

"NO!" The agonizing wail filled the café and everyone turned back to where Bill was helping Kandi stand up. Her chest was dramatically uneven. One giant boob cast an eclipse over its missing twin. The weight of having only one colossal boob was causing Kandi to list to the side as Bill steadied her.

"Thank goodness something good has come out of this," Bill mumbled.

"But I got them for you. Not that it mattered, you still won't touch me," Kandi cried as her mascara mingled with the syrup covering her face.

"They scare me. I could die if I put my face near them. And you look ridiculous. You were perfect before all this. Perfect with stretch marks, a few extra pounds, and your natural brown hair. Now, let's get you to your doctor."

"Oh, Bill," Kandi cried as she wrapped her arms around him and tried to lean in over her still-inflated boob to kiss him. "Will you ever forgive me?"

"Not yet. But you get rid of those death traps and we'll talk. I'm going to move into my own place with the boys for a while, though."

"You're leaving me?"

"Yes, until you can prove to me and the town that you have changed. Now come on." Bill led his sobbing wife out the front door as everyone watched.

"Twenty says she'll reform," Pam Gilbert, PTA president called out.

"Twenty she'll go to Vegas and become an escort," Old Man Tabby said as he scrounged around his overalls looking for the bill.

"It seems as if we are old news. Please, my dear, come home and talk to me," Ahmed whispered into her ear.

"Oh, Ahmed," Miss Lily hailed. "We haven't forgotten about you. Let's hear it."

Bridget almost felt bad for him while he looked around at the town all staring him down again. *Almost.* It seemed she had more friends than she knew.

"Bridget?" he pleaded.

"If you have anything to say, you can say it in front of my friends," Bridget said loudly as the townspeople grinned and some even whistled.

"You go, girl," Dani called out from the back of the room. Bridget looked back and saw Mo sitting there smiling with a huge shiner. Bridget turned back to Ahmed and crossed her arms to wait him out.

Ahmed tried to calm his beating heart as he kept his eyes on Bridget. He loved her, he kept reminding himself. He took a deep breath and ignored Dani's cheers from the back of the café and just remembered what Mo and Cy had told him. He could do this. She was worth this public humiliation, and he did deserve it.

"I'm sorry I was so cold last night."

"Louder," Miss Daisy shouted to the joy of the patrons.

"I'm sorry I shut down last night. I saw how beautiful and full of life you were and I was afraid I'd change that. That my dark side would take its toll on you and you'd end up unhappy and resent that you ever met me." Ahmed kept his focus on Bridget as the people started whispering all around him. He didn't care what they said; he only cared about what Bridget thought.

"You know I understand . . . things. Don't you think if you had this worry you should have been man enough to talk to me about it? Let me decide what I can and cannot handle."

"I thought I was protecting you," Ahmed pleaded. He felt as if he were losing her and that feeling was worse than any torture he'd experienced.

"And how many times have I told you I don't need protecting?" Bridget asked angrily.

"How can I not protect the woman I love more than my own life? How can I stand the thought that my love is in danger from Sergei because of me? What kind of man do you take me to be?" Ahmed shot back.

He saw the shock on Bridget's face and then her eyes softened as she stepped closer to him. "I love you, too. You just need to realize you're not alone anymore."

Ahmed let out a deep breath and unclenched his fists. He was flooded with relief and didn't care how many people were watching. Bridget was his and he'd never be so stupid again.

With one quick move, he grabbed her around the waist and brought her against him. His mouth sought hers and he claimed her lips right there in front of everyone. No one would make the mistake of thinking she was single again. As his tongue ravaged her mouth, he'd be damned if she didn't just mark him as hers forever, too.

"Now I'll come home with you," Bridget whispered when the kiss ended and the town alternately clapped and whistled. Ahmed couldn't stop the reaction that hit him quick and hard.

"Your place is closer," he smiled down to her.

"Oh, Lordy," Miss Lily hollered and then grabbed a paper napkin and began to fan herself.

"I think you may need to stop smiling or the women will be swooning at your feet and then I'll never get you naked," Bridget teased in a low voice.

Ahmed tried to stop the laughter but decided to finally be himself. His head fell back and he gave a bark of laughter as he pulled Bridget to his side. "Nothing is going to get in my way." He smiled down at her while they made their way to the door amid the flutter of napkins and sighs.

Chapter Fifteen

Bridget snuggled against Ahmed's bare chest and rested her arm on his flat stomach. She absently ran her finger up and down the path from his belly button to the small dark trail that disappeared under the sheets. Ahmed had practically undressed her as they hurried down Main Street to her apartment. It had been different this time. They had broken down all the barriers between them and made love with all the passion and love they felt for each other. She closed her eyes as he absently stroked her hair until the sound of her phone alerted her to an email.

"Go ahead and get that, my dear. I'm going to jump in the shower," Ahmed said, kissing her head before sliding out of bed.

Bridget watched him confidently walk to her bathroom completely nude. He had scars on his body — some were thin white lines and some she recognized as bullet holes and knife wounds, but he wore them well. In fact, it only made him sexier.

She stretched out her arm and blindly grabbed her cell phone. She opened her email and saw the new message was from her father. Inside was a secure link to satellite images. There was a short note from her dad reminding her of the deal they struck. Bridget smiled and quickly forwarded the images while removing their source.

The shower turned off and a minute later Ahmed came out with his hair hanging loose around his face and a towel slung low over his hips.

"I have a present for you," Bridget smiled as she drank in the sight of him.

"I think you've already given me a most wonderful present," he smiled and Bridget couldn't believe he was hers.

"Check your email." She giggled when he raised his eyebrow and went to his phone. She saw the moment he realized what he was looking at.

"First, how did you get these?" When Bridget just smiled, she saw his jaw tighten. "Your military source, of course. Second, what did you have to do to get these?"

"I made a couple of promises."

"What kind?"

"The kind I hope you don't mind agreeing to. I promised I wouldn't enter the compound. I also promised that if you used these images and went into the camp that we turned over all intelligence to my source in the military."

"Will I have U.S. military backup?" Ahmed asked as he studied the images.

"You will if you can verify terrorist activity and key targets. Oh, and if you don't get caught. If you can manage that, they'll send in a drone to destroy the compound," Bridget told him as she sat up in bed and watched him study the images.

"If he's there, then he'll most likely be in this building here. See how it's a little away from these smaller tents?" Ahmed pointed. "You do realize I won't wait for the military to blow up the camp. I'm going to be the one to kill Sergei."

"I know. I don't think they'll mind as long as this 'joint' mission has a positive result. They just need the intel to know that they have enough evidence to take out the compound and not get blasted by the United Nations," Bridget explained as she hopped out of bed and started to pull out her tactical gear.

"So, I'll be videoed?"

"Audio, too. I'll make sure it gets edited. You'll never be seen. And you'll have a kill switch on the helmet cam in case you don't want to record something. I'm guessing you know the drill."

"I do. Will I have any boots on the ground?"

"Just me," Bridget grinned.

"You're all I need. You can be my eyes and ears from a safe distance. I'll leave it up to you to communicate with the military. Just try not to get me blown up."

"I wouldn't do that . . . well, I won't do it now that you've apologized," Bridget laughed.

"I need to get my gear. I'll pick you up in an hour. Tell your contact, wheels up in ninety minutes." Ahmed buttoned his shirt and slid on his suit jacket before giving her a quick kiss goodbye. No more smiles, no more laughing. Nope, he was in full soldier mode now and it was sexy as all get-out.

Bridget felt the familiar calm settle over her as she prepared for the mission. They had been supplied a Range Rover with communication equipment, camouflage, an M-60 machine gun, and some other fun equipment upon landing at a private airfield belonging to a expatriate of Rahmi. She and Ahmed had driven three hours south along the coast toward Sudan before turning off the coastal road to bounce along a desert road almost another hour inland. They'd traveled through the rocky red mountains to a spot near the compound.

After studying the satellite images, Bridget and Ahmed picked out her perfect surveillance spot about three-quarters of a mile from the compound, as well as Ahmed's entrance and exit paths. She covered the Range Rover with a camouflaged tarp while Ahmed put on the small lightweight communications device and buckled on the heavy Kevlar helmet with a small camera and night-vision goggles.

He put on his vest and strapped his 9mm Sig and knife to his thigh before slipping the M4 rifle over his shoulder.

"Do you need help?" he asked in a low voice.

"I don't think so," Bridget replied as she put her matching helmet on over her communication device.

"It's going to get dark soon. You need to hurry into position."

Bridget nodded, pulling on the ghillie suit covered with burlap strips and some small desert foliage. "Let's test the communications." When Ahmed gave a barely perceptible nod, she continued, "Eagle to Lion."

"I read you," replied Ahmed.

She gave him a nod acknowledging that she heard him.

"Eagle to base," she said as she waited for a response.

"Base reads you both. Drone has already been launched. ETA one hour and forty-three minutes," she heard back from the U.S. military base in Djibouti coordinating with a ship in the Red Sea that launched the drone.

"Do you need anything?" Ahmed asked her as she put the ghillie rifle wrap around her Tac-338 long-distance sniper rifle.

"Just for you to be safe." Bridget took a deep breath and got accustomed to the heavy suit. She was already getting hot and looked forward to the cooler night temperatures.

Bridget turned away from Ahmed and started toward the mountain. As she approached a cliff, she dropped to the ground and spent the next hour slowly moving the last fifty yards to the spot she picked out. She crawled on the ground before the edge came into sight and moved slowly in case anyone was scanning the ridge.

She kept moving slowly as darkness fell. Night vision goggles were too common now for her to safely move faster. By the time Ahmed was ready to start his mission, she had her rifle set up, the night scope focused on the camp below and blended in seamlessly with the mountain ridge.

"Eagle in position," she whispered into her coms.

"Lion on the move," Ahmed's voice said with no emotion. She scanned the camp that was laid out in a rectangular shape with a campfire close to the target. Ahmed had to come in from the left because there wasn't enough cover behind the target tent. Ahmed said he'd manage it, but she was worried now that she saw the layout.

She took note of the guards' locations and weapons before searching for Ahmed. Bridget knew the path he was going to take to enter the camp, yet she still couldn't find him through her night vision scope. "Eagle," his voice came over the coms again. "If anything goes sideways, I want you to pick up and head out immediately."

"Base seconds that," she heard in her earpiece. She was sure her father had just issued that order. She knew he would be in the war room at the Pentagon listening in with an open line to the command center.

"Copy." Bridget didn't mean it, but it would make the men feel better and allow them to focus on their jobs. "Base, are you getting visual?"

"Yes."

Bridget looked along the mountainside again and spoke quietly into her coms. "I can't see you, but you should be reaching the camp within five minutes. There are two sentries on patrol that you could run into. Their path comes close to your target path, so I would change your course eight degrees north. You'll be able to take the one guard and then meet the other as he rounds Gamma tent."

"Changing course now. ETA three minutes fifteen seconds."

Bridget scanned the mountainside but still failed to see Ahmed. She had to keep her breathing slow and steady in case he needed her to take a shot. Her head didn't move as she scanned the area with an extra scope. The guard walking at the foot of the mountain failed to see her both times he walked by. Her ghillie suit was doing its job. That's when she saw Ahmed. He slid from the side of the mountain and lay still on the ground in a dip on the desert floor as the guard strolled slowly by him, scanning the mountaintop instead of looking at the ground near his feet.

Ahmed controlled his breathing, feeling the footfalls of the guard reverberate though the dry desert floor as he walked by. Knowing Bridget was watching him made this task even more difficult. He would trust her with his life, but the thought of taking a life in front of her made him worry. She would see the true dark beast in action.

"Clear," he heard Bridget's hushed voice say through his earpiece. Silently, he rose from the ground right behind the guard. He only had ten seconds before the second guard would round the tent on the far side of the camp.

He cleared his mind of all thoughts and opened his senses. He heard the man breathing and felt the air his body disturbed as he walked. Not allowing him to take another step, Ahmed wrapped his arm around the guard's throat and against his head. Ahmed pulled and twisted the man tight against him. The guard didn't even have time to gasp before Ahmed broke his neck. He quickly dragged the man against the back of Delta tent and propped him up.

"Second guard in six, five . . ." Bridget counted down as Ahmed raced to lie in the dip in the ground at the base of the mountain once again. "Here's our boy now. Twenty paces. Twelve. Eight."

Ahmed heard the man yell in Arabic for the dead guard to stop taking a piss again and get back on patrol. The other soldier, clearly at the end of his patience, went to grab the dead man when Ahmed made his move.

Bridget watched in silence as Ahmed killed the two guards. She didn't even hear his breathing increase as he dragged the bodies off the main path behind the tents. She scanned the camp once again and knew Ahmed was going to have to pass a clearing on the far side of Beta tent before arriving at Alpha tent, which they hoped was Sergei's hiding spot.

"Okay. You have ten yards between Beta tent and Alpha. Six guards are drinking around a fire in the center of the compound with clear sight of Beta and Alpha tents."

"Copy," was all Ahmed said in response as he disappeared behind Beta tent. She couldn't see him as he made his way toward his target. The wait was killing her. She wished she was down there with him, but she would protect him the best she could from here. Three minutes passed by and the two sentries on the other side of camp had not noticed their comrades missing.

"I'm seeing movement inside Beta tent. The door is opening and someone else is joining the group. There's also movement at Theta camp on the far side of the compound. Three guards, but they have their backs to you."

"I'm going now," Ahmed whispered.

Ahmed pulled the keffiyeh from around one of the dead men's head. He tied the large scarf around his head, leaving just the lens of the camera exposed. He hid the night vision goggles under the keffiyeh and tried to tie it in such a way as to hide the blood. Moving his thigh strap to the left leg to help conceal it, he took off his vest and stashed it behind Beta tent. Without hesitating, he walked straight into the open space between Beta and Alpha tents.

Ahmed strode calmly toward Alpha tent, which he was going to pass until he got behind the men at the campfire. Then he'd duck behind Alpha and cut his way into the tent before the patrol for that side arrived. He relaxed his shoulders and shot a glance to the group around the fire.

"What's going on?" one of the men shouted to Ahmed in Arabic.

"Just watching that idiot get chewed out for pissing while on patrol again. I swear he won't have a dick to piss with if he keeps this up," Ahmed called back as the men laughed and went back to talking among themselves about the guard Ahmed had just killed.

"We got positive ID on two of those men," the base commander broke into Ahmed's coms. "The one who talked to you is Ghali

Yasin. He is responsible for the embassy bombing in Lebanon. The man to his right is Boris Golov. He's a rising star in the Russian Mafia. He started off as a contract killer and murdered the U.S. ambassador to Yemen prior to the embassy closing. Now he's dabbling in the sale of bombs on the black market. It's time to leave, Lion. That's enough evidence for us to authorize the strike."

"ETA of bird?" Ahmed heard Bridget ask while he cut back into the shadows and made his way around Sergei's suspected hiding spot.

"Fifteen minutes. Evacuate now."

"Negative. Wait for my word."

Ahmed smiled in the darkness when he heard Bridget over his coms. His girl was breaking orders to make sure he had enough time to take care of Sergei.

"Lion, forty seconds until the guard becomes visible."

"Get your ass out of there, Eagle. That's an order from the top."

Ahmed stopped and listened for movement inside the tent. Nothing, dammit. He pulled out his knife and cut two of the ropes holding the flap down.

As he rolled under the flap, his eyes widened at the colorful language Bridget used. Who knew this quiet woman could cuss like that. He particularly liked what she told them they could do with that drone if they didn't wait for her order.

"I'm in," he whispered and the voices in his ear quieted. "It's empty."

"Get out," base ordered.

"No. There's things here," Ahmed whispered as he pulled out a small red light to examine the papers on Sergei's desk. "Base, do you see this?" Ahmed asked as he flipped through the pages of the ledger.

"Negative."

"Sergei just bought a bunch of bomb-making material."

"Does it say what it's for?" Bridget's hushed voice came through the coms.

"No, but there are empty cases of new guns as well, courtesy of your Russian friend out there. They're planning an attack," Ahmed said quietly as he scanned more of the room.

"Turn off the light and take cover. The Russian is coming your way. Do you want me to take him out?" Bridget asked in a cold, steady voice.

"Negative. I'll handle it." Ahmed crouched behind the empty crates and waited. He was glad that he'd be able to talk to Boris.

The flap to the tent opened and an oil lamp was lit. The room was encased in a soft glow of light as Ahmed hugged the shadows and watched Boris make his way to the desk. The big Russian moved papers around and started to look worried when he couldn't find what he was looking for.

Ahmed stood and stepped from the shadows. "Are you looking for this?" He held up the ledger stuffed full of documents and a pistol aimed right at Boris's heart.

"You're that guy from before. What are you doing in here with my books?" Boris put his hand on his gun.

Ahmed let his lips curl into a cold smirk. "I'm Ahmed. Now grab your gun with two fingers and toss it here." Boris lost some color and did what he was told. "Where did Sergei take the bomb he made?"

"I don't know. You don't ask too many questions in my business," Boris said as he relaxed and rested on his ego.

"What kind of bomb was it?"

"The kind that goes *BOOM*," Boris smiled cockily.

"It's too bad you can't remember more. I do not give second chances."

"You better hit your mark on the first shot. They'll hear you. You'll be dead in seconds," Boris taunted.

Ahmed shrugged. "Do I look like someone who would miss? Or someone who would care about a few drunken soldiers? Either way you will be dead, so I wouldn't worry about it." Ahmed pulled out a silencer and attached it to his 9mm. Ahmed's lips curled as he saw Boris break out in a sweat.

"Okay. We talk," Boris said as if he were a salesman negotiating a deal.

"Bomb specs and location or you die in five seconds," Ahmed said calmly.

"Seventy-five pounds of Semtex. Like C-4, yes?"

"A half a pound is enough to take down a plane. What's he going to do with that much?" Ahmed held his gun steady even through his shock. He heard Bridget curse in his ear and knew the military would be scrambling for intelligence on this.

"I don't know," Boris shrugged.

"Wrong answer." Ahmed lowered his gun a bit and shot. *Pfft.* The silenced shot hit Boris right in the knee. He screamed and fell to the ground. "Tell me now or I shoot again."

"The scream has gotten you some attention. They're not moving fast, but they're cautiously gathering their arms. Eight total heading your way slowly," he heard Bridget say calmly.

"Boris. Tell me what I want to know." Ahmed strode forward and placed his gun to Boris's head.

"It was to be broken up for multiple smaller explosions set off by remote. That's all I know."

"Drone ETA eight minutes and ten seconds. We're lighting it up. We can't risk anyone getting a phone call off to Sergei to alert him that we know he has bomb materials," Ahmed heard the base commander say into his earpiece.

"Did you kill the U.S. ambassador to Yemen?" Ahmed asked as he dropped his gun to his side.

Boris gulped. "Why do you care?"

"I heard about it and was curious. It was a good shot from what I read."

"Thank you," Boris relaxed and Ahmed felt the anger coiling in his stomach. Boris thought the danger had past. "I'm sure you can appreciate the difficulty of such a shot. It was one of my best jobs. That and the bitch inspector from England."

"The nuclear inspector in Iran? The mother that led to a temporary suspension of further inspections?" Ahmed asked as he listened to the sounds of men's voices growing closer.

"Yes," he smiled. "That shot was taken from almost a mile away."

"This shot isn't nearly as impressive, but I feel pretty good about taking it."

Chapter Sixteen

Bridget set her sights on the man closest to Alpha tent. The guards were armed with high-power rifles and were spreading out to surround the tent. It couldn't wait any longer. "You done with Boris?" she asked as she checked the wind and made a slight alteration to her scope.

"Yes."

"Good, you've got company. Two to the west, one to the east, two to the north and three getting ready to knock on the front door."

"You promised to go. It's time to keep that promise." Bridget heard Ahmed say seriously.

"I lied," Bridget told him as she placed her finger on the trigger.

"ETA six minutes, forty-three seconds. Thanks for the info from Boris, but it's time to clear out now."

"Walk out the front door in five seconds," Bridget ordered him.

"Bridget!" She heard him say her name instead of using code but ignored him as she gently squeezed the trigger. Three quarters of a mile away, Yasin fell to the ground. Moving steadily, she squeezed the trigger two more times.

"Go! Go! Go!" she yelled as she scanned the camp one more time, taking out a guard on patrol rushing toward the fight. Ahmed burst from the tent running full speed past the campfire. "You've got three at six o'clock and two more sleepyheads coming from Omega tent at your eight."

Ahmed turned and threw a fragmentation grenade that had the mercenaries scrambling for cover. Bridget leapt up and grabbed her equipment. "Take the road. I'll pick you up," she yelled into her coms as the rocks and dirt caused her to slide down the path.

The ghillie suit was heavy, but she refused to let it slow her down as she sprinted for the car. She grabbed the corner of the tarp and pulled it off enough to leap into the driver's seat. She looked like a desert ghost sitting behind the wheel as she floored the gas pedal. The SUV took air when she didn't bother to slow down for the little dips and hills.

"I don't have eyes on you. Where are you?"

"A quarter-mile from the camp."

"Base to Lion. Are you being followed?"

"Yes. After the explosion, most stayed but two got into a jeep. They're gaining," Ahmed told them, his breath finally labored although completely in his control.

"I'll take care of it. Be there in thirty seconds. Run faster." Bridget thought she had a heard a chuckle before gunfire erupted.

"Shit," she screamed as she took the turn onto the main dirt road. The car slid on the loose dirt, but she was able to get it back under control in no time.

Up ahead she saw Ahmed coming over the hill with a jeep close on his tail. One man was leaning out the open door shooting at Ahmed with a rifle. Ahmed didn't bother to look over his shoulder. Instead he just raised his M4 and fired off several shots.

Bridget slammed on the brakes as she opened the sunroof. The second the SUV came to a stop, she grabbed the military machine gun and stood up so that the top part of her body was sticking out of the sunroof. She opened the stand attached to the gun and set it on the roof while she locked the ammunition into place.

"Get down," she yelled to Ahmed. He dove to the side of the road and hunkered down against a boulder as she opened fire. The shells spit out the side as she shot at the jeep. The windshield shattered, the tires popped, and when she hit the gas tank, the jeep exploded with a *whoosh*.

Ahmed slammed his back against the rock and ducked his head. Within seconds, the night wakened to the sound of a fully automatic M60. He glanced up and the sight left him speechless. Bridget, still dressed as a desert monster, stood out of the sunroof feeding ammo into the machine gun as she shot at the jeep.

Suddenly, Ahmed felt a little foolish for worrying so much about showing her his dark side. And for telling Bridget he was trying to protect her. He had been a patronizing idiot, he thought as the jeep exploded. She was the most amazingly beautiful warrior woman Ahmed had ever seen.

"Lion, get your ass in the car."

Ahmed pushed himself off the rock and sprinted the short distance to the SUV as she pulled the machine gun back inside. She gunned the gas as soon as he was in the Range Rover. He held on as she spun the car around and took off.

"Time," she said calmly into her coms as her eyes focused on the dark dirt path.

"Sixty-four seconds. Are you clear?"

"Yes. We'll be two miles out by then," she answered. He eyed the speedometer and saw her approaching one hundred miles per hour on the flat dirt road.

"Are there any stragglers?"

"No. Eagle took care of them. I grabbed as much documentation as I could find."

"Roger that. We appreciate the assistance on this. Drive to Quseer. There's a fishing boat ready to bring you to us."

Ahmed looked behind them in the side mirror and saw the camp go up in two explosions. Bridget didn't bother to slow down but did release a breath.

"Visual confirmation of drone strike. We'll see you soon," she said.

"Looking forward to it. Base out."

Ahmed felt like growling. Passion mixed with the adrenaline hit him so hard that he had to have her now. Bridget had seen his dark side and didn't even flinch. In fact, she'd protected him. Ahmed was experiencing freedom for the first time in his life and he didn't want to restrain himself anymore.

"Stop the car," he ordered.

Bridget gave him a confused look but slowed to a stop. "Everything okay?" she asked as he ripped the helmet from his head and tossed it in the back with the communication gear. He grabbed her and dragged her across the console to kiss her hard, causing her to let out a quick yelp in surprise.

Bridget clutched her shaky hands into his chest and held on as their tongues sparred. She felt him release her helmet strap and pull it off along with her coms. Ahmed reached blindly for the door and opened it. In one swift move, he picked her up and set her down outside.

When she reached frantically for him, he lost what little control he had. She was his as he got her out of the ghillie suit. He didn't bother to unbutton her camo but instead pulled it and the T-shirt underneath off in one motion.

"I can't be gentle this time," his voice rumbled.

"Neither can I." She shoved him against the car and attacked his clothing. He'd never needed someone so badly before and he didn't think he could wait one more second to have her. As soon as his clothes were on the desert ground, he had her naked with her legs wrapped around his waist.

"You're mine," he hissed into her ear.

"That may be, but you're mine as well."

Ahmed groaned as she bit his lip and let his beast free.

Bridget couldn't wait to get back to Keeneston. It had taken them almost a day to get to the base in Djibouti where Mo's plane waited for them. It also didn't help that the officers kept hitting on her. She thought Ahmed would snap; instead he seemed at peace while she nearly lost it.

After hours of debriefing and examining the documents, she had had enough. Ahmed excused them from the fluorescent-lit room and ushered her into an empty office.

"Ready to go home, my dear?" Ahmed asked as she sat down on the bare desk in the middle of the room.

"More than anything." She hadn't slept in almost forty-eight hours and the only things keeping her going were Ahmed's gentle touches and stolen kisses.

"Let's go. We've answered all we know and I already made copies of the documents." Ahmed wrapped her in a hug and she rested her head against his chest and closed her eyes for a moment to enjoy the soothing sound of his heart.

"I somehow don't think it will be that easy."

"I'd do anything for you, my love, including breaking us out of this base." Bridget looked up at his smiling face and raised her lips for a kiss. Ahmed immediately complied. His large, slightly rough hands gently cupped her cheeks as he brought his lips to hers. "Let's go home."

Ahmed led her from the room and stopped at the door to the interview room. "Gentlemen, we're going home. Contact the prince of Rahmi if you need to speak with me further."

"You can't go yet," one of the offensive officers said as he stood up, clearly ready to act important.

Ahmed's face hardened and she saw the officer swallow hard. "Yes, we can. If you want to ensure cooperation in the future, then you'll thank us and let us go. Otherwise I'll call the royal family and the media to let them know what really happened and that we're being held against our will. I'm sure King Ali Rahman would gladly take credit for the mission."

"Don't forget I can make a little call as well," Bridget smiled sweetly. "We really appreciate all the help and the hospitality. Goodbye."

She turned and walked down the hall with Ahmed not giving the officers a chance to argue. They wound their way through the base and out to the plane where Mo's pilot was ready to go.

Ahmed held out his hand and helped her up the first step. Bridget felt her body relax, knowing she was headed home. By the time she made it to the top of the stairs, she was half-asleep.

"Come, my dear. Let's get you into bed." As the plane took off, Ahmed helped her undress and slide between the fresh sheets on the bed in the back of the plane. "I love you."

Bridget rolled on her side and felt him kiss her temple. "I love you, too," she murmured. Ahmed slid one arm under her pillow and wrapped the other around her waist as he curved his body to hers. The warmth of his body and the quiet sound of his breathing soothed her to sleep instantly.

Sergei ignored the woman huddling naked in the corner of the room as he pulled up his pants. A message had arrived that had him worried. No one had been able to reach his compound for over a day. He didn't bother putting on a shirt as he stalked over to the trembling woman.

He reached down and grabbed her brown hair in his fist and pulled. Sergei closed his eyes and tried to calm down. This bitch's cries were getting on his last nerve. He pulled her across the marble floor to his door and flung it open to where one of his men stood.

"Get rid of her and hurry back. We have an issue," Sergei ordered as he tossed the woman into the hall before slamming the heavy wooden door.

He strode to his desk and dialed the phone. Anger built as he waited for the phone to be answered.

"Hello, sir."

"What the hell has happened?" Sergei barked.

"I was called this morning when Boris didn't return to Russia. The boss is pissed," Sergei's man told him.

"Screw him. Why can't the compound get in touch with us?"

"We tried everything to find out what was going on, but got nothing. Then just five minutes ago we found out why. Turn on the news."

Sergei grabbed the remote and flipped through the satellite channels until he came to one of the twenty-four-hour news stations. He felt his blood boil as he saw images of Boris and Ghali on the split screen along with an aerial image of his compound decimated.

"Who did this?" Sergei screamed as he smashed his fist into his desk.

"The Americans say it was an undercover operation," his man told him.

"But you don't sound so sure. Why?" Sergei asked as he tried to take a deep breath. He needed to focus and figure out a way to retaliate.

"Because one of our men was in Quseer getting supplies when he saw a man and a woman get out of a Range Rover loaded with weapons. They torched the car and walked to the fishing docks."

Sergei knew who it was instantly. A man and a woman. "Shit," he screamed as he threw the remote control into the plasma television so hard that the screen shattered. "Where are they now?"

"I don't know."

"Listen to the damn bug and find out," Sergei shouted.

"They're down. I mean, they're working, but I think there was a short or something. We can't hear anything clearly enough to make out what's being said."

"Are you stupid? They found them." Sergei looked up at the ceiling and counted silently to ten. "Okay, here's what we are going to do. I'm sending you a picture of the woman involved, Bridget Springer. If she's not in Keeneston yet, then she will be soon. Send some men to pick her up and bring her to me. I don't care what you do to her, just as long as she's alive when she gets here. Barely alive counts."

"Yes, sir."

Sergei hung up and looked down at the devices sitting on his desk. Sergei's mind was spinning with ideas of what to do to her. She hadn't been deemed a threat, but he must have been mistaken if she was with Ahmed at the compound. He had completed five bombs so far and while this was an unwanted distraction, it played into his master plan. One thing he knew for certain. If he got Bridget, then Ahmed would follow.

Chapter Seventeen

B ridget raised her 9mm, took aim, and fired. She smiled in satisfaction as the bullet found its mark.

"Dang, you're a good shot," Annie said as she stared at the bullseye.

Bridget just smiled and stepped back to give Annie a turn at the shooting range on the Davies family farm. She tried to pay attention as Annie fired off a series of shots, but her mind kept wandering to Ahmed. He'd been working nonstop trying to find Sergei since they got back three days ago. In fact, everyone was working so hard that she was glad Annie stole her away today for some target practice.

Ahmed had been getting up early and not getting home until late at night. He would need her then and she was happy to be there for him. After making love, they'd fall asleep as he held her. But come morning, she would awaken to an empty bed. Even her father had only called to make sure she was back on U.S. soil. The knowledge that Sergei had so much plastic explosive had rocked the intelligence world.

Cy had also stepped forward to help when he found out what had happened. Most days, Ahmed and Cy were locked away in the security cottage on Mo's farm with Nabi as they worked with Jamal in Rahmi and some of Cy's contacts. So far they had turned up nothing and Ahmed's mood was turning darker with every passing day.

"I kinda have an ulterior motive for asking you to shoot with me this morning," Annie started to say when she emptied her clip.

Bridget looked downfield and smiled when she saw the big *A* Annie had shot out of the target. "What's up?"

"Well, Noodle is going to a noodling competition in Alabama and Dinky is taking my cousin, Chrystal, to the Smoky Mountains for a romantic getaway . . . so, I'm kinda on football duty tonight and I could really use the help with the bag checks."

"Sure. I can help you. Ahmed's been working late anyway. And there's nothing more fun than messing with some teenagers. I've been practicing the evil glare Ahmed uses." Bridget narrowed her eyes and stared Annie down.

Annie burst out laughing. "You may need to keep practicing." Annie stopped laughing and grew serious. "What do you think Sergei is planning? Do you think he could attack here?"

"I've been thinking about that. He called me the other week and threatened me, so who knows? I hope not. Seventy-five pounds of Semtex could level the whole town."

"He called you?"

"Yeah. He likes to talk to me. Threatened me with a torturous death as Ahmed watched — you know, the normal," Bridget shrugged.

"That's not normal for an international terrorist to be calling you. Did Ahmed flip out when you told him?"

"Actually, I forgot to tell him. I met Sergei in New York but wasn't able to catch him. I didn't think the phone call was a big deal. I don't take it personally like Ahmed does."

Annie thought for a minute and then looked up at her. "I wouldn't tell him. He's got so much going on right now that he'll freak out. Not that I know him very well, but with you I fear emotion may cloud judgment."

Bridget nodded. "Exactly. He would be blinded by anger and that's when mistakes happen."

"But, you're going to be in *t-r-o-u-b-l-e* if he finds out. I'm going to tell on you," Annie sang. Bridget shook her head at her friend's teasing.

"Do you think Sergei will come after you?" Annie asked, growing serious once again.

"I don't know, but I'm guessing I'll find out soon enough." Bridget raised her gun and emptied her new clip into the target.

Ahmed ran a hand through his hair in frustration. No one could find Sergei or figure out what he intended to do with the bombs. He and Cy had been working almost nonstop for days now and still they had nothing.

"No one's talking. We have men trying to get to Boris's boss in Russia, but it's doubtful they'll find him or get him to talk. But we're still working on it," Cy said as he hung up the phone with a contact in Russia.

"Sergei goes where the money is. He could be anywhere." Ahmed slammed his hand on the desk and tried to rein in his temper.

"We'll find him. Everyone is looking for him. He can't elude detection much longer. He must have gone underground, but when he surfaces someone will spot him," Cy tried to reassure him.

Ahmed was starting to get worried. And he never got worried. Sergei had been dangerous before, but with this amount of explosives, it was unimaginable what destruction and death he could bring about.

"Look, we've been working on this nonstop. I promised Gemma I'd take her to the football game tonight. I need to unwind and clear my head. Hopefully, I can actually sleep a little and come up with something new tomorrow. Why don't you and Bridget come with us?" Cy asked as he stood up and stretched.

"He will be going."

Ahmed turned to the door and saw Mo.

"Nabi is taking the night shift. Dani and I need Ahmed with us until Nabi arrives. And we're going to the game."

"I can't. I need to . . ." Ahmed started.

"You need to take a break. You're too emotionally involved in this, my friend. I know what is urging you on, but if you keep going like this, you will be in no position to defeat him once the time comes. Come to the game, relax, go home, and get some sleep. Those are my orders."

Ahmed thought about ignoring Mo, but he was right. He needed to decompress and remove himself from the situation for a bit. Tomorrow he'd look at it with fresh eyes.

Ahmed blew out a long breath and gave Mo a nod. "How much time do I have?"

"We leave in an hour." Mo turned and headed back to the house.

Cy grabbed his coat and rolled his shoulders. "See you there."

"Thank you for all your help. I don't know if I have told you how much I appreciate it."

"That's what friends are for." Cy smiled before heading for his car.

Ahmed picked up his phone and sent a text to see if Bridget wanted to join him. He had hardly seen her since they got back. Yet, she knew he needed her every night. She took away the stress and worry and allowed him a couple of hours of peace in her arms.

His phone beeped and he read that she was on duty tonight at the game. Well, at least he would see her before the game. Maybe she'd need to frisk him. The thought had him smiling as he made his way to his house to feed Zoti and take a shower before the game.

The crowd was at capacity for the game. Upon their arrival, Bridget had cooed over Zain as Ahmed held him in his arms. Unfortunately that meant he didn't get frisked. Instead, women surrounded him, gushing about the cute baby. However, he did get to enjoy the cute eye roll Bridget gave him before he was swept into the small stadium with the crowd.

Ahmed looked into Zain's round little face and smiled down at him. He hadn't held a baby since Kedar. He thought it would hurt too much, but instead he felt excitement. The idea of holding a son or daughter of his own with Bridget had taken root and quieted the darker thoughts. She was a great protector and he respected her for that. She would keep their children safe from Sergei or any other dangers. But, it was her quiet and nurturing side that he knew solidified the idea. She would love any children she had and protect them with her life.

Dani and Mo took a seat next to Kenna and her young daughter, Sienna, who was completely infatuated with the twins. Ahmed handed Zain over to Kenna and took his seat, happy that he wasn't next to Paige. Not that he didn't like Paige. She just got a little excited during games and the last time he sat next to her, his arm hurt for days. He nodded to Cade and Will down on the field as they prepared for the game. Cole shook his hand as he made his way to Paige. Gemma gave him a smile and Cy thumped his back as they took their seats next to him.

Miles helped his wife, Morgan, sit down behind him as they both greeted the crowd. Tammy and Pierce filed in next to Morgan. Tammy leaned forward and gave Ahmed's cheek a quick peck.

"It's good to see you. You're looking much better," she smiled.

He did feel better. Somehow being in the middle of all these people was actually relaxing. The Rose sisters stopped at the edge of the row and handed out brownies as they spread the gossip. He wasn't alone anymore. In fact, he was far from it. He had a best friend — a brother really — and many people who cared for him. It was an odd feeling, but he finally understood what Mrs. Davies had told him.

"How you doing, Ahmed?" Miles asked when Morgan and Tammy turned to talking about their pregnancies.

"Not too good. Cy and I haven't found anything yet," Ahmed told him.

"Well, if you need anything, don't hesitate to ask."

"Thanks, Miles."

"Same goes for me. You know, if you want it done legally . . ." Cole leaned back and smiled, causing Ahmed to laugh. The FBI and Ahmed had different ways of approaching situations, but they could come in handy.

"Come on, Keeneston," Paige screamed and Ahmed knew it was game time. He sat back and followed Mo's order to relax.

"It sounds like the game just started," Annie said to Bridget as they took a seat in the cruiser to stay warm. Winter was coming to Keeneston.

"Sorry you have to miss watching Cade coach." Bridget took a bite of brownie and sipped the hot chocolate the Rose sisters had brought them. She looked up at the back of the bleachers. So far none of the kids had sneaked under them to do whatever teenagers thought was cool these days.

"It's okay. Marshall wanted time with Katelyn and the baby. Plus, I get to stay in the cruiser where it's warm," Annie joked as she picked up a brownie.

"I can't believe all we got were a couple of kids trying to sneak some flasks in."

"I'm more surprised Edna didn't try to sneak her gun in."

"Very true. And it looks like everyone got here early. The parking lot is deserted."

"Good. It gives us time to chat," Annie grinned.

"Is Marcy enjoying babysitting tonight?"

"Sure is. Cade will be, too, after the game."

Bridget laughed as her friend winked. The stadium erupted in applause, and Bridget looked up to see some heads poking up over the top rail as they all stood to cheer. "Guess someone scored."

"It was Keeneston. Paige is practically texting me a play by play. I'm sure whoever is sitting next to her appreciates that her hands are occupied." Annie stopped laughing and leaned closer to the windshield. "Now this looks interesting."

Bridget looked away from the stadium and out into the parking lot. Two tough-looking men were walking quickly toward the cruiser. Bridget knew right away it was trouble. "You thinking what I'm thinking?" Sergei was ready to live up to his threats.

"That it's been too long since I've shot someone?" Annie smiled, not looking worried at all.

Bridget couldn't help but return her smile. "Well, let's go see what they want. After all, we are Southern and our manners dictate it."

Bridget and Annie got out of the car laughing. The men stopped and looked at each other before continuing their stalk toward them. "Good evening, gentlemen. How can we help you tonight?"

Annie had her hand placed on her gun and Bridget followed suit. The men standing in front of them were normal goons. One man reached out quickly and shoved Annie back into the car. "Sergei sent us for you," he taunted as they aimed their guns at her.

Bridget saw red. The stress of this situation, the potential lives that Sergei could take with his bombs, and pushing her best friend were more than enough now. She glanced at Annie. When Annie gave her a little grin, she knew they were ready. Without warning, Annie and Bridget launched themselves on the goons.

Bridget pulled her fist back and used the momentum to land a punch that had the man wheeling backward. He dropped his gun and Bridget kicked it away before she punched him again. In her peripheral vision, she saw Annie jump into the air and kick the gun out of his hand. These poor guys had no idea what they were getting into. Bridget almost smiled as she raised her hands to square off with Sergei's man.

Ahmed had to admit it. He was having a good time. Cade and Will were doing a great coaching job and the players were on their game. Ryan Hall, the sophomore wide receiver for KHS, leapt into the air and came down in the end zone for another touchdown. Everyone jumped up and cheered. Ahmed wasn't a cheerer, but he did clap as Paige jumped up and down screaming like a madwoman. Cole held onto his young son and just shook his head at his wife.

"Hey, Ahmed," Paige called to him after the kick for the extra point was good, "have you heard from Bridget? She and Annie are in the cruiser, and I've been texting Annie, but she hasn't gotten back to me."

Ahmed pulled out his phone and shook his head. "No. I am sure they are just talking. Besides, I think they could hear you screaming to know we scored."

"Ha ha. Look who found his sense of humor," Paige started teasing before she got distracted. "What on earth is Edna doing up there?"

Ahmed turned to look at the little old lady in her orthopedic shoes standing on the bleachers and peering over the side of the stadium. Soon he saw the Rose sisters similarly stand and look over the railing and scream something to whoever was below. Ah, they were talking to Annie and Bridget. But then they turned all as one and started hurrying down the stairs, yelling at the people on both sides of the aisle.

"I told you I should have brought my gun," Edna hollered as they hurried down the metal steps. Miss Violet was trailing behind as she opened her humongous purse and pulled out a wooden spoon.

"What's going on?" Paige called as people from the top of the bleachers all started to leap from their seats and hurry after the women.

"Two huge men are fighting our girls. If I had my gun . . ." Edna shook her head angrily.

"Bridget?" Ahmed asked.

"Is kicking her guy's ass," Miss Lily called out.

Ahmed didn't wait to hear if Miss Lily had anything else to say as he bolted from the bench. Sergei was here.

"Will," Kenna shouted as she picked up Sienna. Her husband turned around and saw the mass exodus of the stadium and hurried over. "Annie and Bridget are being attacked." Will's eyes rounded and he hurried over to Cade and started pointing to the parking lot.

Ahmed and Cade met in the crowded entrance to the stadium. He knew the panicked look on Cade's face matched his own.

"Move," Cade shouted as Ahmed elbowed through the throng of people hurrying to the parking lot. Finally free of the narrow entranceway, the path cleared as people moved to form a semicircle in the parking lot. Cade and Ahmed pushed their way through and finally saw what everyone was looking at.

"I almost feel sorry for them," Cade said with a grin.

Ahmed nodded his head in agreement. The two huge men were getting their asses kicked by Bridget and Annie. "This is the first time I've ever felt useless, but I'm also very proud." Ahmed grinned. The townspeople gasped and cringed when Bridget was grabbed around the throat. Ahmed made himself wait. He knew Bridget wouldn't appreciate it if he rushed in to save her. After saying it for weeks, he had to acknowledge that she could protect herself.

"Did you see that?" Ahmed smiled as Bridget broke the hold and hit the man in the nose. "I taught her that."

"Yeah. That was good. Did you see the way my Annie took out that guy's knee? Now he's really struggling just to stand," Cade said proudly.

Bridget hooked her leg and, with a quick jerk, the man fell to the ground.

"Great sweep, my dear," Ahmed shouted through his cupped hands. Ahmed saw Henry turn and look at him like he had two heads.

"Y'all have a strange relationship," then he looked back as Bridget landed a solid punch to the kidney, "but it's kinda hot. Now, if they were fighting in mud . . ."

173

Ahmed leaned away as Neely Grace's hand arched up and smacked Henry in the head. Annie grabbed her man by the hair and slammed his face into her knee. The man's eyes glazed over and then rolled into the back of his head as he fell to the ground. Bridget blocked a punch with one hand as the other grabbed his arm and propelled him forward into the concrete wall of the field house. The man stumbled back and crashed to the ground — out cold.

Chapter Eighteen

Bridget laced her fingers and stretched them out. She had to admit it felt pretty good to take her frustrations out on the hire-a-thug. Cole and Ahmed had moved in and detained the two slightly dazed men. Annie grinned and high-fived the Rose sisters while giving Edna a sympathetic pat on the back.

"Damn, that was fun." Annie chuckled as she leaned against the side of the cruiser next to Bridget and watched the men being handcuffed.

Bridget felt her shoulders start to shake. "You're going to get me into even more *t-r-o-u-b-l-e.*"

"What do you mean, more?" Ahmed asked as he ambled over toward them with his hands in the pockets of his black wool coat.

Bridget gulped and looked with wide eyes at her best friend who had developed a sudden interest in her fingernails. "Umm," Bridget had been caught off guard. She was just joking with Annie and now Ahmed was giving her *the look* that had men spilling their guts in seconds. "Nothing," she said with a shrug.

"You're a horrible liar. Don't get me wrong; you're the sexiest liar I've ever seen, but a liar nonetheless." Ahmed leaned closer and whispered, "I wonder if your pants will go up in flames. I'd have to get you out of them to save you."

Bridget gulped again as she suddenly felt fire. She noticed Annie staring at them open-mouthed and wide-eyed as she started to fan herself. Ignoring her best friend, Bridget looked up into Ahmed's eyes that had changed in a split second from interrogator to bedroom.

"I might know why these guys were here," Bridget stammered.

"Uh-huh," Ahmed murmured as he ran his hand down her ribcage and cupped her hip.

"Oh gosh, I can't take it," Annie cried as she fanned herself harder. "Sergei called her the other week."

"Seriously? Way to hold out there, Annie?" Bridget said with an eye roll.

"Sorry, Bridget, but he's so freaking hot. I thought if I let him continue you'd be nothing but a puddle of goo stuck against my cruiser."

Cade cleared his throat and cocked his head at his wife. "I think on that note, I'll get back to the game. Dear, we need to make a pit stop at the showers to cool down and jog your memory."

"Isn't there a football game he should be coaching?" Bridget asked.

"Will took over coaching," Ahmed said calmly. "Now, what about Sergei calling you?"

Bridget wasn't fooled by Ahmed's calm "oh, I'm just curious" voice. She looked around to see if she could divert his attention; however, it seemed like the whole town was silently leaning toward them to hear the conversation. "So, what's going to happen to the mercenaries over there?"

Ahmed leaned in closer and traced his finger slowly along her jawline to her chin and gently raised her face to his. "What is this about Sergei calling you?"

"It was no big deal. I mean, it wasn't like it was the first time he . . ." Bridget slammed her mouth shut, but it was too late. Ahmed's eyes flashed with anger and then narrowed before he stepped back and placed his hands on his hips.

"Not the first time he's contacted you," Ahmed roared. Everyone took an instinctual step backward except Bridget.

Cole stepped next to Ahmed to learn what Sergei had said, but Bridget just ignored him. She placed her hands on her hips and glared right back at Ahmed. "You would have known he stopped me in New York if you had just worked with me instead of thinking you are such a badass that you don't need help. But, *nooooo*. You take off in the middle of the night for Rome."

"And you couldn't have possibly found any time between then and now to tell me Sergei talked to you—in person?" Ahmed narrowed his eyes and Father James crossed himself. "What did he want?"

"Oh, nothing important. You know, 'I'll kill you; I'll kill Ahmed. Make him watch . . . blah, blah, blah,'" Bridget said mockingly.

Cole patted Ahmed on the back. "You're on your own for this one," he said before taking a giant step away.

"He threatened you? What did you do?" Ahmed continued to yell. The large, round eyes of the townspeople showed their shock. They didn't even know Ahmed could raise his voice.

"Which time? In New York, I bet him twenty that he'd be the one dead and then I asked him to pick up Marko's poop right before I sent Marko to attack him."

Miss Lily snorted and Edna laughed out loud.

"And when he called you?" Ahmed asked quietly. The crowd went silent and they all leaned forward again.

"Um, let's see. I was very nice. I asked him how hell was and suggested he try yoga to improve his disposition. Then I asked if he didn't get enough hugs as a child as he continued his 'I'll torture you while Ahmed watches talk.'" Bridget paused and then remembered the last bit. "Then I told him I'd save him a cupcake."

"You've been taunting one of the world's most wanted mercenaries and terrorists?" Ahmed's voice was so quiet she almost didn't hear him, but she saw the look he was giving her and felt a shiver go down her spine. The crowd gasped and collectively took a large step away from them again.

Bridget narrowed her eyes. He may scare everyone else, but she'd seen him naked and knew he loved her. This Mr. Tough Guy routine wasn't going to work on her. "I got twenty on Bridget not giving in," she heard Miss Daisy whisper.

"Twenty that she'll start crying," Henry added.

"Twenty Ahmed will start crying," Neely Grace added with a smile and a wink to Bridget.

Ahmed stood ramrod straight and continued to glare while he ignored the betting going on around them. "What was his reaction?"

"I think it's pretty obvious what his reaction was," Bridget gestured to the two handcuffed goons. "But, I did leave him speechless a couple times. I don't think he's used to being talked to like that. It really bothered him that I didn't seem to be afraid of him."

"You should be afraid of him," Ahmed bellowed again. Bridget just shrugged her shoulders and watched as emotion filled his eyes. "Dammit, stop talking to him!" He grabbed her upper arms and dragged her against him. His head lowered and his lips crushed hers. His tongue invaded her mouth as he consumed her.

Bridget felt her head swim as he pulled away from her. The world was blurry and she wasn't quite sure her legs would hold her. "Don't think this means you won," she sputtered breathlessly.

"Well, I didn't see that one coming. No one won the bet. Keep your money," Miss Daisy called out as she put away her little notebook. The men turned to leave, but most of the women stood where they were and sighed. "Come on, come on, we've got a game to cheer for."

The Rose sisters got everyone turned around and headed back into the stadium before Miss Daisy turned back and mouthed "Wow" to Bridget. Bridget started laughing and Ahmed turned around to see what she was laughing at, but Miss Daisy was already herding people into the stadium again.

"I think we need to discuss our relationship," Ahmed said seriously. "You need to tell me when things like this happen."

"Oh, and you're going to tell me where you went the other night on your errand?" Bridget paused and let Ahmed digest that. "Yeah, I didn't think so. When you accept that we make a better team than we do apart, then I'll tell you everything. Now, you wanna have some fun?" Bridget shot him a grin and looked to the two handcuffed men.

"Fine. Let's go have a little chat with them and we'll finish this talk later."

"If you say so, honey." Bridget smiled innocently at him before heading toward the men being held by Cole, Miles, and Cy.

Ahmed reached down and hauled the first man up by his shirt.

"Agent Parker, you have a phone call," Cy said in a tone Ahmed knew well. Gone was Mr. Hollywood and in his place stood one scary man. This was the man he met in New York City a couple years ago when he went with Kenna, Dani, and Paige to protect them during the corruption trial and again when Gemma had been taken.

"No, I don't," Cole glared back. Miles pulled out his phone and dialed. Cole's phone rang and Cole shrugged at the men. "Guess I need to take this." Cole answered his phone and walked off.

"Locker room," Miles said as he grabbed the other man from the ground. Without a word, Bridget reached into the cruiser, pulled out a bag, and turned on her heel to lead them toward the locker room. Ahmed knew Cy and Miles didn't want her there. It would be hard to do the things he imagined with a woman present. But, he was a little worried about asking her to leave. She was like Marshall's dog, Bob. She had a look that could unnerve him.

"In here," Bridget said coldly as she dragged two metal chairs into the tiled shower room. "Easier cleanup."

Ahmed almost laughed at the way the men's faces blanched and Miles and Cy shot a quick grin at each other before tying the first man to the chair.

"Take off their shoes and socks," Bridget ordered.

Cy and Miles immediately went to work removing their shoes and socks, never questioning her. Ahmed leaned back against the wall and watched. He didn't know what she had planned, but the men looked so worried that he decided to see what she had.

"You think you can get us to talk? Sergei will kill you for this," one of the men said with a cockiness that didn't match the fear in his eyes.

"*Think* I can? No. I *know* I can. See, you came into my town and attacked me. You saw how well that went, right? And you think I can't make you tell me everything you know. Well, that means you're stupid and I'll get the info twice as fast." Bridget opened her bag and pulled out a large needle, a smaller needle, and a scalpel from the first-aid kit.

"You're going to let a woman tell you what to do? Do you have no balls?" the one guy managed in a heavy Russian accent.

Ahmed smiled and then laughed coldly along with Cy and Miles. They didn't say a word, just laughed. The men shifted in the metal chairs and looked nervously to where Bridget had laid out her gun, knife, and stun gun. He didn't know what her plan was, but it definitely seemed as though she had one. He was just going to beat the information out of them.

"Gentlemen. Blindfold them."

Ahmed looked around and saw the football team's dirty laundry. He grabbed two sweaty shirts and tossed them to Cy. Cy made a face over the men's heads and Ahmed realized Cy and Miles were completely amused by this scene.

The men gagged as Miles and Cy wrapped the shirts around their heads and then stepped back with an elegant bow for Bridget who sent them a dazzling smile. What on earth was she doing? Ahmed watched her grab the small needle and the stun gun.

"Speaking of balls . . ." She zapped the stun gun and the sound reverberated through the room and the men started to struggle. "I already know you were sent here to get me by Sergei. Where did you plan on taking me?"

"I'll give you something to do with my balls," one of the men grinned. Ahmed lunged, but Bridget's hand shot out and stopped him. She quietly shook her head and gave him a wink.

She zapped the stun gun against the metal chair, giving him a slight jolt and then jabbed the needle into his toe. The man let out a bloodcurdling scream and a string of Russian curse words that had Cy smiling.

"To one of Sergei's men. We were to meet him in D.C. and then they were going to take over. That's all we know," the other man blurted out.

"Wimps," Bridget mouthed to Ahmed and rolled her eyes.

"What about the bomb Sergei has? What is he using it for?"

"I don't know," the man answered as his friend was still cursing in Russian.

"I don't believe you." Ahmed watched as she bent down and before the man knew what was happening, she inserted the small needle under his toenail.

"Tell me," she yelled over the man's screams.

"He was hired to blow up something big. I don't know what. I just know it's a work for hire. A lot of men are being brought in for it."

"Brought in where?"

"From all over. The U.S. contractors met in D.C. yesterday and shipped out. There were similar meet-ups in Russia and Egypt. Sergei is keeping everything close to the vest on this. Only the commanders at those locations know the final destination."

Bridget stood up and shrugged at the guys. Miles looked to Cy and they walked out of the room together.

"They're low-level," Cy said once they were out of earshot.

"I got the same impression. They don't know anything of importance, but at least we got a little more out of them," Miles said as he crossed his arms over his wide chest.

"Unfortunately, I agree. I'll pass along this information to Jamal in Rahmi. Bridget, you should probably tell your military contact."

"You mean her . . ." Cy started.

"Yes, my contact would appreciate the heads-up," Bridget said, cutting Cy off. "Damn," she cursed. "I was hoping for more. Let's turn them over to Cole and get to work."

Ahmed watched her stalk back into the shower and stuff her things back in her bag. Cy and Miles headed in and put their captives' shoes and socks back on before dragging them out of the locker room. They waited as long as possible before taking the smelly shirts off of their heads.

"Why did you do that?" Ahmed asked quietly once they were alone.

"What?" Bridget asked annoyed.

"Take over. It's not like you to torture someone, even if it was only a little prick of the toe."

"To protect you."

Ahmed couldn't believe what he'd just heard. "To protect me? Me?"

"Yes, you. You're too emotionally involved in this. That's when you make mistakes, take things too far, and get into trouble. What did you want to do when you heard Sergei had called me?"

"Kill him."

"Exactly. You two have made this so personal that you can't look at it objectively. That's why I took over."

Ahmed hated to admit it, but she had a point. "It looks like I'm heading back to work," Ahmed said with a sigh.

"And I'll be waiting for you at home." Bridget raised her head and placed a gentle kiss to his lips. "I love you."

Ahmed wrapped his arms around his salvation. She was his everything. Although he knew she was a strong woman, the strongest he'd ever known, it was just hard for him to stop trying to protect her. He knew he'd spend the rest of his life trying to protect her and make her happy. "I love you, too."

Chapter Nineteen

Ahmed took a deep breath as he tried to calm his heavy breathing. His heart was pounding and he wiped a thin layer of sweat from his brow. He turned his head and saw the night sky outside the window before his thoughts overtook him again.

"Hmm," Bridget murmured as she snuggled her naked body closer to his and fell asleep. She had welcomed him into her bed in the middle of the night knowing he was frustrated with the case.

He ran his hand down her bare back and enjoyed the feel of the woman he loved. Finally he felt his body relax and his eyes were just about to drift shut when he heard his phone vibrate. Ahmed reached an arm out and managed to answer it without waking Bridget.

"Hello?" he whispered.

"Ahmed, it's Jamal." He heard his brother's serious voice over the phone.

"Give me a minute." Ahmed pulled the sheet up and covered Bridget's sleeping form before slowly sliding out of the bed. He gave her a quick look and saw her wrap both of her arms around his pillow. He managed a smile at the sweet expression on her face.

"I don't have that much time," he heard his brother say, aggravated.

Ahmed closed the door and walked naked down the hall to the living room. "What is it?"

"Rahmi's been attacked." Ahmed straightened up and his mind instantly focused on his brother. "It was the king's own oil minister! He set off bombs on the oil lines, forcing us to shut down production. We caught him trying to sneak out of the country."

"Why would he do this?"

"I don't know, but he says he wants to talk to you. That he doesn't trust me since I'm part of this fraud."

"Fraud?"

"Yes. But I have no idea what he's talking about. We need to find out if there are any more bombs and if he's working alone. Can you leave Nabi in charge and come out here immediately?" his brother asked.

"Of course. Do you think he's involved with Sergei?"

"We can't find a connection. No emails, phone calls, or anything. It seems he's developed some personal grudge against the king and wants you to plead his case."

"What kind of explosive was used to blow up the pipeline?"

"The one closest to the palace was dynamite. We haven't examined the explosions farther down the line."

Ahmed ran a hand through his hair and nodded. It wasn't Sergei, but it was also the first time his brother had ever asked him for help. "Okay. I'll be in the air in less than an hour. Have you called Mo?"

"Yes. His Royal Highness," Ahmed heard the censure in his brother's voice, "approved your use of his jet. Hurry."

Ahmed let out a breath and wished he didn't have to go. He didn't want to leave Bridget, but he was a Rahmi Guard and it was his duty to protect the country. He went into the kitchen and found a piece of paper and pen. He wrote Bridget a note explaining what had happened and left it in the middle of the island where she'd see it in the morning.

He snuck down the hall and back into the bedroom where he got dressed. He stood next to the bed and looked down at Bridget. He felt the warmth in his heart and decided right then that this was the last time he was going to leave her. Ahmed bent over and placed a feather-light kiss on her cheek. "I love you," he whispered to her. He stood up and gave her one last look before leaving.

Bridget viciously sliced her pecan and chocolate chip pancakes with a knife and looked up at the table of women staring at her. "What? As if you wouldn't be mad if your husband left in the middle of the night for halfway across the world without waking you."

Gemma looked at Dani, Tammy, and Morgan before looking back at Bridget. "Okay, so I'd be upset," Gemma finally admitted.

"Yeah, I don't think I would take that too well. At least he left you a note, though. Surely that means he cares for you and that he didn't really want to leave," Morgan said.

"What I want to know is what were you doing that had you in such a deep sleep that you didn't wake up?" Tammy giggled. Bridget blushed and took a bite of her breakfast as Tammy wiggled her eyebrows.

"Why do I always feel like I'm reminding you that you're married?" Morgan asked with a smile on her face.

"As if you weren't thinking the same thing," Tammy grinned and when Morgan blushed, the whole table started laughing.

"Hi, honey," Gemma said with a guilty look on her face. Cy looked at her strangely before dropping a kiss on her forehead.

"Bridget, where is Ahmed?" Cy asked. The serious tone to his voice caught her attention.

"Rahmi, why?"

"Where's Mo?" he asked, suddenly impatient.

"I'm right here." Mo entered the café and headed to the table. "What can I do for you?"

"I need to have a word if you don't mind. Privately." Bridget couldn't believe that Cy practically dragged Mo to the back of the restaurant. The girls all looked at each other and Bridget shuddered. Something was wrong.

Cy wouldn't look back at the table as he pulled Mo to the back of the café. He had just gotten a call from one of his former CIA counterparts who had caught wind of some troubling news. "What did you hear from Rahmi about the explosion?"

"How did you know about that? We haven't told anyone. We didn't want it to affect the oil contracts," Mo said irritably.

"I just got a call from one of my former buddies. There's chatter that the bombing had nothing to do with oil and more to do with the oil minister's family being kidnapped."

"Kidnapped? Why . . ." Mo's question died.

"Sergei," They both said.

Mo cursed. "It was a ploy to draw Ahmed to Rahmi so Sergei can kill him."

"Not just Ahmed, but all of Rahmi. King Sarif of Surman is working with Sergei again to take over the country."

He hated telling Mo his country was under attack, but he had to. They had to plan. Mo pulled out his phone and dialed his father. Nothing. He tried the landline and waited until he heard the out-of-service message. Communication was down in the small island country. "I need to get to Rahmi."

"Wait. We need to tell her," Cy said as they both turned and looked at Bridget.

Bridget rose from the table. *Please don't let him be dead.* "What is it?" she asked. The café must have picked up on something because everyone became quiet as Mo walked toward her and picked up her hands.

"It's Ahmed. I fear my dear friend is in a battle for his life."

Bridget just nodded her head once as some of the patrons gasped. "Where?"

"Rahmi is under attack. The bombing wasn't an accident and now communications have been cut. I fear there is more danger in store for my country and my friend."

Dani's hand shot up to cover her mouth. "Our family?"

"They're safe as far as I know. I must go. My country needs me."

"No," Bridget said forcefully. "You need to go to D.C. and manage this politically. If Rahmi should fall, you could be the rightful ruler and you would need to get your country back."

"Bridget is right," Cy told him as he placed his hand on Mo's shoulder. "I'll go with her."

Gemma's eyes watered, but she didn't say anything. Instead she placed one hand on her belly protectively and Bridget realized what that meant. She'd seen Kenna and the Davies women do that enough to know she was pregnant. "I can't let you do that. I'll have backup. You know I'll call in favors. And with Mo in D.C., we'll have support there soon."

Cy looked back to Gemma and just nodded as he went to stand by his wife. "I'll call in all the favors I have as well."

"Bridget, please don't go," Tammy cried. The Rose sisters had come up with tears in their eyes and placed a hand on Tammy's shoulders as tears fell.

"She has to, dear," Miss Lily said quietly. "Our boy is in trouble and her heart would never allow her to stay."

"Here, dear. Take this for the trip. You need to eat." Miss Violet handed over a large basket of food as she fought back tears.

"Come back to us. Both of you," the stalwart Miss Daisy said seconds before pulling her in for a tight hug.

Mo kissed Dani hard. "Keep our boys safe. You and Nabi need to go to our safe house. I'll take a handful of the guys and Bridget with me to Washington."

Dani nodded and immediately hurried from the café with a look of sheer determination. She would keep her children safe at all costs.

Bridget looked around the room. Henry had never looked so serious; Neely Grace and several other women sniffled and tried to hold back tears. Bridget felt her throat start to tighten. If she didn't get out of there soon, she'd be a mess. "Thank you all. Let's go, Mo."

The plane landed on the king's private airfield in Rahmi almost fifteen hours after he left Bridget. He could see the oil fires from the air. There had been more bombs detonated on the oil line. He'd talked to his brother when he'd reached London right around the time Bridget would have woken up. He hoped she found his note.

He had been missing her when his brother picked up the phone and told him that they were going to try to get Ameera and Dirar out of the country on a fishing boat, but the king and queen refused to leave. The line went dead before they could say anything more. As Ahmed looked around, he saw why. The bombings had blown up infrastructure and cell towers for as far as he could see.

Ahmed hurried from the plane and made his way to the heavily guarded entrance to the palace. He nodded to one of the guards he knew and flashed his diplomatic identification to another as the heavy metal gate slowly opened.

Flashbacks from that horrible day eighteen years ago crept into his mind. Guards had been stationed on the palace grounds the same way that day. The palace was on lockdown. Come to think about it, there had been no cars or people on the streets either.

Ahmed picked up his pace and hurried into the palace, down the long hallways, and pushed open the door to his father's old office. The room was filled with high-level security officials, including Jamal, standing by a map of the country issuing orders.

"There was another explosion at the five-mile marker of the pipeline. Communications are down still. We need to communicate via two-way radio. I want three teams patrolling the pipeline, but I have a feeling more troops are needed here," Jamal told the men. He looked up and Ahmed bowed his head quickly to his brother. "Ahmed, good; you're here. Men, please excuse us for a moment. I'll call you back in when I'm ready for you."

Ahmed stepped into the office and waited for the room to clear. "What's going on, Jamal?"

"Thank you for coming. I don't know who I can trust anymore. We caught a soldier fleeing the area where a bomb had taken out our communications. He said the same thing as the oil minister — that he would only talk to you."

"How many bombs have gone off and where?"

"Three on the pipeline. Then a massive bomb was set off at the telephone station, knocking out our landlines and the cellular tower. Then one more was set off on the other cellular tower on the island."

Ahmed shook his head. This wasn't right. "This is a coordinated attack on our country. First they cut us off financially and then they took down our communications. They're attacking our infrastructure."

"I think so, too. I checked and Sarif has been quiet since you shut him down at the UN."

"Too quiet?"

"Maybe. The explosions are a mix of explosives, but there's some evidence that Semtex has been used." Jamal let out a nervous breath. "We couldn't get the prince and princess out. There were too many unknown vessels in the area to risk sending them out on the ocean. They are in the new safe room I had built after the last attack on Rahmi. The king and queen are still here and being very visible and offering support to the people."

"Move the guards out of the palace and onto the palace grounds. Only those you personally know are to be inside the palace. Have the king and queen sought help from their allies?" Ahmed asked as he studied the map.

"No. They haven't been able to communicate with them. By the time we thought this was something besides domestic terrorism, it was too late."

"Then let's hope Mohtadi will figure this out and send help. We have to plan as if no one is coming to our aid, though. Do you trust all the men who were in here before?"

"All but one."

"Then dismiss that man. Tell him to go home to his family or occupy him with a nonessential duty. Do the same for anyone you know to be loyal to him."

Jamal took a deep breath and went to his desk to write out orders. After a minute of silence, he went to his door and called the men inside. Ahmed swallowed and pushed the image of Bridget lying in bed waiting for him from his mind. Thank goodness she wasn't here or he wouldn't be able to focus on the operation. He only hoped he would make it back to her.

Chapter Twenty

B ridget followed Mo down the steps of the plane and was met by Agent Woodbury, his men, and Bridget's father. Barking broke out and she grinned as she saw her father let go of Marko's leash.

"Marko," she cried as her dog leapt into her arms and covered her face with kisses.

Mo raised a brow and whispered, "What is your dog doing here? I thought he was with your parents."

Bridget smiled as she stood up and saw her father in his uniform striding toward her. "Daddy!"

"Daddy?" Mo said in astonishment. "Does Ahmed know?"

"I don't think so," Bridget said with a smile before taking a couple steps forward and being enveloped in a bear hug.

"Pumpkin." Her father chuckled.

"Pumpkin?" Bridget heard Mo mumble behind her.

"Daddy, I'd like you to meet His Royal Highness Prince Mohtadi Ali Rahman. Mo, this is my father, General Richard Ward. He's the chief of staff of the Army here in D.C.," Bridget said with a grin at Mo's surprised face.

"Ahmed is really going to wish he'd done the background check on you," Mo whispered to her before he held out his hand. "It's nice to meet Bridget's father. She's a wonderful woman."

"Yes, she is. Now tell me about Ahmed."

"Dad."

Mo smiled quickly, but it faded as he transformed into the prince he needed to be. "After you help me save my country, then I'll tell you everything I know."

"Rahmi is an ally to the United States. What can we do to help?"

"I need to talk to the president as soon as possible," Mo stated instead of asking.

"And I need to get on a military flight to Rahmi," Bridget added. Her voice left no room for argument.

"We have a cargo jet heading with humanitarian supplies to Africa. You can deadhead on that flight and jump into Rahmi. Or you can do the smart thing and wait for His Royal Highness to get approval for troops and go with them."

Bridget just looked at him. "My wife gives that same look," Mo said with sympathy.

"Mine as well." Her father shook his head and then called out. "Woodbury, take my daughter to Andrews. The pilot is expecting you. Your Highness, please come with me. The president is expecting you."

Her father grabbed her up into a tight hug. "I love you."

"I love you too, Daddy."

"Tell Ahmed and my father help is coming. Take care of him," Mo said as he placed a chaste kiss on her cheek.

"Right this way, Miss Ward," Woodbury said with a slight look of shock on his face.

Bridget smiled. Maybe being who she was born to be wasn't such a bad thing. She'd proven herself repeatedly and she really didn't feel the need to anymore. "Thank you."

Woodbury shook his head, "Man, I know a lot of guys who are going to be really embarrassed about the things they said about you. And to you."

"Funny. I don't feel embarrassed at all for the things I said about them."

Mo sat next to General Ward as the SUV raced through the streets of Washington, D.C., heading for the White House. All he could think of was the night before Ahmed was married all those years ago. The way a scared boy had accepted his duty. The way his best friend had told Mo it would be okay, that he would make this marriage work.

Then flashbacks of Ahmed in the hospital battling for life entered his mind. The sleepless nights Mo spent next to the bed begging his one and only friend to please wake up. When he finally did, he wasn't the same. It didn't mean Mo loved him any less; it just meant he was a shadow of the man he used to be. What was being back in Rahmi now doing to him? What was it doing to his whole family? He didn't know if the country had actually been attacked or if his family was still alive.

As they pulled through the iron gates of the White House, Mo decided he would do whatever it took to seal this deal for aid. He was met by multiple men in dark suits as he stepped out of the SUV. Some were Secret Service, some were aides to the president, but they were all shooting off question after question as his own security force stepped in closer to protect him.

With a wave of Mo's hand, his security stepped back with the exception of one man who leaned forward and whispered, "Package has been delivered safe and sound."

Mo didn't acknowledge his man as they walked through the White House to the Oval Office. Dani and his boys were safe. Now he could really focus on saving his country.

"President Nelson, it's so nice to see you again," Mo said with a bow of his head.

"The pleasure is mine, Your Highness. Now General Ward told me this was a matter of urgency so I hope you don't mind that I brought my advisors in order to streamline anything we need," she said with a gesture of her hand to the numerous men and women lining the room.

"Of course. Gentlemen. Ladies." Mo nodded to the group as he sat down in the chair next to the President of the United States and began to plead his case.

Ahmed and Jamal flanked the king, who was dressed in desert camouflage and armed with a knife and gun that Jamal had trained him to use over the years. They made their way along the palace grounds showing the king the security they had in place. They were a small country and it was only now Ahmed realized it had been a miracle they hadn't been overthrown before.

"It has to be Sarif, my good-for-nothing cousin." The king slammed his fist into his hand and took the stairs, where Fatima was waiting stoically.

"What is the news?" she asked.

"We received radio confirmation that fishing boats have been moving toward our shores. I think they are carrying rebels sent from Sarif, but I have no direct evidence. Just a hunch," Jamal told her.

"What did the minister tell you, Ahmed?" she asked pointedly. Ahmed might have smiled if the situation wasn't so bad. Fatima had been quiet and only worked behind the scenes before. But after she started spending time with Dani and the new Ameera, Fatima had become more outspoken. Surprisingly, the king seemed to appreciate the support and was giving his wife more and more duties.

"It's strange," Ahmed started. "He just seemed relieved that I was there. He didn't say anything except that he was sorry. Although, he kept glancing at one of his guards. I think that guard was there to make sure the minister didn't say anything else."

"Very strange. I don't like it."

"I didn't either, wife. I stopped to talk to him and asked him to give me a tour of solitary. I had Jamal shove the guard in a cell and lock the door. If he was working with someone, then he won't be able to communicate with him now. Ahmed is heading back to talk with him now."

Fatima smiled. "Very good. Let us know what you learn."

Ahmed bowed his head respectfully and headed back to the prison. He made his way down the brown-tiled floor to the interview room holding the oil minister. "I'd like to have a word with the minister alone," Ahmed said as he sat down. The two armed guards walked out of the room and closed the door.

"Where is my guard?" the older man asked in a shaky voice.

"In solitary. He is working for Sarif, isn't he?"

"What?" The man looked wildly around as if someone might be listening.

"We're alone and please save us the time of pretending you don't know anything," Ahmed said as his patience wore thin.

What he wasn't expecting was the minister to break down in tears. "I am so very sorry. It wasn't Sarif, but his man Sergei. They have my family."

"Sergei is back with Sarif, of course. But why were you to ask for me?"

"Sergei wanted you here. He's coming to kill you during the rebellion. Please, save my family. They were taken on a fishing boat. They . . ."

Ahmed cut him off as he stood up. Sergei was here. "I can't promise, but I will look for them after we secure Rahmi. What else do you know?"

"Nothing, that's all I was able to overhear. Please . . ."

Ahmed didn't wait to hear the rest. He hurried from the room and ran across the palace grounds. Jamal was with the king and queen as they rallied their troops against the impending rebellion.

"It's Sarif. He's leading the rebellion," Ahmed said as soon as he reached them. "Come, we need to get you to safety." Ahmed reached for the queen's arm as the ground shook and the world crumbled around them.

Bridget checked the straps of the harness that held Marko tight against her body. He was completely relaxed as he waited for the jump. "Two minutes," the pilot's voice rang out in her headset. The cargo ramp of the plane slowly opened. Bridget stood up with Marko in her arms and walked closer to the ramp.

She looked out and saw the blue ocean. She'd be able to see Rahmi in less than a minute. She knew jumping into the palace would be risky, so she was aiming for the village surrounding the palace instead. Rahmi came into sight inch by inch. The bright blue of the ocean mixed with the sandy coastline full of boats. When the palace finally came into view, Bridget couldn't hide her surprise as black smoke swirled upward.

"Are you sure you want to jump into this?"

"I'm sure," she answered as she secured her weapons and prepared to jump from thirteen thousand feet.

"Then get ready."

Bridget took a breath and moved closer to the end of the ramp. The wind whipped her cheeks and pushed at her, yet Marko stayed as relaxed as if he were hanging his head out the car window.

"Jump!"

Bridget held Marko tight against her and was freefalling toward Rahmi at one hundred twenty miles per hour. Marko was wrapped tight against her body as they fell almost nine thousand feet before she pulled the parachute cord. As she grew closer to landing in the village surrounding the palace, Bridget just prayed Ahmed would still be alive. She could see multiple columns of smoke across the beautiful island. Buildings had crumbled, pipelines had been damaged, towers were down, and oil was burning. Panicked people ran around the streets not knowing if more explosions were coming.

Marko stayed relaxed in his harness as they approached the ground. With a thud, her feet hit the ground at a run. Marko began barking as people screamed at them. Bridget detached the parachute and unhooked Marko from his harness before she peeled the goggles from her face.

She ignored the people staring at her in fear and swung her gun around into position. She found the palace and looked to see which streets she needed to take to get there. "Let's go," she said to Marko as she took off at a jog in the direction of the palace.

Ahmed tucked Fatima's head under his arms as a piece of stone fell from the palace and hit his shoulder. The multiple blasts had rocked the palace, sending decorative pieces of stone falling on them. When the rumbling stopped, he raised his head to see Jamal helping the king up.

"I am safe, Ahmed," Fatima's voice said from where she was buried beneath his body. He stood up and pulled his queen to her feet.

"You two need to get to the safe room. Now," Jamal ordered. Fatima nodded, but the king shook his head.

"My wife, go. Please. But this is my cousin and I will take care of him."

"Your Highness, I can't work with you here. I need to make sure you are safe in order to be able to defend your crown," Jamal pleaded as one of his guards ushered Fatima into the palace.

"No. I am king and I will fight with my men. I have plenty of heirs now, so do not worry about the crown. I must find Sarif—if that coward even had enough guts to come himself."

Ahmed saw the rebels pouring in a massive hole in the wall toward the coastline. He quickly shoved the king behind him. "Fine, just stay behind us. Come, brother."

Jamal stood shoulder to shoulder with Ahmed. He wasn't the same boy he was the last time Sarif tried this. And knowing Sergei was leading this charge angered him so much that he was having trouble controlling his beast within. This moment was what he'd spent the last eighteen years preparing for.

"Colonel," Jamal yelled. "Flank from the east. You . . . take your team from the west."

"What are we going to do?" the king asked as he peeked over their shoulders.

Ahmed looked at his brother and they both smiled. "Go right up the middle," Ahmed answered.

Ahmed and Jamal strode into the crowd of rebels while unloading their firearms. The Rahmi soldiers had joined the fight on all sides, forming an effective barricade to the palace. They were systematically pushing the rebels into a tight group close to the wall and away from the palace. Smaller skirmishes had broken out on all sides of the palace, but Jamal's troops were doing their job and suppressing them.

Ahmed saw the man running at him with a knife, but before he could strike, a loud gunshot temporarily deafened him. The man fell and he looked back to the king and gave him a nod. The king had taken up position behind the wall Ahmed and Jamal formed.

As they approached the hole in the palace wall, fighting turned to close quarters and guns became useless.

"Do you see him?" the king yelled.

"Not yet," Jamal answered back. "Oh no, look!"

Ahmed glanced into the sky at the fighter jets and cursed. He couldn't see who it was, but he guessed Saudi Arabia had changed their minds and decided to back Sarif. "Get the king back to the palace," Ahmed ordered as he turned and started shoving the king back.

"Wait," Jamal called over the noise of loud explosions in the distance. "They just hit the boats. They are friendlies."

"My son! Mohtadi must have found out we were under attack and gathered our allies. Push forward, men." The king's cry rang out as his soldiers cheered and doubled their attack.

"Sarif's men are wavering and if I am not mistaken, that is Sarif in the back," Jamal yelled.

"Sarif," the king bellowed over the noise of fighting. Ahmed and Jamal shoved ahead, pushing through fighters as they surged forward. "SARIF," the king's deep voice caught his cousin's attention and they locked eyes with each other.

The fighter jets flew by again, taking out more of the rebel boats and surveying the fighting. Ahmed caught a glimpse of different countries' flags and knew Rahmi would be saved. However, that was Jamal's end game, not his. He fought forward with the king holding onto the back of his shirt as to not be separated.

"We end this right now, Sarif. Unless you're too much of a coward to fight me for my country," the king yelled as more and more Rahmi soldiers finished fighting and cleared a path through the destroyed wall.

"It was never your country. It's mine! All of this should be mine. Instead I'm stuck with a title that holds no power while my wife rules," Sarif spat. His balding head and pointed white beard gave him a menacing look.

"Then fight me for it. Save all these men's lives and fight me for it. It doesn't concern them. This is between you and me." The king pushed past Ahmed and Jamal and dropped his gun to the ground. "I'm not afraid to die for my country. Can you say the same?" The king pulled his curved dagger and pointed it at Sarif.

"I always knew you were old-fashioned, but please. A battle with the daggers of our fathers?"

"I thought you would appreciate the tradition. It's their birth that's in dispute. Let's end this fight between brothers with their own knives. Order your men back." The king gave Jamal a nod and his men started to clear a circle.

Ahmed looked around and saw the soldiers and rebels pausing to see what would happen. Kings never fought their own battles. A quick glance at the palace and Ahmed saw Fatima standing tall and proud on a balcony watching the action. He didn't know how she could stand there so quietly waiting to find out if she would become a widow. All he could do was be thankful Bridget wasn't here to watch him battle Sergei.

It was then that Ahmed saw him—Sergei. He stood a short distance behind Sarif who was now making his way forward with a knife. However, Sergei did not follow his employer. He stood in the back of the crowd waiting to see the outcome of the fight before deciding to retreat like a weakling or advance. Ahmed took a step toward him, but Jamal's arm stopped him.

"Not yet, brother."

The sound of metal against metal brought Ahmed's attention to where the two royals fought. Dust and sand filled the air as they lunged and retreated with their attacks. The king had never seemed like the athletic type, but his form and mind for strategy were clear to Ahmed. Jamal had trained him well.

"You are not the only one with a vendetta. The king has been waiting and preparing for this for eighteen years as well," Jamal whispered.

Ahmed was floored. All this time he had felt alone in his mission, alone in his training, alone as he hardened his heart and body, and alone as he dreamed of revenge. Yet, here was his king doing exactly what Ahmed wanted to do—and doing it well. With a spin and a slice of the king's sword, blood blossomed across Sarif's upper arm. His knife dropped to the sand and he found the blade of a knife pressing against the delicate skin of his neck.

The group of men fell silent and Ahmed held his breath. The king had Sarif dead to rights, but he wasn't moving. "I told you this ends today. Your men either turn themselves in as enemy combatants or they face being killed. You will be taken into custody and tried for treason."

"I can't be tried for treason when this is *my* country," Sarif shouted.

"You can plead your case in court. But I think we both know that you will die for your crimes against Rahmi. When the time for that decision comes, it will be at the hand of her people, not me. Jamal, take him away."

Ahmed stood speechless. The king had his revenge in hand but didn't take it. His brother rushed forward with six guards and Sarif's hands were cuffed. It was then the king slid his knife back into its sheath and turned toward the palace. He bowed to his wife who bowed back in kind. It was over. The rebels closest to the palace walls dropped their weapons and held up their hands.

But Sergei ran. Ahmed saw the movement as Sergei's four comrades turned to run into the village. Ahmed pushed people out of his way as he gave chase. There was no way he was going to let him get away. He would not allow him another chance to go after the woman he loved. As the king said, it ended today.

Chapter Twenty-One

Sergei cursed to himself. Sarif had been defeated. He looked to his men and they took off. He hated running, but the battle was lost. He had planned this to perfection, but Sarif wasn't as strong as he liked to think he was. Sergei had wanted to turn the palace to nothing but a pile of rubble. Sarif wanted the wealth and status of the palace and wouldn't let Sergei destroy it. Now Sarif was going to spend the rest of his days in a jail cell. Sergei wasn't going to end up like Sarif, so he ran, too. No, when it was his time to go, he wanted it to be in battle, not rotting away slowly in some prison.

In the end, he didn't need Sarif installed as king of Rahmi. It had just fit his plan better. Ahmed would have become an enemy and lost all the power he had. But, that was okay. Sergei could still take Ahmed out regardless of who was in power.

Sergei cut through a small alley and made his way through the town. He had a contingency plan just in case Sarif lost. There was a boat waiting for him on the opposite side of the island from where the rebels landed. He just needed to make it out of the center of the city where a car waited to take him to the far coast.

The town was easy to get lost in and that was exactly what Sergei had counted on. The town was nothing but a network of small streets and alleys crammed with houses, markets, and businesses. Soon he had wound himself onto a side street that ran parallel to one of the main ones. All he needed was to follow the route another half-mile and his car would be waiting.

A blonde-streaked red ponytail and camouflage caught his eye between buildings for less than a split second, but it was enough to cause him to skid to a stop. "Stop!" Was he hallucinating? Could the answer really have literally run right by him? His heart beat with excitement as he pushed past his men and started running back toward the palace. He cut through a backyard and a smile crept onto his face. He knew this house. It was where he killed that lying, cheating bitch and the son that represented her betrayal. He might have lost the battle, but as he saw Bridget skid to a stop, he knew he had just won the war.

Bridget controlled her breathing as she jogged up the street toward the palace. Her pack weighed a ton, but luckily she had kept up with her training even after her final deployment.

Marko ran silently by her side as the palace grew closer. Bridget stopped and pulled out a map to figure out where the fighting was. She had seen the fighter jets and knew Mo had been successful in talking with not only the president, but also other allies of Rahmi. During her descent, she had seen the British naval forces entering the water surrounding Rahmi. Several shots from the big ships' guns and the fire from the jet fighters left the rebel ships crippled.

Marko growled and Bridget turned her head just in time to see a man launch himself at her from behind a tree. She took the hit hard and went down with the weight of the man on her. He raised his arm back to punch her, but he didn't have time. Marko was on him. The man howled in pain, giving Bridget enough time to raise the gun she was carrying and crack it down on his head.

"*Brava,* Miss Springer." Sergei clapped condescendingly with a man standing on each side of him and one behind him. Bridget scrambled to her feet and Marko positioned himself between her and Sergei.

"Sergei. You'll have to forgive me, but you took too long coming for me. I ate that cupcake I promised you."

"I guess I'll just have to kill you for it," Sergei smiled. He flicked his wrist as the three men moved forward. "And kill that damn dog."

"You touch my dog and I'll kill you," she threatened as she raised her gun at the men. They stopped moving forward at the sight of the gun, but it could have been because they heard the animalistic cry that rang out.

"Take care of her. He's all mine," Sergei ordered.

Ahmed had chased after Sergei through the streets and alleys. He knew he had a chance when he saw Sergei cut through his old backyard. It was fate bringing him back to where it all began. It was appropriate that one of them die here. But when he made his way around his old neighbor's house, he saw Sergei with three of his men stalking toward Bridget. The cry had been wrenched from his heart.

Without thought, he sprinted for her. He would protect her this time. He wouldn't fail. He couldn't fail. It wasn't his life he was fighting for any longer. It was hers.

"Sergei. I should have known you would be such a . . . what's the word you used? *Weakling*. You're such a weakling that you ran when your army was defeated," Ahmed mocked as they faced each other with guns raised and pointed at each other.

"I was never weak. You, on the other hand, have always been. Let's see if you have the nerve to back up that insult. You and me — no weapons," Sergei challenged. With Ahmed's silent acceptance, they held out their guns and tossed them to the side. "Knives, too, even though I love them so much. I'll save them for her."

Ahmed saw Bridget and Marko holding the three men at bay but knew it wouldn't last. "I have everything under control. Don't even look this way," she shouted as Ahmed and Sergei tossed their knives next to their guns.

"I would. After all, my men are going to kill her. Go ahead and have one last look at yet another woman you couldn't protect." On the implied command, the three men lunged at Bridget. She got a shot off and took down one man before a second man knocked the gun out of her hand.

Marko snarled and attacked the third man right as Sergei made his move. Ahmed felt Sergei's punch connect with his chin and his head snap back. He didn't hear the man scream as Marko's jaws closed so hard that it snapped his wrist. Instead, Ahmed made himself focus on the man in front of him. Bridget had told him over and over again that she could protect herself. She had flown halfway around the world to help him and he needed to trust her to do that. She loved him enough that she was taking on two men in order to give him the chance for revenge that had waited eighteen long years.

The blow to Bridget's face was enough to have her sink to her knees and see stars. But she refused to let it affect her. She needed to keep this man focused on her and unable to stab Ahmed in the back. She heard the scream come from the man Marko had a grip on and knew he had things under control. Once Marko latched onto a mark, he wouldn't let go. That left the ugly Russian in front of her.

In her peripheral vision, she saw Ahmed and Sergei circling each other. She needed to end this fast so she could make sure Sergei didn't cheat. She didn't trust him for one second to not have another weapon on him.

Bridget made herself start to cry. The man in front of her laughed.

"Stupid woman. Thinking you could beat a man? Pathetic." He stopped in front of her and aimed a gun at her head. Bridget took a deep breath and sobbed again. She planted the balls of her feet on the ground and with a quick combination of moves that Ahmed taught her, she knocked the gun from his hand and launched herself upward.

The weight of her body knocked the man in the chest and left him stumbling backward. Bridget grabbed hold of his shirt with one hand and used the other to slam her open palm against his nose. Blood splattered as the cartilage crunched, but the man refused to go down.

He roared in pain and reached for her. She moved faster, though. She boxed his ears and grabbed his hair before cracking her head into his face.

The head-butt did it. The man fell to his knees with blood pouring down his face and his eyes rolling back. Bridget moved quickly and managed to get his hands zip-tied. She would have to thank Kenna for the crying tip when she got home. Bridget picked up her gun along with the one the man dropped from the ground. Marko still held onto his man as she took a slow step forward. She talked to Marko as she approached so he knew who she was. She placed her hand on his collar and ordered him to release his hold on the man. As soon as he released, she had the man's hands in zip-ties and the gun leveled on him. Marko sat by her side with his tongue hanging out and his tail thumping.

"Over there," she ordered. The man looked as if he were going to protest, but he grudgingly moved next to his comrade. With her gun in her left hand aimed at the men sitting ten feet in front of her, she aimed the gun in her right hand over their heads to where Sergei and Ahmed were battling. She wouldn't interrupt unless Sergei made her.

Ahmed blocked a punch and countered with a jab followed by a cross. Sergei stumbled backward before they circled each other again. Relief flooded him when he saw Bridget standing with guns in hand and two men cuffed on the ground as Marko stood guard over them. Instead of stopping him, she was allowing him to lay his demons to rest.

Sergei shot daggers at him as they faced each other. Ahmed could feel Sergei's anger radiating from him. His whole being was dark with rage. Blood dripped from Sergei's split lip, and Ahmed felt his bruised ribs that throbbed.

"Why? Tell me why you killed my son?" Ahmed demanded.

Sergei roared and charged Ahmed. His shoulder slammed into Ahmed's bruised ribs and they went down hard on the ground. "You don't even honor the wife you took against her will by asking about her?" Sergei shouted as he pummeled Ahmed's midsection in a flurry of punches.

The pain was searing. His midsection was on fire as he absorbed the punches. Ahmed placed his hands on Sergei's shoulders and pushed hard, sending him falling back onto the ground. Ahmed scrambled away and got back to his feet. "I would never do that to a woman. True, I didn't want her as a wife, but I would never do that to her."

"Don't lie," Sergei shouted as he balled his hands into fists. "I know you did; Paulina would never willingly lie with you. She belonged to another."

"The man she got those notes from?" Sergei was so surprised he dropped his hands and Ahmed attacked.

Ahmed snapped Sergei's knee with a sharp kick. Sergei cried out in pain as he fell to the ground. Ahmed quickly moved behind his crippled foe and put his forearm across Sergei's throat. He squeezed and Sergei gasped for air. Retribution was at hand and power surged through Ahmed's body. He looked down at the top of Sergei's head as he clasped his fist and tightened his grip.

Sergei kicked out with his good leg and clawed at Ahmed's arm. "This is for killing Kedar. For killing the only person I loved then."

"You . . . took . . . *my* . . . wife," Sergei gasped.

Ahmed loosened the chokehold only slightly and Sergei sucked in air. "I didn't take your wife."

"Paulina was my wife."

"She was my wife. She loved some man named Mikhail, but she was a virgin when *she* demanded our consummation," Ahmed said with confusion. Was Sergei just trying to save his life? Ahmed tightened his grip again. He wouldn't be fooled.

"I . . . married Paulina. Her father . . . stopped us. Took her. She swore," Sergei choked and gasped.

Ahmed stood stunned. "Swore what?" Ahmed asked, loosening his hold once again.

"Swore she'd always love me. Swore her love and her life to me. Swore that the only way you'd touch her was if you forced her. She promised to wait for me to rescue her. Her father forbid us to talk and brought her here when he discovered us at the church. But it was too late. We had been married before God. He threatened me with death, but it did not matter. She was mine!"

"I don't believe you. She's the one who forced me. The wedding had to be consummated," Ahmed argued.

"But then she told me that she'd fallen in love with you. That she was pregnant with your child. That she didn't mean any of those things she swore to me. That it was just foolish puppy love. She denounced our love, our marriage, and me. I died that night. But I got my revenge on her and that brat."

"Shows how much you know. She hated me. She hated our child. She mourned the man from the notes. And since you don't know what I am talking about, then you are just lying to save your sorry life."

"Mikhail!"

Ahmed had been ready to complete his vengeance until he heard Sergei scream the name. "What did you say?"

"My name was Mikhail."

"I don't believe you," Ahmed said, stunned.

"I told you. That adulteress bitch was my wife. Mrs. Mikhail Sergei Petrov. You are not the only one to conveniently drop parts of your name when you felt as if you had died, Ahmed Mueez. Of course, I only died of a figurative broken heart. You on the other hand," Sergei laughed at Ahmed. Laughed at killing his wife. Laughed at killing his son. Laughed at almost killing him.

Anger filled Ahmed. It pulsed through his blood and pounded his head as he choked the life from Sergei. It was coming soon—vengeance. He looked up to heaven to tell Kedar his death had been vindicated. Instead of seeing the sky, he saw his brother, the king, and guards surrounding them. He saw Bridget and Marko holding them back. She was giving him time to complete the one thing that had motivated him for eighteen years. Her eyes were filled with determination, but sadness, too.

He could tell she pitied him, pitied his need for retribution. Yet she was holding back Jamal and others, using her body and her life to let Ahmed have his moment. For what? For a wife who turned out to not be his? For his child—yes, but would he want death to shroud his beautiful son's name? He was killing Sergei in his son's name, after all.

No. Ahmed shook his head and loosened his hold on Sergei. His son deserved better than that. He deserved to be remembered as the precious boy he had been, not for the terrible things Sergei had done. He saw that when he looked at Bridget. She was the future. She would love him—all of him. Bridget would love Kedar and celebrate his short life. She would be by his side always because they were partners and they loved each other.

Ahmed dropped his arms to his side and Sergei fell to the ground gasping for breath. Bridget smiled and dropped her guns. Ahmed felt the darkness crack and fall away from him. "You deserve far worse than a quick death. You deserve to rot in a cell as you are transported from country to country to face the families you robbed of loved ones. Kedar has his justice. You'll never be a free man again."

He stepped around Sergei's gasping body and found himself filled with hope. Bridget's smile dropped and he quickly wondered if she thought he was weak for not killing Sergei. She raised her gun toward Ahmed and squeezed the trigger. Ahmed felt the burning pain of skin being torn as he collapsed to the ground.

Bridget was running toward him along with his brother and the guards. The king was yelling orders to get him, but it was Bridget who reached his side first. With the look of an avenging golden-haired goddess, she kicked out hard. Ahmed felt the weight lift from him as Sergei flew backward with the force of the hit.

"Ahmed may have decided to let you live, but I'm not so forgiving," Bridget said in a cold voice as she leveled her gun at Sergei.

"No," Ahmed called out. The pain from the knife lodged in his back had him struggling to talk. "It would be torture to him to be locked in a cell for the rest of his life. A quick death would be too good for him."

"I'll kill you the second I escape." Sergei spat at her with blood blossoming where her bullet had hit his shoulder.

Ahmed drew in a painful breath as Bridget smiled down at Sergei and pulled the trigger.

Bridget had never experienced a kind of fear like she had the moment she saw Sergei pull the hidden knife from behind his back and lunge forward. The knife had been buried in Ahmed's back as her bullet lodged in Sergei's shoulder. The shocked look on Ahmed's face would haunt her nightmares as both men fell to the ground, with Sergei landing partially on top of Ahmed.

The kick had felt good. She thirsted for revenge against this man who dared take so much from the man she loved. And when he threatened her, she knew what she had to do in order to secure her future with Ahmed. So she pulled the trigger.

Sergei screamed and she pulled the trigger a second time. No one had moved. The king and Jamal stood shocked, but then Ahmed smiled at her. She moved to stand over Sergei. "I hope you don't mind if I don't bother saving anymore cupcakes for you." Sergei's eyes rolled back and he hit the ground with a thud.

"You didn't kill him?" Jamal asked as he motioned men to take Sergei into custody.

"Nope. But he sure as hell will never be able to walk well again. Can't escape without a good pair of knees." Bridget tucked her gun away and turned to where Marko had crawled next to Ahmed. He whined and nuzzled Ahmed's hand with his nose. "Are you okay?"

She kneeled beside him and examined the knife sticking out of his shoulder. "Yes, I think it stopped when it hit my shoulder blade. He was too weak from our battle to do any real damage. Now come here and kiss me," he ordered.

Bridget leaned forward and placed her lips on his. It was a soft kiss. Tender and loving, but filled with a promise of their future. "Now, let's go get you stitched up."

Chapter Twenty-Two

Bridget finished talking to her dad and hung up the phone just as Ahmed exited the king's private study. Ahmed, Bridget, and Marko had been hastily driven back to the palace. While Ahmed was stitched up, she and Marko had walked the exterior of the palace grounds as well as the main areas of the palace. She had just stopped to call her father and check in on Ahmed before finishing the rest of her sweep.

"Feeling better?" she asked.

"Yes. The king briefed me as the doctor sewed me up. The Americans gave us the name of a company with explosion detection dogs to help clear the pipeline of any remaining Semtex. It seems he wanted to blow up the palace but didn't get the chance to plant the explosives. There are already people at work fixing the damaged pipes, so I hope we won't be shut down too long."

"How are you feeling? And what's happening with Sergei?" Bridget tossed the tennis ball for Marko and laughed as he skidded on the marble floor.

"I just need stitches, some antibiotics, and a tetanus shot. More interestingly, I was informed that countries are already fighting over extradition of Sergei. The newspapers and gossips are most appalled by the fact I was stabbed in the back. Within hours Sergei will be known for that and not as the world's top mercenary." Ahmed laughed as he put his arm around her. "Did you get your calls out of the way?"

"Yes. Here's one of the satellite phones. I'm sure Mo would like to hear from you and the king." Bridget handed him the phone and leaned against him. She was a mess. Dirt mixed with sweat had turned to mud and dried on her. Blood from her fight with Sergei's men was splattered in places, and she was having a serious case of helmet hair.

"I am sure my husband would like that very much." Fatima smiled and held out her arms. Bridget clasped her hands and kissed each cheek. "Thank you for your help today. I have a bath ready for you and I want the doctor to make sure you are well. Ameera and I will take you up."

"I need to finish my sweep," Bridget said with a sigh. She was exhausted and a bath sounded like heaven.

"A team from Saudi Arabia has already arrived. Mohtadi called his sister and she told her husband who informed the sheik. The sheik was devastated; he was coming for a visit next month and sent a team to help so he would not need to postpone the trip." Queen Fatima smiled at Ahmed. "Funny thing, we never invited him. Good thing the king remembered you did and made sure to tell the sheik all the impressive, manly things he had planned already. Because of you, our relationship with that country is getting stronger by the day."

Ahmed bowed his head respectfully. Bridget was excited to see Dani's sister-in-law hurry over to them with her slightly rounded belly almost hidden under her flowing sari.

"It is so nice to see you again. I want to hear all the gossip from Keeneston," Ameera giggled.

"I don't know, it sounds as if the Keeneston grapevine has extended to your sister and the sheik," Bridget laughed and soon they all joined in.

Fatima laced her arm through Bridget's while Ameera did the same with the other arm. "Go have your man-time while we take care of your Bridget," Fatima called over her shoulder to Ahmed. "We'll see you at the celebration. It is time for our country to rejoice and begin the healing process."

Ahmed watched as Bridget was escorted to the suite of rooms Fatima had prepared for her. He looked down at the phone and turned toward the king's study. He quickly scribbled down the last number called. His first call was to Mo. His best friend was relieved to hear that they were well and Sarif and Sergei had been captured.

"How did you do it, my son?" the king asked, full of pride.

"I might have told the President of the United States a story of love and told her that only she could ensure a happy ending. Then I invited the prime minister to our box at the Kentucky Derby. The British love the races," Mo said happily. Ahmed almost laughed. Not only had Mo received aid, he'd probably worked out a deal for some more horses to race in the U.S.

"You got them to help with just that?" the king asked.

"I also let them know how important it was that our countries remain allies. It seemed they agreed and gave the orders for aid from their men stationed nearby. They looked good helping a small country and they didn't risk any boots on the ground. It was a win-win for them. And for us. I just can't believe you challenged Sarif like that, Father."

Ahmed had watched it and was still in disbelief. He couldn't wait to get home and tell Dani and Nabi all about it. Ahmed waited impatiently as the king and Mo finished their talk.

"I am going to go get ready for the party. Tonight we open the doors to the palace and celebrate peace in our great country." The king rose and handed the phone back to Ahmed. "You are a great warrior, Ahmed. Your father would be proud. However, your father would have killed Sergei."

Ahmed hung his head. Even in death, he could not please his father.

"You are like a brother to my son and therefore a son of mine."
The king patted Ahmed's shoulder and looked seriously down at
him. "And as my son, I am proud of you for not killing him. Now go
get cleaned up for tonight."

The king left Ahmed alone in the room. He stared at the number
he had written down and felt ashamed when he called Nabi. "I need
you to run a number for me." He rattled off the number that Bridget
had just called and waited for Nabi to run a trace.

"That's just her father, sir," Nabi told him. Ahmed let out a
breath he knew he shouldn't have even been holding.

"Do you have his address?"

"Of course."

Bridget slid into the beautiful gown and felt like a princess. Ameera
and Fatima had been so kind to her. The bath had been exactly what
she needed to feel refreshed. While she had cleaned up, the women
had gone through their dresses and found the perfect one for her.

"You look wonderful," Fatima beamed.

"And right on time. Here he comes." Ameera giggled.

Bridget saw him in the mirror. Ahmed leaned against the door in
a black tuxedo and held a narrow rectangular box in his hand. "And
he bears gifts. We will see you at the celebration." Fatima linked her
arm with Ameera and they hurried from the room with their heads
bent together whispering.

"You steal my breath every time I see you. But tonight you make
me even more thankful that I am yours. I brought you something."
Ahmed placed a reverent kiss on her cheek and handed her the box.

She opened it and found an intricate gold chain with a single
pearl in the middle. Thin gold leaves surrounded the pearl making it
appear to be set within a flower. "I saw this in Italy before you
arrived. It reminded me of you and I've been waiting for the right
moment to give it to you."

Bridget refrained from leaping on him and covering him with kisses as he came to stand behind her to fasten the necklace. "It's stunning. Thank you." She reached up and let her fingers trace it while she looked in the mirror.

"Can I show you where I grew up before heading to the celebration?" Ahmed asked.

"I'd love that."

Ahmed walked her down the long hallway of the third floor. Thick Persian runners ran the length of the hall. Vases filled with flowers sat on the small tables under the colorful works of art on the royal family's private floor. They had honored her tonight by having her stay with them.

She followed Ahmed to a hidden door behind a fake bookcase and then down the narrow steps behind it to the bottom floor. This was for servants to move around undetected, Ahmed had told her. The cooks, maids, and butlers hurried through the rooms and hallways. The first door they came to was locked, but Ahmed pulled out a key after knocking. "They must be at the party already. This was where I grew up. It now belongs to Jamal and his family."

He pushed open the door to a small living room. Off to one side was a kitchen and to the other side was a narrow hall leading to what she assumed were the bedrooms. "We had to be near the royal family always. My father, like his father before him, was the head of the guards. I was different. I wanted to take photographs, like this one." Ahmed pointed to a picture Jamal had framed on the wall.

Bridget took a step closer and looked at the teenager in the picture with his head bent over his father's desk. Their father stood looking proudly down. The shadows of the image, the clear look of joy on his father's face, and the adoration of the son was both moving and telling. The son the father was so proud of was Jamal.

"Your picture is amazing. It actually reminds me of the pictures at your home."

Ahmed smiled and Bridget could see him fill with pride. "Thank you. Those are mine as well."

"You're amazing. You need to take more pictures."

Ahmed nuzzled her neck and placed his lips near her ear. "I have a wonderful idea for a series of nudes."

"Ahem."

Bridget jumped in surprise, but Ahmed just held her in place and winked.

"Yes, Jamal?"

"The king is requesting your presence at the celebration. I believe the two of you will be honored tonight."

Ahmed held out his arm to lead her to the party. "Shall we?"

Ahmed kept Bridget's hand tucked in the crook of his arm as they stood next to his brother on the royal family's dais. The palace gates were open and everyone from state officials to fishermen stood dressed in their best while waiting to go through the security line to get inside to celebrate Sarif's capture and the return of safety to Rahmi.

However, there was no one there who could come close to the image that was Bridget. She was simply stunning in the cobalt-blue dress that hugged her curves and flared at the knees—and she was his. Ahmed had never felt so much pride before. Not only was she breathtakingly beautiful, but she was also kind and gentle. The royal family loved her as much as the old woman who had encountered her right after she landed in the village. She had a smile and a kind word for every person who approached her.

Marko was eating up the attention as well as he sat beside Ameera with his nose pressed to her belly. The dog could sense the child inside of her and was refusing to leave her side. He was worse than a mother hen. Ameera was delighted and already begged Bridget to let Marko spend the night with her.

"In conclusion, thank you to my security, our soldiers, and to our allies for helping keep Rahmi safe. We're a small country but full of pride and unlimited possibilities if we work together. To the people of Rahmi and our future!" The king raised his arms in triumph and the crowd erupted.

The king nodded to the band and music surrounded them. "Ahmed, a word with you and Jamal, if you don't mind." The king ushered them toward Mo's oldest brother.

Reluctantly Ahmed followed his brother to the stand next to the king and his son. "Ahmed, I have talked to Jamal, and I want to offer you a way to come back home. You have trained Nabi well. His father is most impressed. I want you home now to work side by side with your brother. You two will both work as our two chiefs of security."

Ahmed opened his mouth to respond, but the king held up his hand. "It is a big honor and one you should speak to my son about. Go back to Kentucky and talk it over with Mohtadi. Get him used to the idea, for this is not a request."

He couldn't stop looking at Bridget. Desperation clawed at him. Ahmed couldn't leave her. Not after how hard he fought to be with her. She laughed and he stepped from the shadows. If his time was limited with her, then he needed to make the most of it.

"Excuse me," he said, interrupting her discussion with Jamal's wife. "Care to dance?" The music slowed and Ahmed held out his hand for Bridget.

She smiled radiantly at him and his heart broke. He was going to talk to Mo and then he'd be leaving. He was bound to the family by duty. After all, he was a Mueez, and they served the king.

"I'd love to."

Ahmed slid his hand around her waist and cupped her hand with his other. He pulled her tight against him and slowly led her around the floor. He didn't say anything. He couldn't. Instead he listened to her happy chatter and heard the hitch in her voice when he slid his leg between hers on a turn.

He smiled down at her when she automatically leaned into him with her breasts molded against his chest. He couldn't stand the thought of being halfway around the world from her. The desperation overtook him as he bent his head to kiss her, not stopping until they were both breathless.

He rested his forehead on hers and knew he needed her. Every fiber of his body called out for her silken touch. "Bridget," he pleaded.

"I know," she smiled up to him as she cupped his face. "Take me to bed, Ahmed."

"Now that's an order I don't mind following."

Bridget stood nervously behind him as he pushed open the large door to her suite of rooms. The golden room glowed in the low light of the lamps. The sheer fabric covering the windows glittered as she followed Ahmed across the open living area to the bed.

A light gold bedspread covered the massive bed. Pillows in every shade, from ivory to dark gold, were piled against the arched headboard. The bed seemed to float like a cloud above the rest of the room. Ahmed took one of the three steps to the bed and stopped. Bridget swallowed hard when she saw him looking down at her. Love shone from his eyes, but so did something else. He dropped her hand.

"Wait here." He climbed the remaining steps and sat slightly above her on the edge of the bed. She felt her breathing become shallow as need filled his eyes. "Let your hair tumble down," he said in a rough-edged voice.

Bridget reached up to release the clips and shook out her hair as pins fell to the floor. Ahmed's dark eyes blazed with desire as he shifted on the edge of the bed. She was doing this to him. "The dress. I want it off," his voice rumbled.

A heady feeling of womanly power gave her confidence as she watched him restrain his arousal. He may not be moving to touch her, but the hunger in his eyes was clear. Bridget reached to her side and unzipped the dress slowly. She held it in place with one arm across her chest and tossed him a teasing look of disobedience.

"I said I wanted it off," he demanded as his jaw tightened.

"Jacket and tie. Off," she ordered. Bridget grinned at the surprised expression on his face.

Ahmed relented, though, and his eyes darkened even more. He stood and shrugged out of the jacket while never taking his eyes from her. He pulled the bow tie from his neck and looked at it, then to her with a smile. "Drop the dress, my dear."

Bridget dropped her arms to the side and allowed the dress to pool at her feet, leaving her standing in her red strapless bra, matching panties, and nude silk stockings.

"Shirt." Bridget licked her lips as he slowly unbuttoned his shirt and pulled it from his arms. His broad chest melded into rippled abs and an impressive erection straining against his pants. She felt her face flush and tried not to stare.

"Bra and panties. Slowly remove them," he ordered.

She reached behind her and unclasped the bra. She felt his eyes raking her body, taking in every small movement. Her breasts swelled with excitement and her nipples hardened in anticipation of his hands on them. When his strong jaw clenched, she dropped the bra to the floor.

Ahmed tried to take a deep breath but couldn't. He'd wanted to control her. He'd wanted to prove he still had power in his life when he felt it being taking away by the king, but it was clear she had other plans. They were partners in the field, in life, and in the bedroom. Sharing the power with her was exhilarating. The excitement of her pushing him just as he was doing to her had ignited his desire even further.

"Panties." His voice was so rough he hardly recognized it. He sat back down and watched her hook her thumbs into the waistband of the red silk. She moved her hips seductively as she slowly peeled them off.

"Stockings?" she asked as she stepped from her panties.

"No, leave them on." He had ideas for them. He stood up, no longer being able to wait to touch her. He wanted nothing more than to lose himself in her.

"Stop," she held up her hand and took a step closer to him. He looked down at her head as she dropped to her knees in front of him. Ahmed was drawn to the valley between her breasts and ran a finger down the silken path before she stopped him. "Pants. Off."

He throbbed as she slid his pants from his hips. Ahmed felt her warm breath on him a moment before she took all control away from him.

Chapter Twenty-Three

Ahmed placed her bag on the floor and gave Bridget a tight smile. It felt odd being back in Keeneston knowing he wasn't able to stay. Marko, however, was thrilled to be home as he ran from room to room making sure nothing had changed since he was last there.

"I'm sorry I'm going to be busy for a while. I need to meet with Mo and I have some things to do for the king. I'll call, but it may be a couple days until I can see you again."

Bridget smiled at him. She could tell something was wrong. After their scorching night together, he'd started to withdraw. "Okay. Do whatever it is you need to do and then come back to me. Understand?"

Ahmed felt his smile tighten. If only she knew he could never come back to her. "Of course. I love you." He bent and kissed her cheek. Oh, how he loved her. Then he did the most painful thing he'd ever done—he left.

"My father ordered what?" Mo yelled so loudly Dani rushed into the office with a concerned look on her face.

"Is everything all right?" she asked, full of worry.

"No," Mo yelled as he slammed his fist on the ornate desk.

Ahmed sat quietly in the chair across from Mo and didn't say a word. He knew his best friend would be angry. Neither of them could ever dream the king would order him back to Rahmi.

"My father has ordered Ahmed back to Rahmi to share chief of security duties with his brother," Mo said agitatedly. "He's taking my best security officer and my best friend from me to serve him and my eldest brother."

"How can he do that? Why would he do that?" Dani asked, astonished, as she dropped into the chair next to Ahmed.

"Because Ahmed is part of the Royal Guard and, as king, my father's orders must be obeyed. He probably thinks this is an honor after what happened eighteen years ago," Mo said without thought. Ahmed closed his eyes. Mo was so angry he had lost his ability to filter his thoughts.

"What happened eighteen years ago?" Dani asked.

"When Sergei killed Ahmed's wife and newborn, then almost killed Ahmed. My father let Ahmed leave the country with me after that because he embarrassed his fam . . ." Mo stopped mid-rant and snapped his eyes to Ahmed's. "I am so sorry, my friend. I wasn't thinking."

"What?" Dani jumped up. "And you didn't tell me this?"

"I'm sorry, but it was, and is, none of your business," Ahmed said quietly.

"Well, now everything makes sense. You got your revenge, found new love, and now the king is taking it away from you thinking he's doing you a favor," Dani recapped more for herself than for him.

"That's right. I need to meet with Nabi and review some things before I leave," Ahmed stood up. He had accepted his fate. He just didn't know if he could live with it.

"No," Mo and Dani cried at the same time.

"Sit down and give me a minute," Dani ordered. She started pacing the room while mumbling to herself. "How much money do you have?" she asked after a minute. "I mean, I always see you in fancy cars. But do they belong to you or to us?"

"Me, why?"

"How can you afford them?" Dani asked, not really trying to hide her bluntness.

"It pays well to keep the prince of Rahmi and his family safe," Ahmed said with a bit of annoyed sarcasm. "Besides, I have no expenses. I live here on the farm. Eat most of my meals here. I don't have anything to spend my salary on. So, I might have bought a couple nice cars and a couple of Mo's racehorses. But that's all."

"You like racehorses?" Dani smiled and looked between a confused Ahmed and Mo.

"Yes," Ahmed answered hesitantly. "Mo got me hooked when we lived in England."

"He's great with the stud books, too," Mo put in. "I always get his advice on breedings. Why?"

"Because I have a way for Ahmed to stay in Keeneston," Dani grinned.

It was almost done. Bridget put her hands on her hips and looked up at the structure taking shape on her property against the twilight sky. The training facility was framed and the roof had just gone on the apartment above the kennel. By next week, the cement walls would be up and painted. Then the kennels could be installed.

Her butt started to vibrate and Bridget pulled out her cell phone hoping it was Ahmed. It had been two days since she talked to him and she was missing him terribly. She recognized the number and smiled. "Hi, Daddy."

"How you doing, pumpkin?" her dad's deep voice asked over the phone.

"Good. My kennel is almost done," Bridget said proudly.

"That's wonderful. I can't wait to see it. Your mother and I will have to make a trip out there soon. We are actually going to discuss it when we sit down to dinner in a minute."

"That would be nice," Bridget said as she waved to Pierce and Tammy who pulled their truck to a stop in front of her.

"It would be nice to see the guys again," her dad started to say.

"Look, Daddy, Pierce and Tammy just . . . what's up, guys?" Bridget interrupted herself.

"Hey, pumpkin, someone's at the door. I gotta go."

"Me, too. Pierce and Tammy are here. Talk to you soon. Give Mom my love."

"What about me?" her father joked.

"You, too. Bye." Bridget hung up the phone and waited for Pierce to help Tammy out of the truck. "Hey, guys. What are you all doing here?"

"I wanted to see how the kennels were coming," Pierce said as he looked at the progress.

"And I'm here to invite you to dinner at the Davies. Marcy wants to hear all about Rahmi. I think we all do," Tammy said excitedly.

"Sure. I'll be there."

The house smelled great. Aromas from fresh breads, pork chops, and key lime pie filled the air and made Bridget's stomach rumble as she told the Davies women about Rahmi. When she was finished, the women were all determined to go visit.

"Oh! Did you hear the latest about Miss Lily and John?" Paige asked in a conspiratorial whisper.

"No. What's happened now?" Morgan asked as she put her feet up on the couch.

"Well, after the Roger Burns incident, apparently Miss Daisy and Miss Violet confronted Miss Lily. You know they've all had a thing for John at one point or another," Paige told them.

"That's right. For the longest time we all thought he'd end up with Daisy Mae," Marcy explained.

"Well, he might still. Miss Lily broke down and told them she couldn't move on from the past."

"That's so sad. Poor John," Tammy sniffled.

"Don't feel too bad. I don't think he'll be lonely for long," Paige continued. "Apparently there was a pitcher of ice tea involved and Miss Daisy declared that her sister was an idiot."

The women gasped.

"What happened next?" Gemma asked as she scribbled down notes. There was no doubt that this story was going in the *Keeneston Journal* next week.

"Miss Lily started to cry and said she was scared. The heartbreak she suffered all those years ago was too much to get over."

"I'm stunned," Katelyn said as she swayed with baby Sydney in her arms.

"Wait, what heartbreak?" Gemma asked.

"It's very sad. All the Rose sisters had someone special in their lives when they were younger. I don't know the specifics about Miss Violet. I know something happened, but no one ever knew what it was. However, Miss Daisy's high school beau joined the Army and Miss Lily was involved with her neighbor. They were very serious and then suddenly he was gone. The family moved and she never saw him again," Marcy told them.

"So, what is Miss Lily going to do?" Annie asked her sister-in-law.

"She's trying to win him back."

"Oh, this should be very interesting," Gemma muttered as she finished taking notes.

"I thought you all could use some food to go with your gossip." Jake set down a bowl of cheese dip and tortilla chips.

Bridget watched as Gemma's eyes went wide and she quickly placed her notebook down. Her face turned a slight greenish color and her hand covered her mouth. She shot up and dashed to the bathroom.

"Cyland," his mother yelled with tears in her eyes.

"Yeah, Ma?" Cy asked as he joined them.

"I'm finally able to die happy and you keep it a secret from me? Your own mother? Oh, Jake, we're going to have another grandbaby!"

"Geez, Ma, you're a walking pregnancy test," Cy said with a roll of his eyes, but the huge grin on his face showed how excited he was.

Gemma walked from the bathroom with a half-smile on her face. "Sorry, I guess I ate something that didn't agree with me."

Marcy gave a hiccupped sob and embraced her in a tight hug.

"The gig's up, babe. You might as well tell them everything." Cy slipped his arm around Gemma and they suddenly had the whole family's attention.

"Well, we're ten weeks along. Due at the end of May, but I probably won't make it that far."

Cy gave her a squeeze and Jake wrapped a supportive arm around Marcy.

"What's the matter, sweetheart?" Jake asked.

"I've been told to expect . . ." Gemma paused and took a deep breath. "I've been told to expect an early arrival since we're having twins."

The women were all happy for Gemma and Cy, but it was nothing compared to the happy and shocked sobs coming from Marcy. Everyone laughed as Jake, much to his embarrassment, got misty-eyed at the news.

"We're going to have eight grandbabies, honey." Jake hugged his wife and then his daughter-in-law before wrapping Cy up in a great big bear hug.

"At least eight," Cole said as he wrapped his arm around Paige. "We have grand plans for the future."

"Well, we can't be outdone by them," Marshall teased.

"Oh, Jake. Why do you keep talking about dying happy? We have too many grandbabies to play with to think about that," Marcy cried as she wrapped her family up in a huge group hug.

Bridget suddenly felt like she was intruding. She also felt lonely. She checked her phone. Nothing. After falling so hard in love,

Bridget was worried she'd never have this. Ahmed was clearly putting up walls and retreating again. She had the horrible feeling she wouldn't have the happily-ever-after that her friends had.

Ahmed stopped in front of the large rectangular house and swallowed hard. He had to do this. It was the right thing to do, he told himself. He opened the door to the sports car he had driven from Kentucky and got out. He buttoned his black suit coat and shut the door.

His footsteps echoed through the sleepy neighborhood as he walked up the dimly lit sidewalk to the front door. It was dinnertime, almost six at night, and Ahmed hoped that the light spilling into the yard meant he was home. Ahmed wrapped his fingers around the brass knocker and banged it against the navy-blue door.

He dropped his hands to his side and took a deep breath. He heard voices behind the door and tensed for battle. The door unlocked and the knob turned. Ahmed tried to put a smile on his face to appear less frightening but decided it would look insincere.

The door opened and Ahmed felt his mouth drop open.

"You," they both said at the same time.

There was no hiding his shock. All the training he'd received had not prepared him for this. He didn't bother to hold out his hand. Ahmed knew the gesture would be ignored.

"Oh my goodness," the soft voice said from inside the house. Ahmed glanced into the hall and saw a woman with dark-blonde hair cut short wearing an apron over her tan slacks and standing with her hand on her heart. "Are you here to kill us?" she asked.

"No, ma'am." Ahmed looked at the tall, dark red-haired man in front of him dressed in full military attire, and more importantly, at the four stars across each shoulder. "I'm here to ask permission to marry your daughter."

Chapter Twenty-Four

"**N**o." "Richard, let him in," Bridget's mother said as she pushed her large and intimidating husband out of the way. "You must be Ahmed. I've heard a lot about you."

"Obviously he hasn't heard a lot about us," General Ward snapped.

Ahmed cleared his throat. "Actually, I have. Bridget just seemed to leave out one very important detail about you."

"Come, sit down. Bridget said you were a nice young man. I find it so romantic that you would ask our permission. Let me bring you something to drink. Water? Ice tea?" Patty Ward looked from her husband to Ahmed, both unflinching. "Bourbon it is."

Ahmed smiled at Bridget's mother. He could see where Bridget got both her sweetness and toughness.

"Oh my," she blushed as she hurried from the room.

"Stop wooing her to your side. Let's go to my office and have a nice long talk," General Ward said as he buttoned his military jacket and started down the hall.

"Let's call it like it is, sir. There's nothing like an interrogation to get to know someone." Ahmed followed behind the general and noted that he seemed to have scored a small chuckle.

Ahmed had thought meeting Bridget's parents was going to be nerve-wracking, but that was before he knew the man was one of the most powerful generals in the United States Army. Shoot, he'd be lucky to get out alive. And as soon as he did, he was going to have a few words with Nabi. How could he not have told him? Ahmed felt like banging his head . . . because Ahmed hadn't asked. Why did he think knowing less about Bridget would have stopped him from falling in love? Well, if he knew General Ward was her father, it might have worked. Who was he kidding? He'd go through a hundred generals if it meant he could marry Bridget.

"Take a seat." General Ward motioned to one of the deep-red leather chairs in front of an immense desk. Ahmed chose one and watched the general take a seat behind his desk in a classic power play. A quick glance around the room left Ahmed more nervous and completely envious. If General Ward agreed to let him marry his daughter, then Ahmed had a feeling he and his father-in-law would get along great.

A huge cavalry sword hung behind the desk. Books on military theory, philosophy, and psychology lined the bookcase. Pictures of the general and Bridget wearing camouflage in the desert sat on the table. Pictures of his family hung on the wall. Right next to it was a picture of the general and three soldiers. He narrowed his eyes to get a better look, but the general started talking.

"So, I assume you know who I am."

"General Richard Ward. You're the man who refused Mohtadi Ali Rahman's request for aid when I was taken hostage by Sergei."

The general shrugged his massive shoulders. "I think I made up for it. I take it my drone and fighter jets came in handy recently."

Ahmed tossed back his head and laughed so hard he startled Patty when she walked in with the drinks. She smiled, thinking things were going well, and happily headed back out, closing the door behind her.

"You find that funny?"

"Yes, very funny," Ahmed said as he smiled. "See, I thought Bridget's military source was a man she was romantically involved with previously. To learn it was you looking out for her makes me very happy indeed."

"And what would you say if I told you there *were* other men trying to date my daughter?"

"Let them try. I love your daughter more than I have ever loved anyone in my whole life. She's the most remarkable woman I've ever known. I want her watching my back during a fight and then by my side every night for the rest of my life. I don't know what I did to deserve this second chance at happiness, but Bridget loves me. Those men, and I don't doubt there are some, can try all they want, but they won't have any luck."

"You're a ruthless murderer. I don't know what my daughter sees in you." General Ward narrowed his eyes at Ahmed.

"Some would say you are, too. We all do what we need to survive. I'm not denying anything from my life, but I will say they were all necessary to protect my country, my prince, and my king. And I wouldn't hesitate to do that and worse if anyone tried to hurt Bridget. Of course, they would have more to worry about from her than from me."

General Ward sat back in his chair. "She is very determined. I guess I have to take the blame for that. She gets it from me. Someday when you're the father of a little girl, you will understand how hard it is to have a man known for his harsh interrogation techniques and ruthless killing ability sitting across from you and asking to marry your precious baby."

"I understand I'm not what you hoped for. But I promise I will love your daughter better than anyone else. I promise to keep her safe, to encourage her in her pursuits, and to not let any children we have marry anyone like me."

"How do I even know what 'anyone like me' means? For cripes sake, you don't even have a last name. There's not enough information out there for me to know anything about you beside your military record. Which, by the way, is outstanding," the general admitted reluctantly.

Ahmed sat back in his chair and looked at him. "Then let me tell you about myself. My name is Ahmed Mueez and I was born to serve the royal family," Ahmed started.

Bridget tried to pretend she was too busy to notice that Ahmed had finally pulled up to her apartment. She'd been busy with Annie on patrol the last couple of days. They'd become something of a spectacle together since the night they took those goons down. While Marshall was requested at the PTA meetings, Annie and Bridget were big hits at the Farmers Association and the tractor pulls. Bridget didn't mind. In fact, they both thought it was hilarious. But that morning, Ahmed had called and said he was almost finished wrapping up business and wanted to see her in the afternoon. Her shift had ended and she'd hurried home to get ready.

What happened in Rahmi seemed magical. Dancing at a palace, girl talk with the royal women, and the passion that had consumed them. The night in his arms had come to an end and the dream seemed to be just that, a dream. Which was why she was so focused on not paying attention to the fact he paused before knocking on her door.

Bridget took a deep breath. Something had shifted inside Ahmed that night in Rahmi. She just hoped he would tell her. They could handle anything as long as they were together. She reached for the door and nervously opened it.

"Hello, Ahmed. It's good to see you again."

Ahmed leaned forward and placed a kiss on her cheek. Her heart sped up when she saw how lovingly he looked at her. But it was still there. Something just wasn't right.

"I missed you," his voice rumbled.

Bridget smiled up at him and relaxed. "I missed you, too. Do you want to come in?"

"Actually, I thought since the winter weather gave us a break, it would be nice to take a stroll out at the farm. The colts and fillies born this spring are very playful today."

"That sounds fun. Marko, you stay here. I don't want you scaring the babies."

Ahmed gave Marko's ears a scratch. "We can drop him off at my house and he and Zoti can hang together."

Marko barked and wiggled around with approval. "Okay, get in the car." Marko shot past Bridget and Ahmed to race down the stairs. He danced impatiently around the black Mercedes.

Ahmed slipped his hand into hers and laughed as Marko spun in circles. "He's going to get your car all dirty if he's out running on the farm with Zoti," Bridget said as she smiled at her dog's antics.

"That's okay. It's leather. It'll clean. I'm just happy he's not like Marshall's dog, Bob. I get this eerie feeling whenever I'm over there that he's watching me. It's more than that, even. It's like he's judging me and coming to the conclusion he's smarter."

"Big Bad Ahmed, scared of a dog looking at him." Bridget giggled.

"Just wait. You'll see." Ahmed opened the passenger door for Bridget and soon enough they were on their way out of town on the curving narrow country roads heading to Desert Sun Farm.

The leaves had long ago changed from their lush green to shades of orange, red, and yellow and had fallen to the ground. The grass was turning brown as it hunkered down for winter, but the rolling hills were outlined with warm colors in the sky. Pinks, purples, and oranges streaked the sky as the sun started to set for the early winter night.

The unique fence design of Desert Sun Farm came into view and Ahmed had been right. The horses were enjoying this break from the cold weather as they romped in the pastures, stretching their legs.

Stallions tossed their heads and ran the fence line as they drove by. Ahmed made his way through the farm to his house and opened the back door for Marko. "I'll be right back."

Bridget's heart swelled as she watched Mo open the door to his house and then bend down to rub both Marko and Zoti as they wiggled around him. She relaxed against the seat and smiled. She was happy and she was spending the day with the man she loved. She didn't think she could be any luckier than she was now.

Ahmed strode toward her and smiled. The jacket to his suit hung open and fluttered in the wind. The fitted dress shirt molded to his flat stomach and Bridget found herself flushed as flashes of their night in Rahmi passed through her mind. Definitely couldn't get any luckier. Well, maybe tonight she could.

"Okay, the boys are happily running through the house playing with that long rope toy. Is everything okay? You have a funny look on your face." Ahmed sat in the seat and cocked his head at her.

"Just happy," Bridget smiled. "And thinking about what you could do with that tie . . ."

She saw Ahmed's breathing hitch and the instant reaction he had in those great tailored slacks. "Don't worry, I have plenty of ideas, too." Ahmed leaned over the console, his fingers threaded into her hair as he pulled her toward him for a kiss. His tongue pushed past her lips and thrust into her mouth. He pulled away and Bridget was left breathless.

"I'd been thinking about it, too," he purred. "But let's take advantage of this beautiful day. Tonight I'll strip you naked and . . ." Ahmed placed his lips next to her ear and whispered exactly what he was going to do to her.

Bridget flushed again and it wasn't from embarrassment. It was with arousal as his hot breath caressed her ear and images of what he had planned filled her head. "Okay," she stammered. Yep, she was very lucky indeed.

Ahmed sat back with a satisfied smile and started the car. "I want to take you to the yearling barn. The weanlings just moved in this week. I thought you'd like to see them and I have someone special for you to meet there."

Ahmed drove through the farm and stopped in the small parking lot outside the barn that was nice enough to be a house. The ivory-painted barns were accented with green trim on the windows and doors. The angular, green-shingled roof with spires enhanced the house-like appearance. He opened the door and they walked in on soft rubber floors made to look like brick.

Bridget peeked into the luxurious office as they passed it. It had a desk, computer, and a leather couch against the wall. In front of her was the long row of pristine stalls made from glowing yellow pine. Dark-green steel bars made up the top quarter of the sections between each stall, and also at the door, giving the stable a bright and open feel. It also allowed the horses to stick their heads out into the aisle and see what was going on. Bridget loved it. She approached the first stall and read the nameplate, *Winning Desire*.

"Well, aren't you a sweetheart?" She laughed as the young horse nuzzled her hand and lowered her head for more scratches.

"Do you like it?"

"Yes. I've always thought Desert Sun was a beautiful farm. But these stables are absolutely gorgeous."

"Thank you. Mo and I worked hard on them. Same with these little guys."

"You and Mo?" Bridget asked. She thought the farm was all Mo's project.

"Sure. He made me fall in love with horses when we were in England together. I helped him out when he got this place started. We looked at farms all over the United States together. When we found this place, I helped with the breeding program while Mo handled the business and crops on the farm. I handled the foals, weanlings, and yearlings. I even designed this barn," Ahmed told her as he pulled out a bag of apple chunks and fed one to the cute filly.

"I had no idea." Bridget was amazed. Though she wasn't all that surprised. Even though Ahmed was quiet with other people, he was very good with animals. Marko and Zoti worshiped him and it would only make sense he would be the same with horses.

"Actually, it's something I wanted to tell you, the real reason I've been so busy these last couple of days."

Bridget didn't know what to say; she felt by the way his body tightened next to hers that it was serious. "Yes?"

"The king was so pleased with my service that he ordered me back to Rahmi to serve as co-chief of security."

Bridget felt as if the world had dropped out from under her. He was going back to Rahmi. "Well, um, congratulations. You deserve it." Bridget felt the tears pushing on her eyes. Her nose started running and she had the strongest desire to leap into his car and speed away for dear life.

"Thank you. But I didn't take it."

Her head shot up and she looked into Ahmed's smiling face. "You didn't?"

"I didn't. I resigned from the Royal Guards. Nabi will now be in charge of security for Mo and his family. Of course, I'll be around if he needs an extra hand."

"What will you do then?"

"Well, I'm now a co-owner of a horse farm. This horse farm," Ahmed held out his arms to show off his stables. "I'm in charge of the breeding program and all the foals and yearlings we have and will have. And I do plan to have lots of these little guys running around here with the best bloodlines in the world."

"I can't believe it," Bridget managed to say. She was shocked. Ahmed out of the security business and working with Mo at the farm . . . it seemed so strange, yet so right. He'd been through so much, seen so much, and now he could have a place of his own out of danger. "Oh, that's wonderful. No one's going to be shooting at you anymore."

Ahmed grabbed her as she jumped into his arms and laughed. He spun her around and set her down before placing a soft kiss on her lips. "Let me show you the colt I'm really excited about. His mother won numerous stakes races at Ascot in England. The farm bought her last year and then she was bred to one of the best turf racers here in the United States."

"Can't wait to see him then. You're a good man, Ahmed," Bridget said with emotion building inside her. He was showing her the soft side he had buried so deeply all those years ago.

"Thank you, my dear." Ahmed pulled her close to his side and led her past the stalls until he reached one with a small white cloth hanging over the brass nameplate on the stall door.

The colt, with a pretty white diamond right between his eyes, eagerly stuck his head out as she and Ahmed approached his stall. He whinnied and stomped his hoof as Ahmed laughed.

"He's demanding an apple. Here, you give it to him." Ahmed handed her a thick slice of apple to feed to the colt.

Bridget held out her hand and the colt eagerly took the apple and then spun around in his stall showing off. Bridget laughed at his antics. "You're a handsome boy, aren't you?" The colt whinnied again and tossed his head at the compliment. "What's his name?"

Ahmed gestured to the small white sheet covering the nameplate. "This just came in today. Why don't you do the honors?"

The colt's soft nose hit her arm, demanding more attention. She turned away from Ahmed to rub the horse's nose and was rewarded with a happy whinny. "Well, let's see what your name is, handsome."

Bridget lifted the white cloth from the nameplate and stared in confusion. *Will You Marry Me?* What a strange name for a horse. She turned around to ask Ahmed if that was right when she saw him behind her on one knee. She whipped her head around to the nameplate again and then back to Ahmed.

He smiled up at her, but she just stood frozen to the spot. He looked so strong and sexy on one knee holding out a tiny black box. A diamond sparkled from its cushion and all Bridget could do was put a hand to her chest and stare in shock.

"There was a time in my life that I didn't care if I lived or died. My only thought was revenge until I met you. You have helped me out of the darkness. You changed my life and showed me there was a whole future out there waiting for us. You're the most remarkable woman I have ever met. You're strong and compassionate. Every day, I think I can't possibly love and respect you any more. But then I'm with you and my love just continues to grow. Bridget, will you do me the greatest honor of becoming my wife?"

"Yes! Yes! Yes! Oh, I love you."

Ahmed stood up and she jumped into his arms. He kissed her and it was then she realized why he'd been so nervous. His hands were strong, yet a little shaky as he slid the ring onto her finger.

"I love you, too," he said as he rested his forehead on hers and looked into her eyes. "Always and forever, but with you forever won't be long enough."

Bridget lost her battle with tears as she wrapped herself around him and kissed him with all the hope of the bright future ahead of them.

Chapter Twenty-Five

A hmed wrapped his arm around his fiancée's waist and led her out of the barn. He had one more surprise for her. Thank goodness she said yes or this would have been very awkward. He pushed the barn door open as Marko and Zoti bounded forward.

"I still can't believe it," Bridget said as she continued to stare at her ring.

"You'll have the rest of your life to look at that ring because it's never leaving your finger. But right now, why don't you look up," Ahmed grinned, giving her hip a little squeeze.

Bridget elbowed him teasingly and finally looked up right in time for Marko and Zoti to come skidding to a halt in front of her. Big white bows were tied to their collars and she smiled at how cute they looked. But how did they get here? She looked into the small parking lot and grinned at the happy faces there.

"Dani, you knew about this and didn't tell me?" Bridget finally laughed when she saw Mo, Dani, and Nabi standing shoulder to shoulder with matching smiles.

"I know. I also didn't tell you about this." Dani and Nabi stepped apart as her father and mother got out the car they had been hiding in.

"Dad? Mom? What . . .?" Bridget looked to Ahmed and kissed him. "Thank you," she whispered before running to her parents.

Her father engulfed her in a bear hug and her mother dabbed the tears from her eyes. When his soon-to-be father-in-law handed Bridget over to Patty's embrace, Ahmed stepped forward and held out his hand. "It's good to see you again, sir."

"You too, son. Turns out my daughter was right the whole time. She said you were a good man and you are. Congratulations to you both." General Ward grabbed his outstretched hand and shook it.

"Wait, you all met?" Bridget asked from her mom's embrace.

"Oh yes. He was so romantic and came all the way to Virginia to ask us for permission to marry you," her mother told her.

Bridget pulled away from her mother and walked over to him. Ahmed looked down at her eyes shining with happiness. "Thank you." He'd never felt more like a hero than he did now. "I will show you how happy you made me later," she whispered. He'd live the rest of his life trying to be her hero if this was his reward.

"We are both so happy for you two. Now, we have a party to go to," Mo said as he shook his best friend's hand.

"A party?"

"Yes, Dani arranged the whole thing. We have two things to celebrate today — my partnership with Ahmed at Desert Sun and your engagement. I hate to rush, but when we left, Miss Lily was about to hit Edna over the head with an empty casserole dish for talking to John. And Miss Violet was trying to tell Anton, my chef, how he should fix his pastries. Needless to say, it was a good thing the Davies crew arrived. They're my only hope there will be no bodies when we get back," Mo told them as he hurried Dani into their car.

"We will see you there. We'll take Marko and his new brother back to Ahmed's and feed them. Sorry to have gone into your house, but Mo gave us the key. And we're family now," Patty said apologetically.

"I don't mind. And I know the boys won't mind either," Ahmed said gently.

As the group dispersed, Ahmed realized he had a general calling him *son* and a sweet woman telling him they were family. It touched him deeply. He discovered what a real father should be like after his long talk with General Ward in Virginia. Hard, but supportive. Tough, but compassionate. He'd been slightly jealous of Bridget's upbringing with a loving mother and father, but now he had a second chance at family. They were his family now, too. And he hoped he and Bridget would have their own children.

"I can't believe you did all this since we got back. And I love you for it and so much more, but I gotta see if Miss Lily took out Edna," Bridget teased as she hurried to the car.

"I see I'll just have to prove to be more interesting that the granny gang. I can think of a few ways." Ahmed pinned her against the car and rocked the slightest bit to give her an idea of what he had planned. "If the pastries aren't up to par, then I'd better have my dessert now."

Ahmed popped the button to her jeans and showed her why he was definitely more interesting than the senior showdown.

Cars were everywhere. Ahmed had said to invite some of their friends, but it looked like Dani took that to mean the entire town. Ahmed parked and opened the door for Bridget. All he could think about right now was how long they needed to stay before he could get her home and finish what he'd started against the car.

They made their way toward the wide stairs leading to the front door when Ahmed stopped. "Do you hear something?"

"No. Wait. It's . . ." Bridget turned her head toward the sound and they crept around a truck to see what it was.

"My dear, can you tell me if I've gone crazy? I think I see Mr. Tabernacle's pig dressed in a white tutu with a veil attached to her collar eating some apples on the prince's lawn."

He felt her body shake as she stared at the pig happily eating while her tutu shook with each snort. Soon they were leaning on each other as laughter overtook them. "There are no words, but bless his heart," Bridget said.

The front door opened and their friends spilled out onto the stairs. Bridget hurried to where Annie and the rest of the girls were and they immediately surrounded her with squeals of joy as she showed them her ring.

"Come inside. We have champagne ready to be popped as soon as Bridget's parents arrive," Mo called as he gently guided everyone except Cy inside.

Ahmed climbed the rest of the stairs and shook hands with the man who had quickly become a close friend. "Congratulations. Mo told me about the king. It's going to be strange for you to leave that life behind, but you have one hell of a person to move forward with."

"Thank you, Cy. You are a good friend and I don't know how I can repay you."

"Shoot, you jumped out of a plane to help me save the woman I love. I think I still owe you. Come on, let's get a drink and talk about the good ol' days of fighting, guns, and secret missions."

Ahmed laughed and followed Cy into the house. The party was in full swing and soon the women turned on him. "We knew she'd be perfect for you," Miss Daisy said as she patted his hand.

"We're so happy for you both," Miss Lily said with half an eye on John talking to Will.

"Oh, bless your hearts." Miss Violet grabbed Ahmed and before he knew it, his face was buried in her billowy bosom as she hugged him tightly to her chest.

"Don't smother him before the wedding," Kenna teased. "Congratulations, Ahmed." Kenna rose up and kissed his cheek. "I'm so glad you found your love."

"Me, too," Tammy sobbed. "I'm so happy for you. Damn pregnancy hormones. I swear these are happy tears."

Ahmed wrapped the closest thing he had to a little sister in his arms and kissed the top of her head. "Thank you, Tammy."

Bridget finally broke free of Morgan, Pam Gilbert, and Neely Grace and made her way to his side right before her parents were escorted in. Her father looked imposing, except for the big smile on his face.

"Holy . . ." Miles started to say before Miss Lily swatted the back of his head.

"I can't believe it." Marshall stopped bouncing Sydney from where he stood between Miles and Cade.

"General Ward? What are you doing here?" Cade questioned in surprise.

"You know him?" Bridget asked the Davies brothers.

"Know him? Shoot, we went to war with him," Miles joked before the three brothers surrounded her father.

"I can't believe you came all this way to see us. Especially now that you're a big shot in Washington." Marshall shifted Sydney to his left arm and shook the general's hand.

Cade pinched his lips. "He has diplomatic immunity. Whatever laws he broke, you can't arrest him."

"I'm not here to arrest Ahmed."

Ahmed almost broke out in laughter as he watched his future father-in-law fight a grin as they both remembered their first meeting.

"Then why are you here?" Miles asked. "Not that we aren't glad to see you again."

"I'm here to welcome Ahmed to my family. The man *is* marrying my daughter."

This time Ahmed couldn't stop the laughter when he looked at their faces. Miles, Marshall, and Cade all had their brows furrowed. They looked first to him, and then to Bridget, and back to the general.

"Bridget is your daughter?" Miles was in shock.

"Sure is. And Ahmed's going to be my new son."

"Oh shit." Cade paused as Miss Daisy hit him up against the back of his head for cursing. "Does the president know?"

"And the CIA? FBI? Homeland Security?" Marshall added.

"They have all been informed and were relieved to hear about his career change," General Ward laughed as he reached over and grabbed Ahmed by the shoulder. "Very relieved. Although I think our president has a sweet spot for you after His Highness told her about your love story. She sends her congratulations. Patty?"

"It's right here, honey," Patty pulled out a bottle of very expensive bourbon. "There's a note, too."

"Good luck with your green card application," Ahmed read out loud. "You can use me as a reference. Signed, President Sheila Nelson."

Everyone laughed and soon people started breaking into groups as the champagne was popped and poured. Bridget made her way over to her parents and Ahmed, who were now surrounded by the Davies family.

"Dad," she interjected, "I can't believe you didn't tell me you knew the Davies family?"

"I may have wanted you to find a nice place to call your own. And I knew you would be safe here."

"Wait, back up. You wanted me to find? What did you do?" Her voice raised and everyone stopped talking and looked at them.

"I may have suggested Marshall's sheriff's department could use a K-9."

"Suggested to whom?"

"That would be me," Cy said proudly.

Ahmed turned and looked at his friend. "You?"

"Yep," Cy grinned as he rocked back on his heels. "I'm the one who hired her after her father suggested it. I looked into her a bit. And yes, I knew he was her father and I knew he had been my brothers' commander. I am a spy, after all."

"Way to help a friend out. It would have helped if you'd told me who her father was *before* I showed up at his house asking permission to marry his daughter," Ahmed said as he gently punched Cy in the shoulder and they laughed.

The champagne was handed out and Ahmed slid his hand onto the small of Bridget's back. She smiled up at him and rested her head against his shoulder for just a moment.

The general cleared his throat and raised his glass. The room quieted as they waited for his toast. "Thank you, Your Highness."

"We're practically family now. Call me Mo."

"Well, thank you. To Mo, and your beautiful wife, Danielle, for hosting this party. And to all of you for loving and caring for my daughter," he tilted his glass toward the packed room. "My dear wife of thirty-eight years and I only had one child. Who could top perfection? We knew it would take someone special to make her fall in love. Now, Ahmed isn't exactly what we expected, but we've seen them together and we've heard them talk about each other. We know our prayers have been answered. The man she fell in love with will cherish her. And we all know he'll keep her safe."

"And she'll keep him safe," Annie called out over the laughter.

"True," her father bellowed. "But most importantly, he'll love her and that's all her mother and I could ever want. To Bridget and Ahmed."

"To Bridget and Ahmed!"

Chapter Twenty-Six

Summer in Keeneston . . .

"Take it off," Katelyn told Bridget as baby Sydney crawled around the room.

"Yes, take it off." Tammy laughed as she set her daughter, Piper, on the play mat.

"But I don't want to." Bridget almost stomped her foot in defiance.

"I like it," Annie grinned.

"Well, of course _you_ like it. But come on. Take it off," Morgan ordered in her fierce negotiating voice as she bounced her daughter, Layne, on her knee.

"I don't know . . . He might like it. I mean, it is Ahmed we're talking about," Gemma giggled feeding her newborn daughter, Reagan, in one arm and dangling a rattle in front of Riley, Reagan's little sister by sixty-four seconds, with her other hand.

"See," Bridget grinned.

"I'll bring you up on weapons charges if you don't take that knife out of your garter," Kenna threatened as she glanced at her son, Carter, staring wide-eyed at Piper on the play mat. The two were only a month apart and were fascinated by seeing other babies. Her three-year-old daughter, Sienna, twirled around the room in her flower girl dress, totally oblivious to the argument going on.

"While the knife is lovely," Dani started diplomatically as she tried to tie the little bow ties around Zain and Gabe's necks, "it might cut him when he goes to pull off the garter at the reception. Blood on that beautiful white gown would be a shame."

Bridget huffed and with a roll of her eyes pulled the beautiful knife from her garter. "It even had blue on it," she said wistfully as she placed the knife with the beautiful blue handle back in its case.

"Something that doesn't involve weapons." Her mother clapped. "That I can do." She dug around her bag and came up with a little box. "I wore this at my wedding."

Bridget felt her heart swell as her mother pulled out an aquamarine necklace and slipped it around her neck. "It's beautiful. Thank you, Mom."

"You're welcome, dear. Now, let's go get married. We're seventeen seconds behind schedule," she laughed and hugged her daughter.

Ahmed tightened his bow tie and took a sip of the bourbon Cade brought. The women were holed up in Mo's house as they got ready for the day.

Will stared at him and shook his head. "Is it not straight?" Ahmed asked.

"It's not the bow tie. Are you planning on shooting someone?" Will raised his chin to indicate the gun Ahmed had tucked in the small of his back.

"You never know," Ahmed shrugged.

"Ahmed, really?" Mo asked as he shook his head. "Nabi and all the other guards will be there. Secret Service is swarming all over the place since the president is here. On top of it all, it's your wedding day. Take the gun off."

"Who wears a gun to a wedding?" Will chuckled.

Cy quickly buttoned his tuxedo jacket, but not before Ahmed caught a glimpse of Cy's own weapon. The door opened and his soon-to-be father-in-law, Miles, Marshall, and Cade walked in wearing their blue dress uniforms with sabers attached at their waists.

"Why do they get to wear a weapon?"

The general just smiled and looked pointedly at Ahmed's gun.

"Fine," he sighed as he placed it in his drawer and locked it.

"Patty just called. The women are ready," the general informed them.

"Nabi has the limo ready to take us to the barn," Miles said as he drank down a shot of bourbon.

"What's gotten into you?" Marshall asked. "You look kinda white."

"You all haven't thought about it?" Miles asked anxiously.

"Thought about what?" Cade and Pierce said at the same time.

"All of us brothers have daughters. Someday we'll be doing this," Miles looked to the general. "How can you give your daughter away? Even the saying 'giving her away' is horrible. I'm not giving Layne away."

"I'll kill the first boy to touch one of my girls," Cy said as he absently touched his gun through his tuxedo jacket.

Cole just grinned and rocked back on his heels. "I don't have to worry about that. We just found out the baby due in January is another boy."

"You're lucky you're family and we don't have to worry about your boys. Ryan is already a rogue," Pierce joked.

"Hey, I heard Ryan's been putting the moves on Sienna at their play dates. You better teach him the word *Friendsville*," Will said as he pointed at Cole.

"Gentlemen," the general said as he raised his glass. "To the women in our lives."

"To our women," the men toasted.

"But, if you hurt my baby girl, I will hunt you down and kill you slowly," General Ward whispered to Ahmed before slapping him on the back and smiling. "Now, we have a wedding to get to."

Ahmed stood beneath the glowing lights decorating the yearling barn with Mo and Cy at his side. Annie and Dani made their way down the aisle, followed by Sienna who gleefully tossed flower petals straight up into the air and twirled around. Beautiful golden-yellow carpet had been put down in the parking area leading up to the barn. Soft padded chairs filled with guests in black-tie attire filled the transformed parking area. The scene was topped off with white paper lanterns, lining the aisle for Bridget and her father, who held her tenderly on his arm.

Bridget's dress was made of delicate lace. The bodice was fitted and hung gently from her body. Ahmed had never seen a more beautiful sight. She smiled at him and he fought the urge to run to her. It seemed to take forever for her to make it down the aisle, but then her father was placing her hand into his and Ahmed was finally able to touch her. He ran his thumb over her knuckles, and it barely registered when Mo handed him Bridget's wedding ring or when Annie handed his ring to Bridget.

Before he knew it, he was kissing his wife. How he had gotten so fortunate he didn't know. But he intended to show her how much he loved her every day. The crowd cheered and soon they were laughing as they ran down the aisle hand in hand.

A white silk tent with a dance floor stood in the grass not far from the barn where they had just been married. Bridget looked into her husband's eyes and knew this was just the beginning of a wonderful life together. He picked up the knife to cut their wedding cake, and she reached out to stop him.

"Here." Bridget reached under the sweetheart neckline of her dress and into her cleavage. "Use this," she smiled as she handed him a Gerber folding knife.

"Am I the only one not armed?" Ahmed complained as Annie whooped her approval of Bridget's hidden weapon.

"We tried, ladies," Katelyn said with a long-suffering sigh.

"You have anything else hidden down there?" Ahmed whispered in her ear while he cut the cake.

"You'll have to wait to find out." She opened her mouth and Ahmed placed a small piece of cake on her tongue.

"I think I'll save a piece of this cake for later," he said in a low voice. Bridget flushed with excitement. Oh, yeah, she was one lucky woman.

Miss Lily hurried across the crowded dance floor trying to get to her sisters at the microphone. "Move out of my way," she called as she burst through Henry and his new wife, Neely Grace. They'd been married just a month and were still in the honeymoon phase. Lily Rae should have felt bad, but she didn't. Not when one of the biggest bets of the past year was about to be resolved.

Her Easy Spirit shoes slid to a stop as Dinky and his wife, Chrystal, blocked her way while gazing lovingly into each other's eyes. They had married on New Year's Day and still acted like goofy, love-struck teenagers. She tried to move around them, but Noodle and Dr. Emma danced by and cut her off. And that's when she saw it . . . John Wolfe huffing and puffing as he ran along the outskirt of the tent. He tossed her a wink and she tossed him a smile. Bless his heart, he thought he was going to win. It had taken a lot of chasing, but they had settled into a playful relationship where beating each other for nuggets of gossip was foreplay. Someday her heart would heal and someday he might be ready for something more. Until then, they were having more fun than any of the kids in town.

"Get out of my way — gossip coming through." She pushed past the lovebirds and caught Violet Fae's eye. She nodded toward John. Her sister grabbed a piece of cake, and bless her heart, threw it right at John's face. The cake hit its bullseye and John was forced to stop and wipe the frosting from his eyes. It gave her the extra time she needed to reach the microphone first.

"What is it?" Daisy Mae asked as Lily tried to figure out how to turn the blasted thing on.

"Why did I need to take out John with a piece of cake?" Violet asked.

"Look." Lily pointed to the parking lot. Her sisters gasped and Daisy dug around in her purse for her notebook.

"Ladies and gentlemen, Madam President, and Royal Highnesses, may I have your attention?" Lily asked excitedly into the microphone. The music turned off and soon everyone was looking right at her. "We have a little Keeneston news to share and then dancing will resume. I'd like to be the *first* to give you the results of the most hotly contested bet of the year. I can now tell you that Kandi Rawlings is back."

The townspeople immediately started gossiping.

"Married to a ninety-year-old millionaire?" Bridget called out from where she stood next to the President of the United States. That had been her guess. After the incident at the café, Kandi had disappeared. Bill said she had gone to their lake house, but no one believed it.

"Sorry, dear. But I can now tell you those who bet that Kandi went off to become a stripper were wrong," Miss Lily stated as some of the people groaned.

"Yes, it has to be escort," Old Mr. Rogers called.

"No, mud wrestler," Henry stated matter-of-factly.

"Alien abduction?" Pam Gilbert asked with her fingers crossed.

"Nun," Father James called out and then crossed himself. "Come on, has to be a nun. We need some new pews."

Miss Lily raised her hands and quieted them down. "No, I just saw her in the parking lot. She's coming in with Bill and the boys. The bazongas are gone and she's in a dress past her knees and not exposing any of her much-smaller cleavage." The crowd gasped, but Lily hurried on. "They've reconciled and she went back to school. She got her associate's degree in business accounting and is working in the back of Bill's auto dealership. Unfortunately, no one guessed that occupation. However, half the pot will go to the winners who placed bets that Bill and Kandi would reconcile. The rest we decided would go to a charity of the president's choice."

The crowd clapped and Miss Lily looked into the shocked and confused face of President Nelson. "It's such an honor to have you here, dear." Then she looked back out into the crowd. "And thank y'all for placing bets. We're now opening the book on the arrival of Baby Mueez." Miss Lily turned off the microphone and people hurried forward to place their bets with Miss Daisy.

"What kind of town is this?" President Nelson asked with horrified curiosity.

"The best," Bridget answered as she grabbed Ahmed's hand and led him to the dance floor. "One last dance, husband?"

"Anything you wish, I will make happen." Ahmed wrapped her in his arms and pulled her tight against him. She rested her head on his shoulder and he knew true happiness.

Epilogue

Keeneston, three years later . . .

B ridget lifted her face to the sun and enjoyed the warmth on
her face. It was the beginning of June and the humidity had
yet to set in. The grass in the pasture had just been cut; she
closed her eyes and breathed in the fresh smell. She smiled as she
heard the clicking of the camera.

"I didn't know you were ready yet."

Ahmed stood with his camera to his eye and snapped some more
pictures of his beautiful wife enjoying the outdoors. She lounged on a
blanket while Will You Marry Me, fondly called Willie, munched
grass behind her. Ahmed knew the picture he'd taken of his very
pregnant wife would be placed on his ever-growing photo wall in
the living room.

She smiled at him, and he took a couple more shots before setting
the camera on the tripod. They had decided to wait a couple of years
before having a child and now their little bundle of joy was due
anytime. Ahmed had needed time to get used to being a civilian and
a married man. Bridget had needed the time to wrap up all her
contracts with Marko and get the training facility up and running.
The training facility had become so popular in the last year that she
bought another twenty acres from Pierce and Tammy, built some
houses, and hired two full-time trainers. Ahmed couldn't be prouder

of his wife. She'd just landed a contract to supply trained dogs to the Secret Service.

"What a perfect day," Bridget sighed as she closed her eyes again and relaxed. Her parents were to arrive in a couple hours for the birth of their grandchild, so Ahmed had suggested taking some pictures while they waited. Bridget had been so happy when he'd picked up his camera on their honeymoon. He found joy in his photography. The farm was growing, the upcoming stock of foals and yearlings was the best yet, and most importantly, they managed to fall a little bit more in love with each other every day.

"Okay, it's ready." Ahmed pushed the button for the timer and hurried over to his wife. He sat down behind her and wrapped his arms around her, resting his hands on their child.

He got up and checked the picture. Perfect. "Let's do one more and then have lunch." He pressed the button again and resumed his position, except this time they looked at each other with eyes full of love.

"Oh," Bridget gasped as the camera continued to click. "I think I'm going into labor."

"Okay, okay, we practiced this. Five minutes apart for an hour. We've got this," Ahmed said with a calm he really didn't feel.

"Let's just stay here for a bit and take a walk. Emma said that would help."

"You shouldn't be walking. You should be still and . . ."

"Ahmed," Bridget said slowly. "It's okay. Let's just walk the pasture and then we can head to the hospital. I feel great."

Ahmed looked at her. She was glowing. "You know, you kind of look like you did after you beat the crap out of those guys with Annie."

"I feel like it. This is a rush to know we're going to be meeting our baby soon."

Bridget gripped her stomach and screamed. "Why the hell didn't you take me to the hospital?"

Ahmed looked around and felt completely helpless. Forty minutes ago, Bridget had been happy and excited. Now, not so much. Unfortunately, the contractions sped up and intensified when they were across the pasture from the SUV. "I'll run and get the car."

"And leave me here?" Bridget gripped his hand so tight that he thought she would break a bone.

"I can run very fast, my dear. We need to get you to the hospital." Hearing the commotion, Willie trotted over to check them out. Ahmed looked from his wife to the horse and across the pasture. "Bridget, I will be right back. Don't move."

"You'd better be back by the next contraction or, so help me, there will be no more sex . . . ever!"

With a quick kiss to her cheek, he grabbed Willie's mane and pulled himself up. He squeezed his thighs and Willie took off. Ahmed bent low over the horse's neck and urged him faster. His heritage did him well and they were back to the gate in no time. Ahmed gave his horse a pat on the neck as he slowed down and leapt from his back before Willie even stopped.

"Back," he yelled and then opened the gate. Willie looked fascinated by the idea of an open gate, but took a couple steps back and just watched Ahmed run for the SUV. He knew it was a cliché, but when they found out they were going to have a child, he turned in one of his sports cars and bought a Range Rover. He was very glad of that now. His little sports car could go a hundred and forty miles per hour without missing a beat, but it had no chance in the fields.

Willie reared up and tossed his head as he shot through the gate. Thinking it was a race, the horse took off after him. They charged across the pasture and he'd never been more relieved than when he saw his beautiful, pissed-off wife.

"The quickest way to the hospital is to take Route A at this time of day. The bag is in the car. I'm sending out the text to everyone now. See, calm and orderly. Everything will be fine." Ahmed felt the kind of excitement bordering on panic that made leaping out of a plane pale by comparison. He was about to become a father.

He helped Bridget into the car and went across the pasture as fast as Bridget could handle. Willie had grown bored of the game and trotted slowly behind. He shot through the gate and barely remembered he had to close it. "Gate," he said as he was already jumping out of the car.

"Hurry up," Bridget cried as another contraction hit.

"We're good. Your contractions are three minutes apart. See, we're on our way," Ahmed said cheerfully.

"*We're* good? Oh, I'm so glad *we're* good," Bridget said between clenched teeth.

Recognizing the tone of his wife's voice, he kept his mouth shut and sped up. Being married for a couple of years had taught him well. The countryside flew by and the outskirts of Lexington came into view as Bridget's cursing grew worse. It was a sudden reminder that his sweet wife spent time with soldiers and could curse with the best of them.

"Give me a gun, sweetheart," Bridget growled. "If this traffic doesn't start moving faster, I'm taking out their tires." His sweet, kind wife rolled down the window and stuck out her head. "Hey, you — bald guy in the Miata convertible . . . The light is green! That means you press the gas pedal now. It's the skinny one on the right."

Ahmed slowly slid his hand to the door and pressed the window button. As soon as it closed, he engaged the child safety lock for the protection of the other drivers. Luckily, a contraction overtook his loving wife and she didn't realize he'd locked her in the car.

"We're here," Ahmed said with relief as he came to a stop at the hospital. He hurried around the car and helped Bridget into a wheelchair.

"Hi, Bridget, Ahmed. Are we excited?" Emma asked happily with her curly hair bouncing as she walked toward them.

"Bite me," Bridget snapped.

"Oh, does someone need drugs? And here I was worried about hotshot over there fainting before he could get you here."

Bridget literally growled.

"Yes, drugs would be good," Ahmed answered for his compassionate wife who had suddenly turned into a woman who could put a blush on a sailor's face.

"Okay, off we go. I'll get her some happy juice while you get her signed in. The nurses will want to know if Miss Violet is going to bring those red velvet cupcakes again." Emma shot him a confident smile and disappeared down the hall while the most amazing woman in the world threatened to have him castrated.

It seemed as if it had been days, but it had only been eight hours since her labor began. Bridget grabbed her husband's hand and squeezed for all she was worth as she pushed.

"Great," Emma called from down below.

"Don't look. Can't faint," she ground out when she caught Ahmed turning toward Emma.

"For the last time, I don't faint. I've removed a bullet from my own arm."

"Right. Do I need to show you the video Miss Daisy posted from the last birth you swore you didn't faint at?" Emma asked. "We have a game plan and we're keeping to it. Ahmed, don't you dare look down here. Smile at your wife and here we go. One more good push, Bridget."

Bridget smiled down at the perfect round face in her arms. Ahmed sat on the corner of the bed and took a picture of their daughter's sweet face as she peacefully slept.

"Here. I bet she would love to snuggle with her daddy for a while." Bridget handed her over to Ahmed and watched with more love than she could have imagined as Ahmed cradled their daughter.

"Hello, Abigail. I'm your father and I will love you and protect you all of my life. You and your mother are the most precious gifts in the world to me." When Ahmed kissed Abby on her head and then looked at Bridget, her heart managed to find room to love him even more.

Lily Rae, Daisy Mae, and Violet Fae sipped their glasses of special iced tea under the large leafy tree. Mo and Dani were hosting a Labor Day cookout at their farm. After a full day of activities, the sisters were enjoying some time relaxing in the shade.

"How precious is little Abigail?" Miss Lily asked her sisters.

"She looks so exotic with those blue eyes, dark hair, and lightly tanned skin. Poor Ahmed is going to be in trouble with that one when she gets older," Miss Daisy said before taking a sip.

"And Tammy and Pierce are here with little Dylan," Miss Lily clucked. "Piper just loves being a big sister, bless her little heart. You forget how small they are. They just grow so fast. Look at our boys there—all in their thirties now. It was just yesterday they were Ryan's age. I still can't believe he's already five."

"Paige is having a time keeping those two boys in line. Ryan is a rascal, that's for sure. And his little brother, Jackson, is a sweetheart," Miss Violet pronounced.

"True, but there is mischief in those Davies hazel eyes they all inherited. I still can't believe every Davies boy's firstborn were girls. It serves them right for all the hell they raised as young men," Miss Daisy chuckled.

"And look at little two-year-old Wyatt toddling after his big sister, Sydney. How sweet it was of Katelyn and Marshall to name him after her grandparents. Ruth and Beauford are so proud," Miss Lily said.

"And these twins. They just wear me out watching them. Zain is so responsible and takes his role as oldest very seriously, even though he's just four. See how he's trying to keep Gabriel from pulling Reagan and Riley's pigtails," Miss Violet laughed.

"Oh my." They all gasped as little three-year-old Riley narrowed her eyes at Gabe. Reagan bent down behind Gabe, and Riley pushed, sending Gabe tumbling backward over her sister and leaving Zain grumbling in exasperation.

"Well, bless her heart," the sisters cooed as Layne, now three and a half, made her way over to Zain and patted his back understandingly.

"Look over there." Miss Lily pointed to the older kids, playing hide and seek. Sienna, the oldest at six, was with Ryan and Sophie. Sienna had her hands covering her eyes and was counting out loud. Sophie took off and started to climb a tree, but Ryan just smiled and crept toward her. Sienna finished counting and dropped her hands. That was when Ryan made his move. He leaned forward and kissed Sienna before she opened her eyes.

"Cole," Will yelled as the women dissolved in laughter and the other men looked nervously around at their daughters.

"These poor girls are going to need our help with such over-protective daddies," Miss Daisy said, looking at her sisters.

"And these boys need to have an eye kept on them," Miss Violet advised.

"I think we did a pretty darn-tootin' good job with this first batch," Miss Lily told her sisters while she looked around at all the happy couples sitting on blankets watching their children play. "But I bet we can do even better with this group," she said with a mischievous glint in her eye.

About The Author

Kathleen Brooks is the bestselling author of the Bluegrass Series. She has garnered attention as a new voice in romance with a warm Southern feel. Her books feature quirky small town characters you'll feel like you've known forever, romance, humor, and mystery all mixed into one perfect glass of sweet tea.

Kathleen is an animal lover who supports rescue organizations and other non-profit organizations whose goals are to protect and save our four-legged family members.

Kathleen lives in Central Kentucky with her husband, daughter, two dogs, and a cat who thinks he's a dog. She loves to hear from readers and can be reached at Kathleen@Kathleen-Brooks.com

Check out the Website (www.kathleen-brooks.com) for updates on all of Kathleen's series. You can also "Like" Kathleen on Facebook (www.facebook.com/KathleenBrooksAuthor) and follow her on Twitter http://twitter.com@BluegrassBrooks.

Other Books by Kathleen Brooks

The **Women of Power Series** will begin in April of 2014. The first book in the series will be called *Chosen For Power*. You can catch a sneak peek of this book beforehand by downloading the multi-author box set *Hot, Sexy & Bad*. Here is the description for Kathleen's sneak peek novella:

> *Elle Simpson's days revolve around expanding the family business into a global conglomerate. Work has left her no time to find Prince Charming.*
>
> *Drake Charles hosts a masquerade ball each year in hopes of finding true love. This year's event is unlike any other when a mysterious masked beauty steals his heart and ignites his passions.*
>
> *Will this night of romance lead to a happily ever after?*

Bluegrass Series

Bluegrass State of Mind

McKenna Mason, a New York City attorney with a love of all things Prada, is on the run from a group of powerful, dangerous men. McKenna turns to a teenage crush, Will Ashton, for help in starting a new life in beautiful horse country. She finds that Will is now a handsome, successful race horse farm owner. As the old flame is ignited, complications are aplenty in the form of a nasty ex-wife, an ex-boyfriend intent on killing her, and a feisty race horse who refuses to race without a kiss. Can Will and McKenna cross the finish line together, and more importantly, alive?

Risky Shot

Danielle De Luca, an ex-beauty queen who is not at all what she seems, leaves the streets of New York after tracking the criminals out to destroy her. She travels to Keeneston, Kentucky, to make her final stand by the side of her best friend McKenna Mason. While in Keeneston, Danielle meets the quiet and mysterious Mohtadi Ali Rahmen, a modern day prince. Can Mo protect Dani from the group of powerful men in New York? Or will Dani save the prince from his rigid, loveless destiny?

Dead Heat

In the third book of the Bluegrass Series, Paige Davies finds her world turned upside down as she becomes involved in her best friend's nightmare. The strong-willed Paige doesn't know which is worse: someone trying to kill her, or losing her dog to the man she loves to hate.

FBI Agent Cole Parker can't decide whether he should strangle or kiss this infuriating woman of his dreams. As he works the case of his career, he finds that love can be tougher than bringing down some of the most powerful men in America.

Bluegrass Brothers Series

Bluegrass Undercover

Cade Davies had too much on his plate to pay attention to newest resident of Keeneston. He was too busy avoiding the Davies Brothers marriage trap set by half the town. But when a curvy redhead lands in Keeneston, the retired Army Ranger finds himself drawn to her. These feelings are only fueled by her apparent indifference and lack of faith in his ability to defend himself.

DEA Agent Annie Blake was undercover to bust a drug ring hiding in the adorable Southern town that preyed on high school athletes. She had thought to keep her head down and listen to the local gossip to find the maker of this deadly drug. What Annie didn't count on was becoming the local gossip. With marriage bets being placed, and an entire town aiming to win the pot, Annie looks to Cade for help in bringing down the drug ring before another kid is killed. But can she deal with the feelings that follow?

Rising Storm

Katelyn Jacks was used to being front and center as a model. But she never had to confront the Keeneston Grapevine! After retiring from the runway and returning to town to open a new animal clinic, Katelyn found that her life in the public eye was anything but over. While working hard to establish herself as the new veterinarian in town, Katelyn finds her life uprooted by a storm of love, gossip, and a vicious group of criminals.

Marshall Davies is the new Sheriff in Keeneston. He is also right at the top of the town's most eligible bachelor list. His affinity for teasing the hot new veterinarian in town has led to a rush of emotions that he wasn't ready for. Marshall finds his easy days of breaking up fights at the local PTA meetings are over when he and Katelyn discover that a dog-fighting ring has stormed into their normally idyllic town. As their love struggles to break through, they must battle to save the lives of the dogs and each other.

Secret Santa, A Bluegrass Series Novella

It wouldn't be Christmas in Keeneston without a party! Everyone's invited, even Santa . . .

Kenna's court docket is full, Dani's hiding from her in-laws, Paige and Annie are about to burst from pregnancy, and Marshall is breaking up fights at the PTA Christmas Concert. The sweet potato casserole is made, the ham and biscuits are on the table, and men are losing their shirts – and not because of bets placed with the Rose Sisters! All the while, the entire town is wondering one thing: who is the Secret Santa that showed up with special gifts for everyone?

Acquiring Trouble

As a natural born leader, Miles Davies accomplishes anything he puts his mind to. Upon returning home from his special forces duties, he has become the strong foundation of the Davies family and his company. But that strong foundation is about to get rocked in a big way by the one woman that always left him fascinated and infuriated.

Keeneston's notorious bad girl is back! Morgan Hamilton's life ended and began on her high school graduation night when she left Keeneston with no plan to ever return. As a self-made businesswoman, Morgan is always looking for her next victory. Little did she know that next victory would involve acquiring the company that belonged to the one man she always wanted for herself.

With their careers and lives on the line, will Miles and Morgan choose love or ambition?

Relentless Pursuit

Pierce Davies watched as his older siblings fell in love – something this bachelor was not ready for. After all, he was now the most eligible man in all of Keeneston! Though Pierce enjoys the playboy lifestyle, his life is his work and that hard work is set to pay off big time with the unveiling of a big secret. However, this work hard, play hard attitude may have also landed him in hot water as he finds himself arrested for a brutal murder with all evidence pointing to him.

Tammy Fields has been suffering from the crush to end all crushes. But her flirtations have fallen short as Pierce Davies always ended up in the arms of a Keeneston Belle. Having waited long enough, Tammy decides now is the time to grow up and move on. She has a good job as a paralegal and a hot new boyfriend. But everything changes quickly when Pierce is arrested and Tammy is called upon to help with his case. While working closely with Pierce to prove his innocence, she realizes her crush is something far more meaningful as she risks everything to save him.

Will they finally find love or will the increasing danger prevent their happily ever after?

Secrets Collide

After spending the past few months wrapping up his life outside of Keeneston, the mysterious Cy Davies is finally coming home. And he's not coming alone. After rescuing a sassy investigative reporter for a gossip magazine in a dark alley, he takes her to the one place he knows he can keep her safe — Keeneston.

Gemma Perry was having the worst week of her life. Now she finds herself in a small town where gossip is the currency, a place where she should fit right in. During the most difficult time of her life, Gemma must trust the man that came to her rescue to unlock the clues to bring down a dangerous criminal intent on silencing her.

With their lives in danger, will Gemma and Cy be able to discover themselves and true love?

Final Vow

As the ultimate bodyguard, Ahmed's focus has been protecting the lives of everyone he cares about. When the darkest part of his past resurfaces, Ahmed knows he must go on the offensive to protect his future . . . a future with the one woman that can match his toughness and return the love that was once robbed from him.

Bridget Springer's private security work involves training with a mysterious man feared by many in her line of work. She finds herself drawn to Ahmed despite his attempts to remain distant. Bridget vows to help Ahmed in his pursuit of justice, not knowing the full danger that she would find along the way.

As Bridget and Ahmed's passion heats up, so does the threat from Ahmed's oldest enemy. Can they defeat him and finally be free to pursue their chance at love?

Make sure you don't miss each new book as they are published. Sign up email notification of all new releases at http://www.Kathleen-Brooks.com.

Made in the USA
Lexington, KY
05 June 2014